itty bitty
MASK ®

itty bitty MASK ®

ART BALTAZAR & 'FRANCO

WRITER & ARTIST   WRITER

THE MASK CREATED BY
MIKE RICHARDSON

DARK HORSE BOOKS

Digital Production **CHRISTINA McKENZIE**
Designer **KAT LARSON**
Assistant Editors **IAN TUCKER** & **JEMIAH JEFFERSON**
Editor **BRENDAN WRIGHT**
President and Publisher **MIKE RICHARDSON**

Published by
Dark Horse Books
A division of Dark Horse Comics, Inc.
10956 SE Main Street
Milwaukie, OR 97222

First edition: June 2015
ISBN 978-1-61655-683-9

This volume collects issues #1–#4
of the Dark Horse Comics series *Itty Bitty Mask*.

1 3 5 7 9 10 8 6 4 2
Printed in China

NEIL HANKERSON Executive Vice President • **TOM WEDDLE** Chief
Financial Officer • **RANDY STRADLEY** Vice President of Publishing •
MICHAEL MARTENS Vice President of Book Trade Sales • **SCOTT ALLIE**
Editor in Chief • **MATT PARKINSON** Vice President of Marketing • **DAVID
SCROGGY** Vice President of Product Development • **DALE LaFOUNTAIN**
Vice President of Information Technology • **DARLENE VOGEL** Senior
Director of Print, Design, and Production • **KEN LIZZI** General Counsel •
DAVEY ESTRADA Editorial Director • **CHRIS WARNER** Senior Books Editor
• **DIANA SCHUTZ** Executive Editor • **CARY GRAZZINI** Director of Print
and Development • **LIA RIBACCHI** Art Director • **CARA NIECE** Director
of Scheduling • **TIM WIESCH** Director of International Licensing • **MARK
BERNARDI** Director of Digital Publishing

CHAPTER ONE

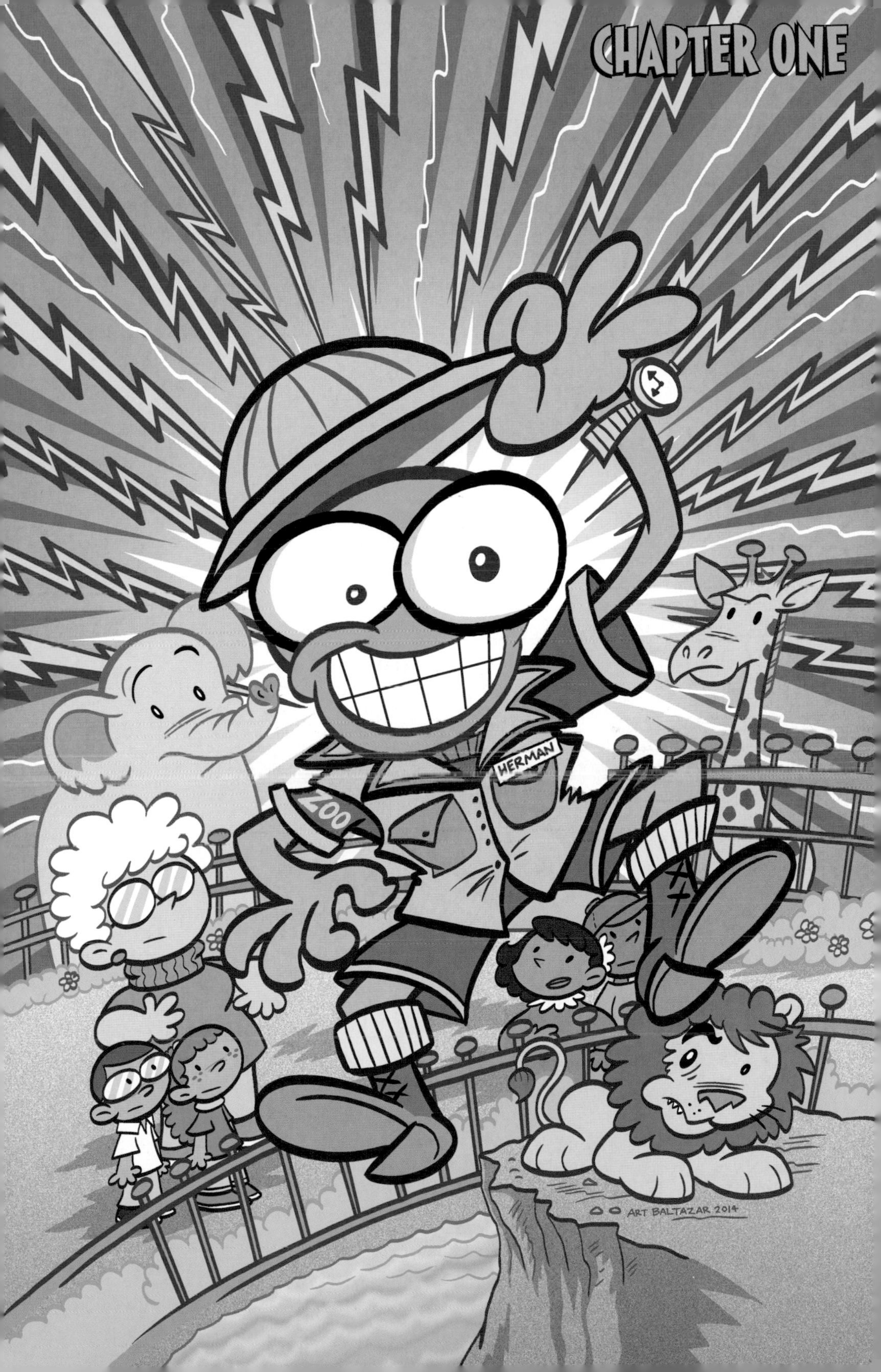

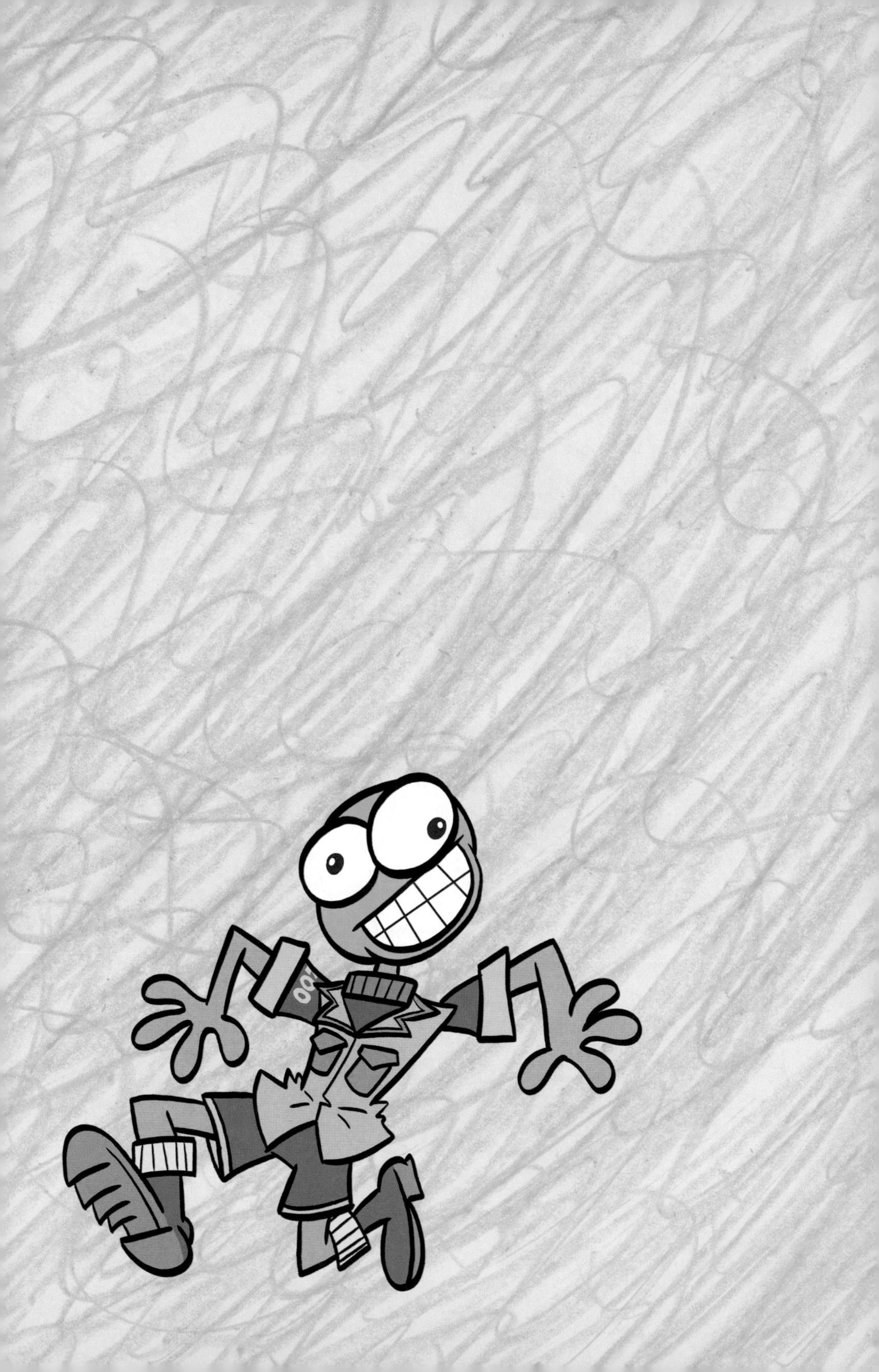

DARK HORSE COMICS PRESENTS...

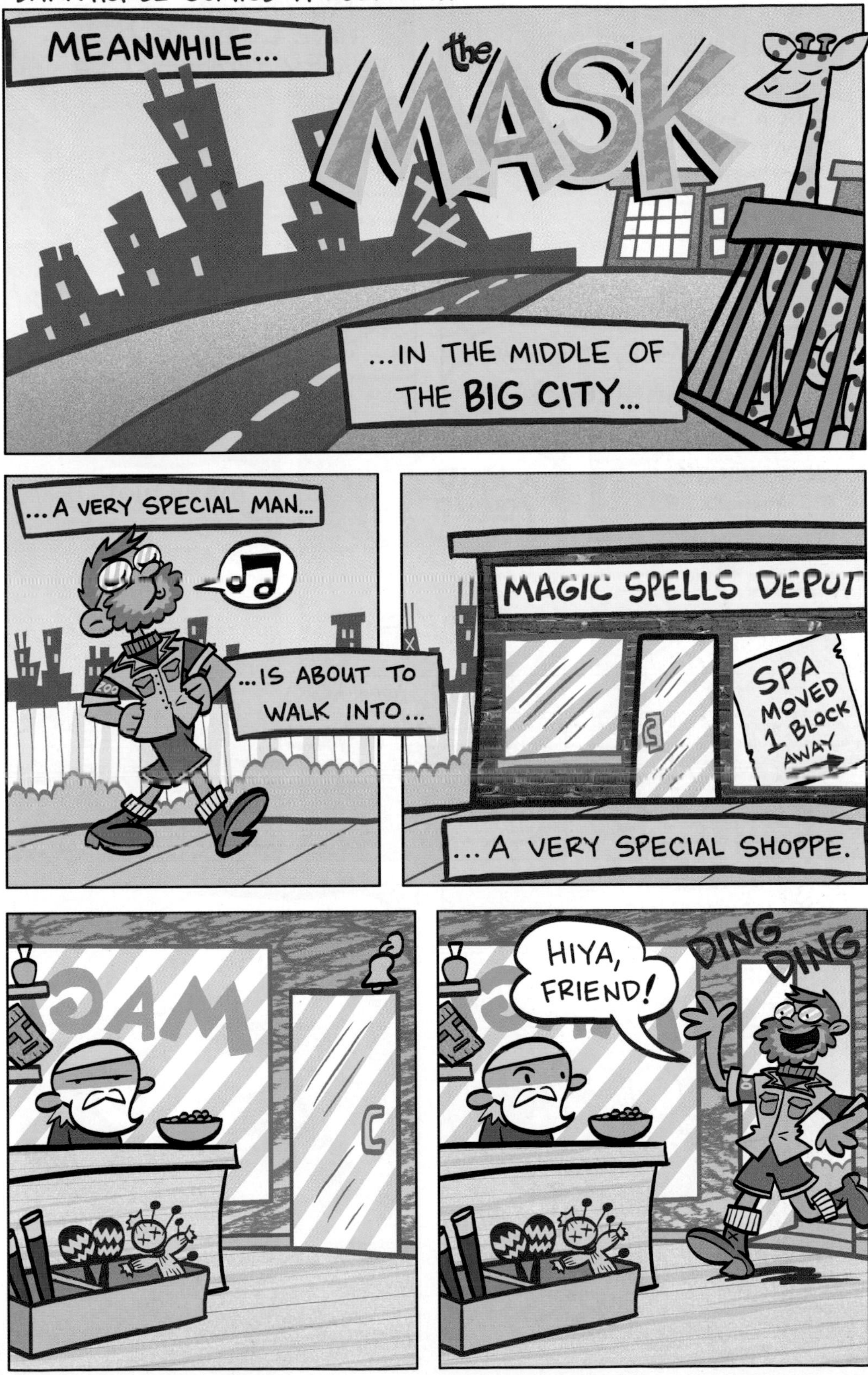
MEANWHILE...
the MASK
...IN THE MIDDLE OF THE BIG CITY...
...A VERY SPECIAL MAN...
...IS ABOUT TO WALK INTO...
MAGIC SPELLS DEPOT
SPA MOVED 1 BLOCK AWAY
...A VERY SPECIAL SHOPPE.
HIYA, FRIEND!
DING DING

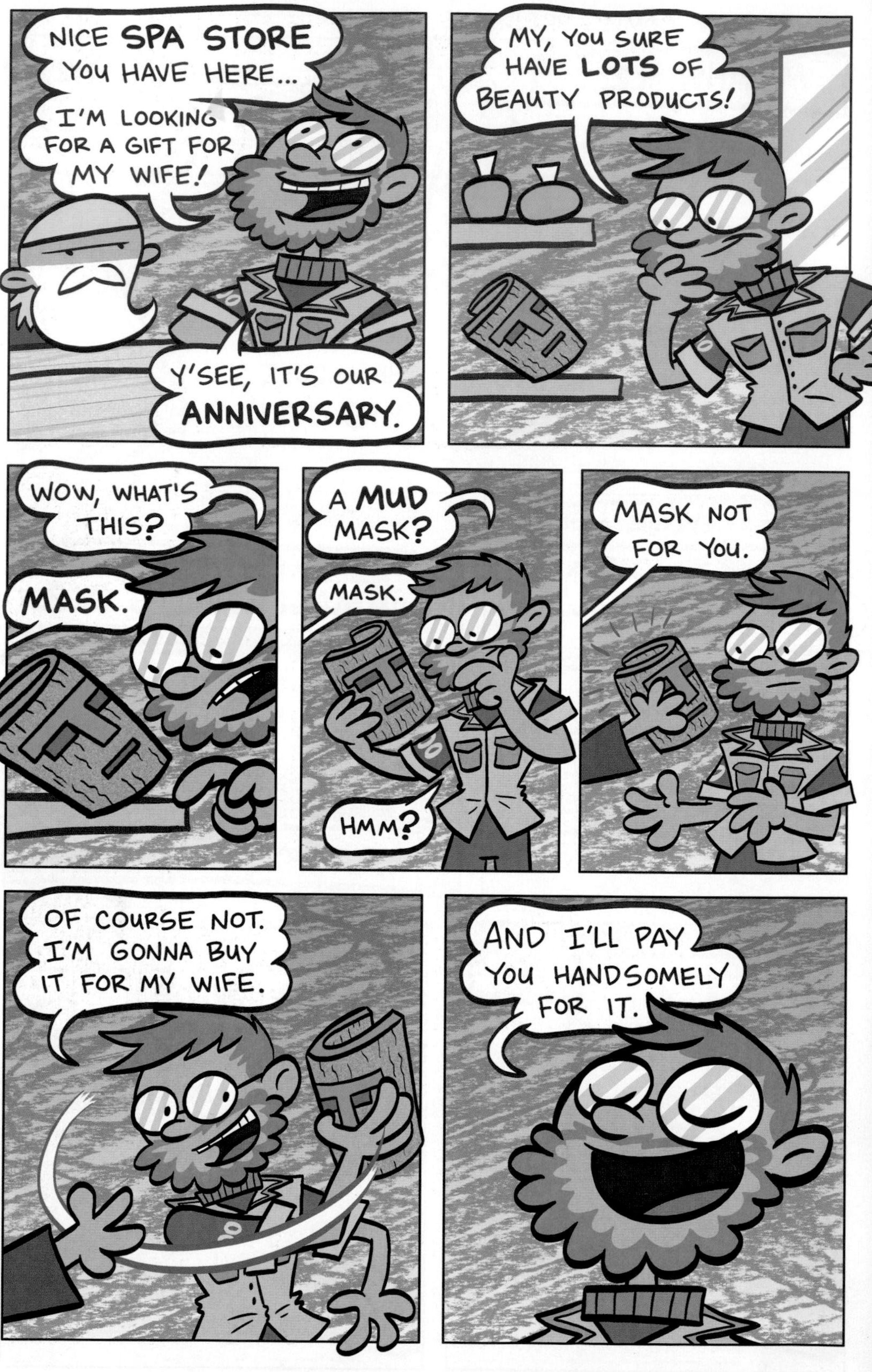
NICE SPA STORE YOU HAVE HERE...
I'M LOOKING FOR A GIFT FOR MY WIFE!
Y'SEE, IT'S OUR ANNIVERSARY.
MY, YOU SURE HAVE LOTS OF BEAUTY PRODUCTS!
WOW, WHAT'S THIS?
MASK.
A MUD MASK?
MASK.
HMM?
MASK NOT FOR YOU.
OF COURSE NOT. I'M GONNA BUY IT FOR MY WIFE.
AND I'LL PAY YOU HANDSOMELY FOR IT.

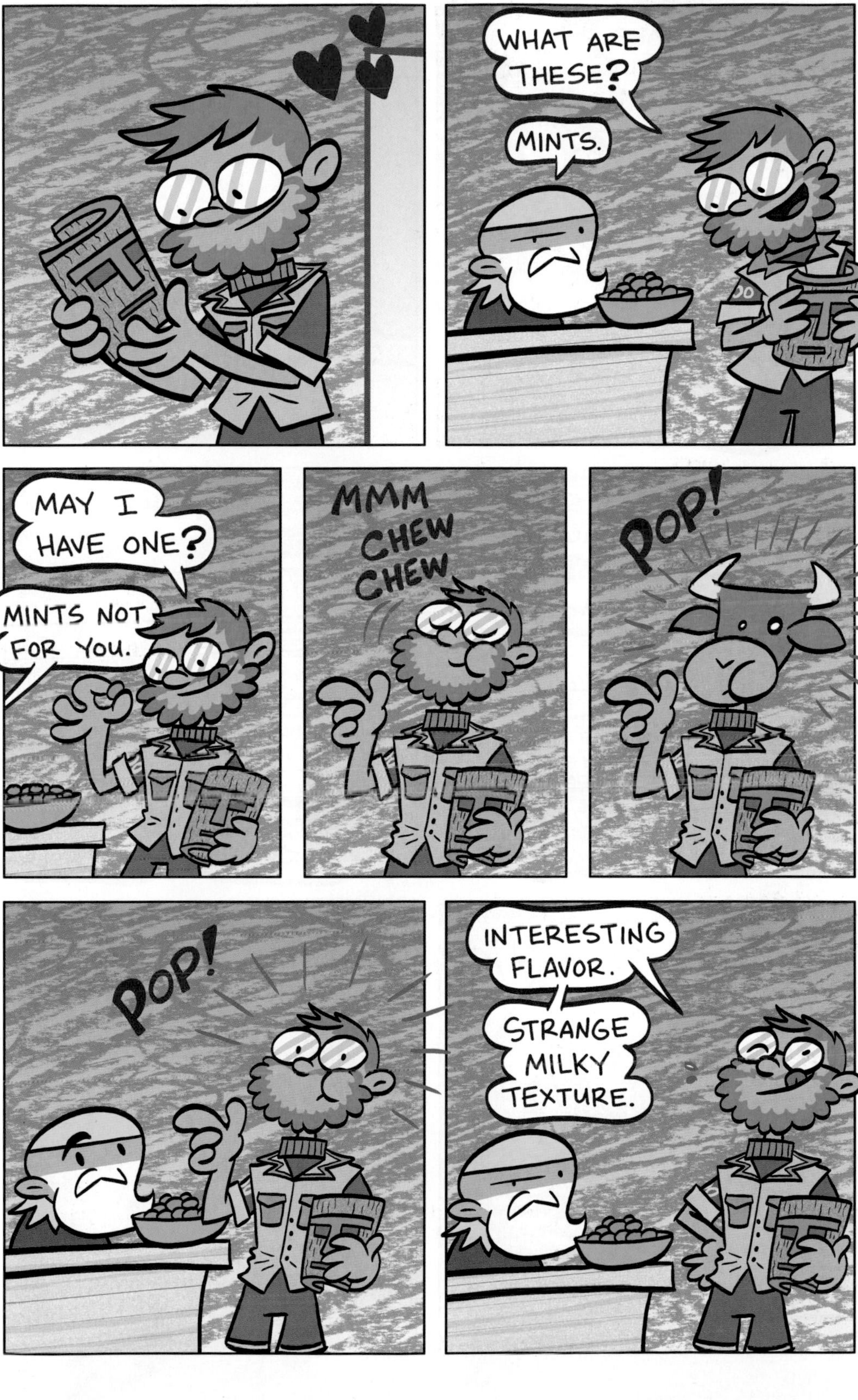
WHAT ARE THESE?
MINTS.
MAY I HAVE ONE?
MINTS NOT FOR YOU.
MMM
CHEW CHEW
POP!
POP!
INTERESTING FLAVOR.
STRANGE MILKY TEXTURE.

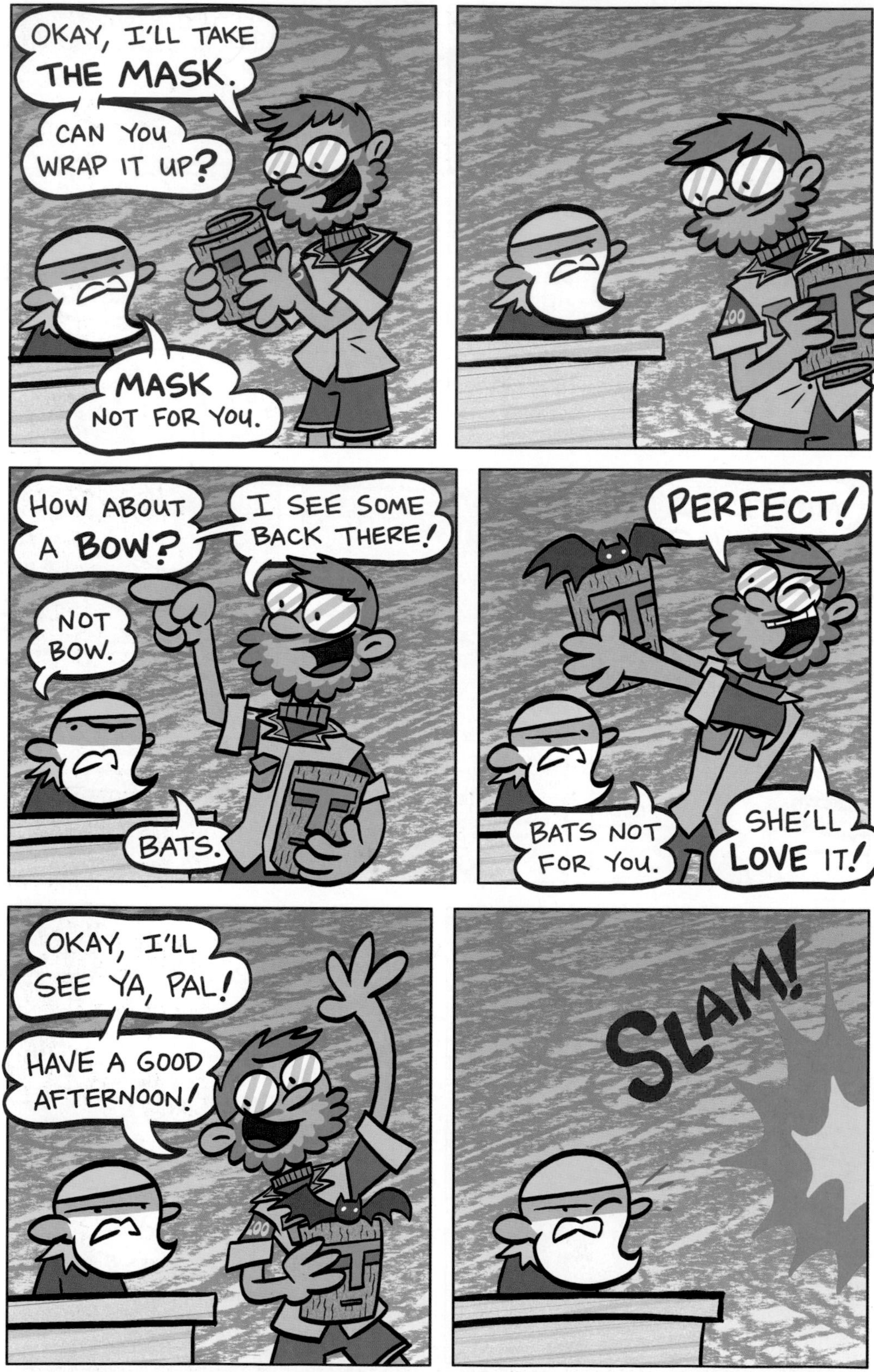
OKAY, I'LL TAKE THE MASK.
CAN YOU WRAP IT UP?
MASK NOT FOR YOU.
HOW ABOUT A BOW?
I SEE SOME BACK THERE!
NOT BOW.
BATS.
PERFECT!
BATS NOT FOR YOU.
SHE'LL LOVE IT!
OKAY, I'LL SEE YA, PAL!
HAVE A GOOD AFTERNOON!
SLAM!

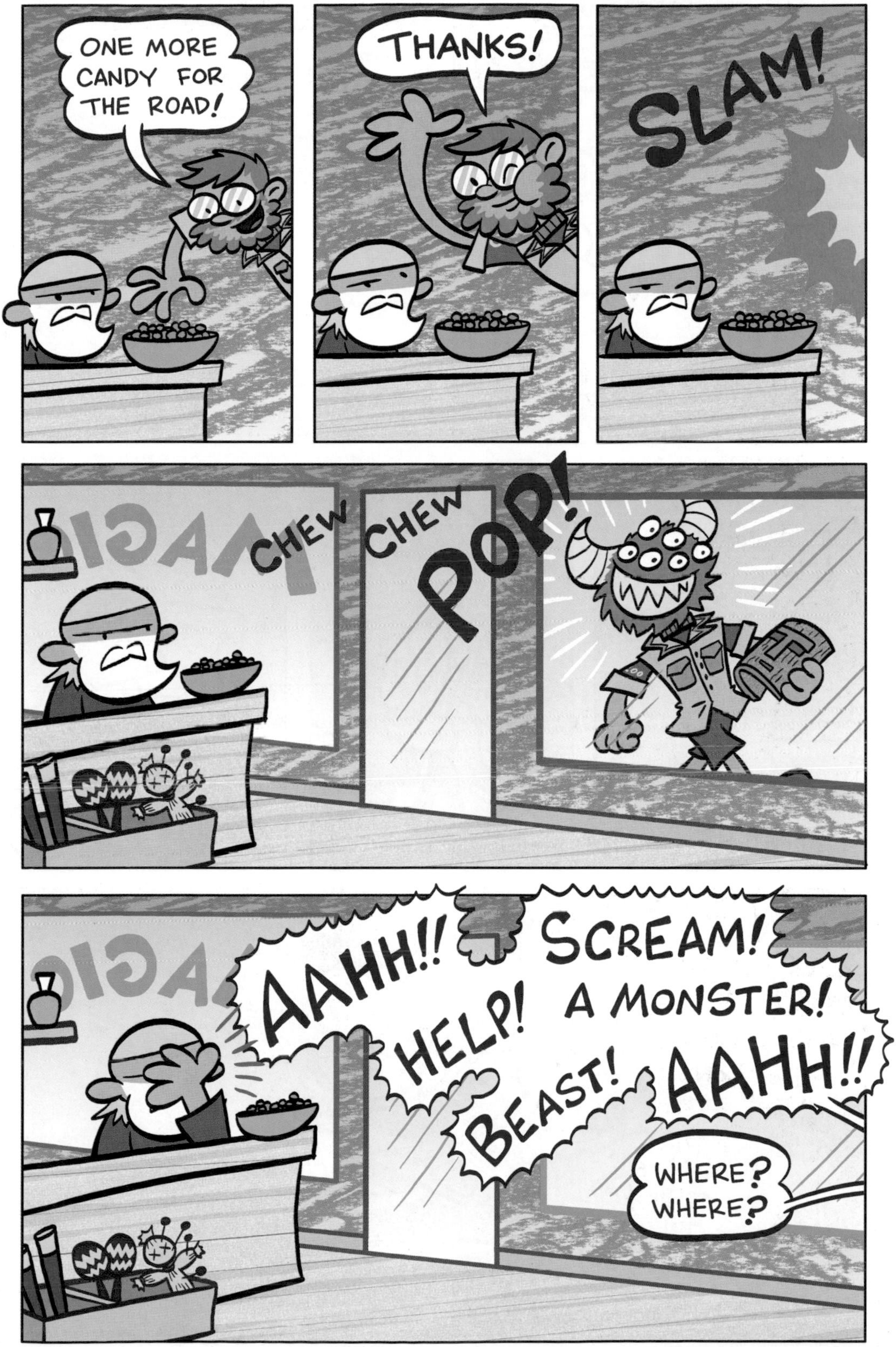
ONE MORE CANDY FOR THE ROAD!
THANKS!
SLAM!
CHEW
CHEW
POP!
AAHH!!
SCREAM!
HELP!
A MONSTER!
BEAST!
AAHH!!
WHERE? WHERE?

—AND SO IT BEGINS...

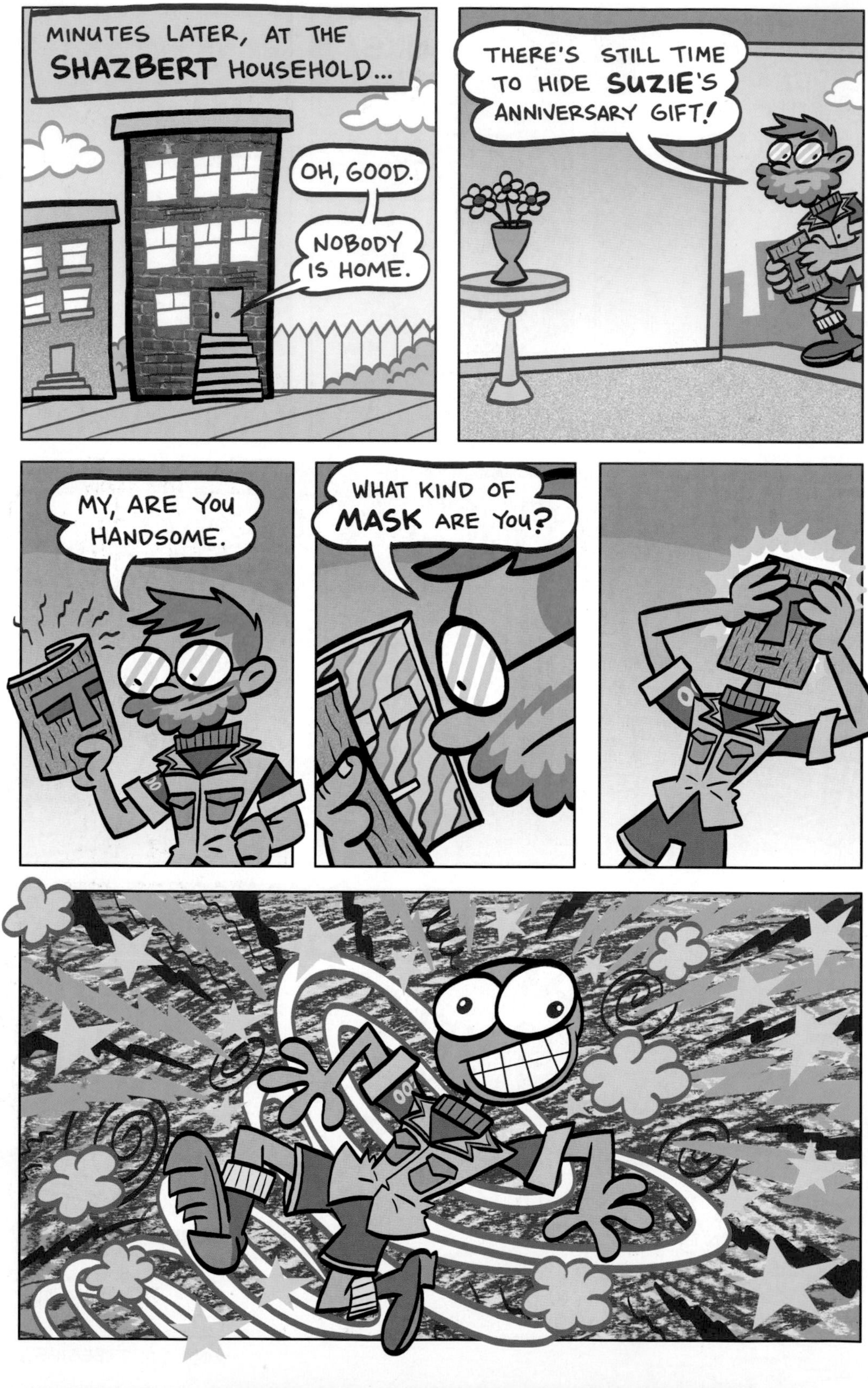
MINUTES LATER, AT THE SHAZBERT HOUSEHOLD...
OH, GOOD.
NOBODY IS HOME.
THERE'S STILL TIME TO HIDE SUZIE'S ANNIVERSARY GIFT!
MY, ARE YOU HANDSOME.
WHAT KIND OF MASK ARE YOU?

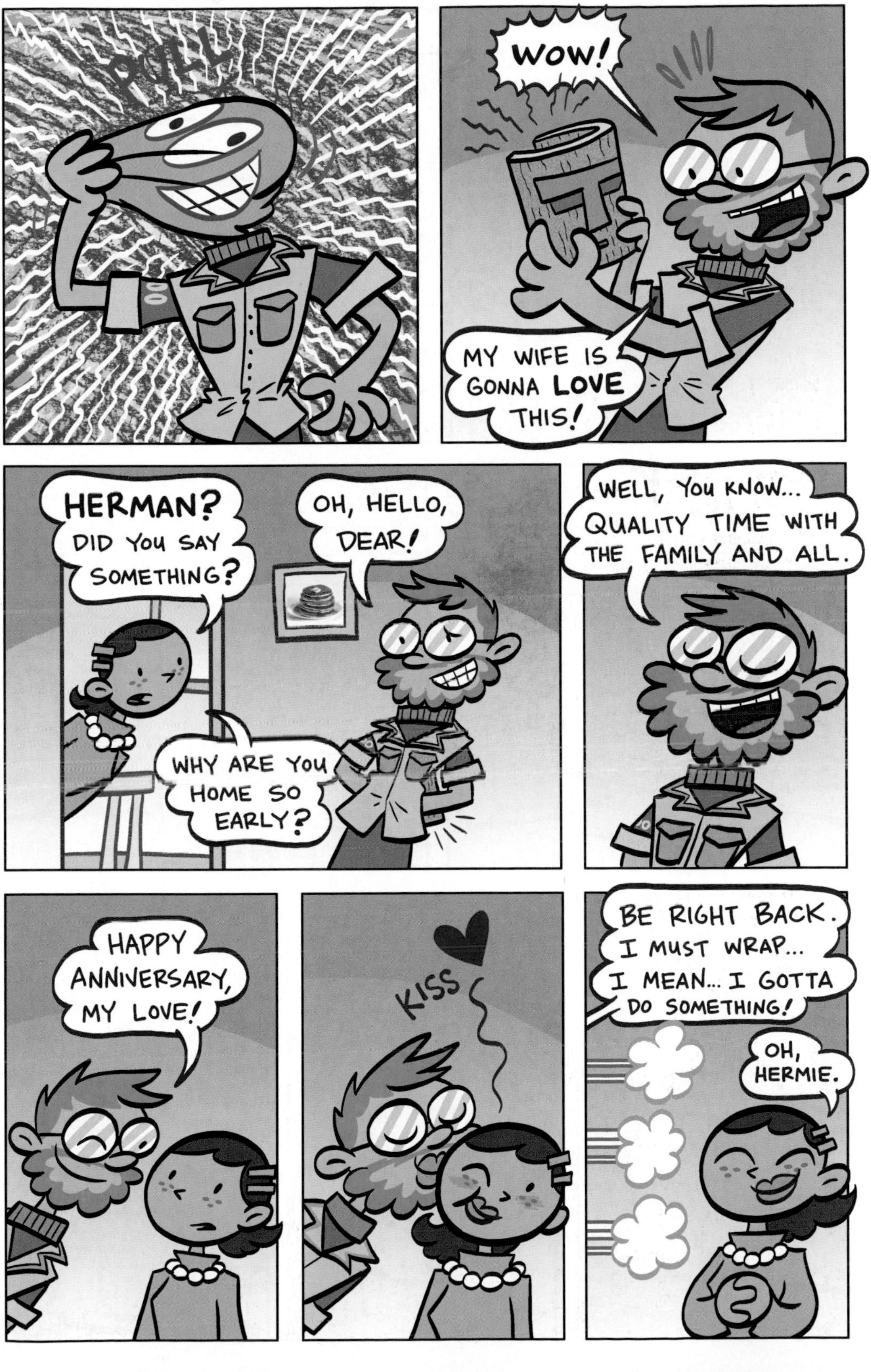
PULL
WOW!
MY WIFE IS GONNA LOVE THIS!
HERMAN? DID YOU SAY SOMETHING?
OH, HELLO, DEAR!
WHY ARE YOU HOME SO EARLY?
WELL, YOU KNOW... QUALITY TIME WITH THE FAMILY AND ALL.
HAPPY ANNIVERSARY, MY LOVE!
KISS
BE RIGHT BACK. I MUST WRAP... I MEAN... I GOTTA DO SOMETHING!
OH, HERMIE.

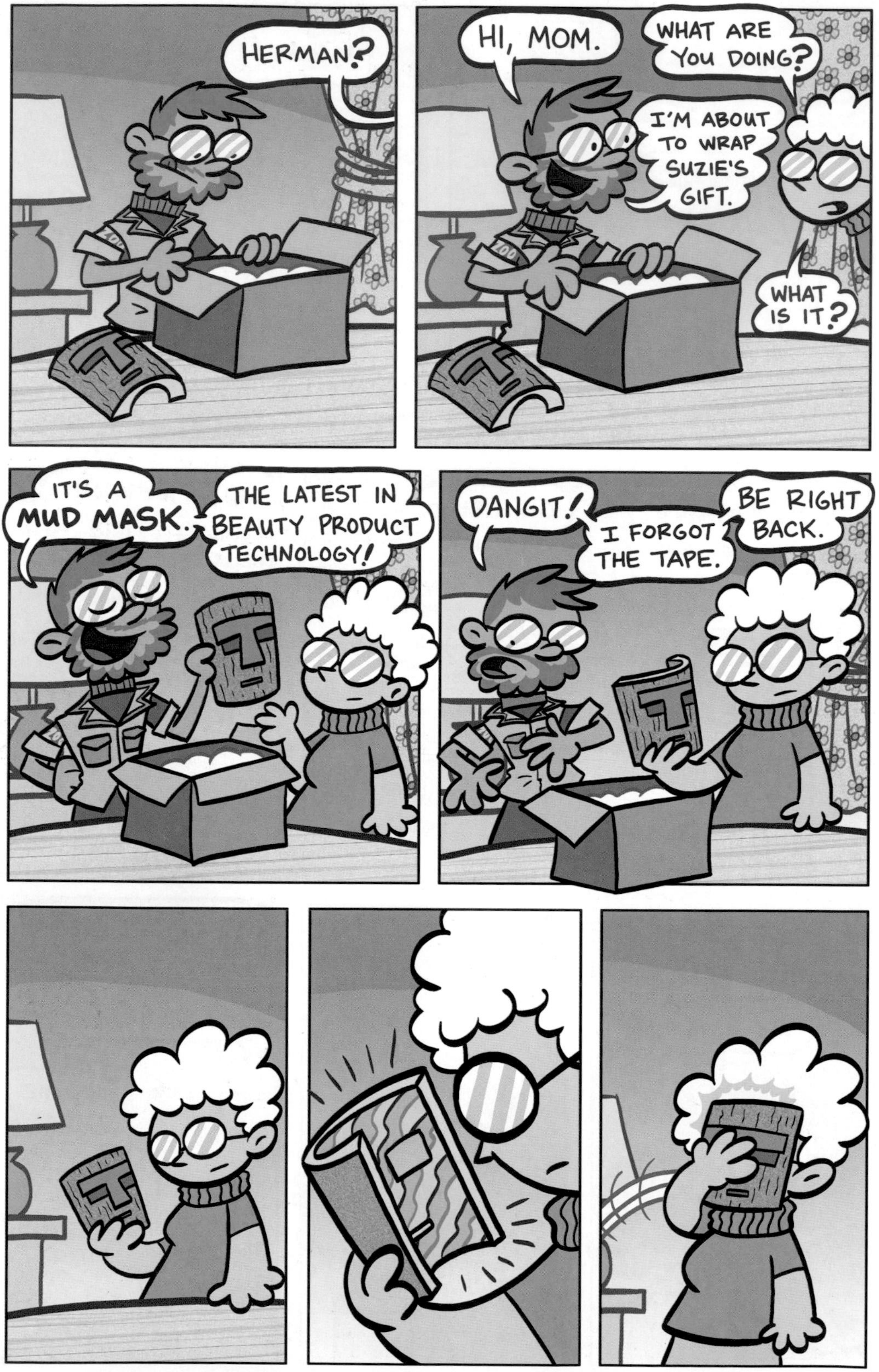
HERMAN?
HI, MOM.
WHAT ARE YOU DOING?
I'M ABOUT TO WRAP SUZIE'S GIFT.
WHAT IS IT?
IT'S A MUD MASK.
THE LATEST IN BEAUTY PRODUCT TECHNOLOGY!
DANGIT!
I FORGOT THE TAPE.
BE RIGHT BACK.

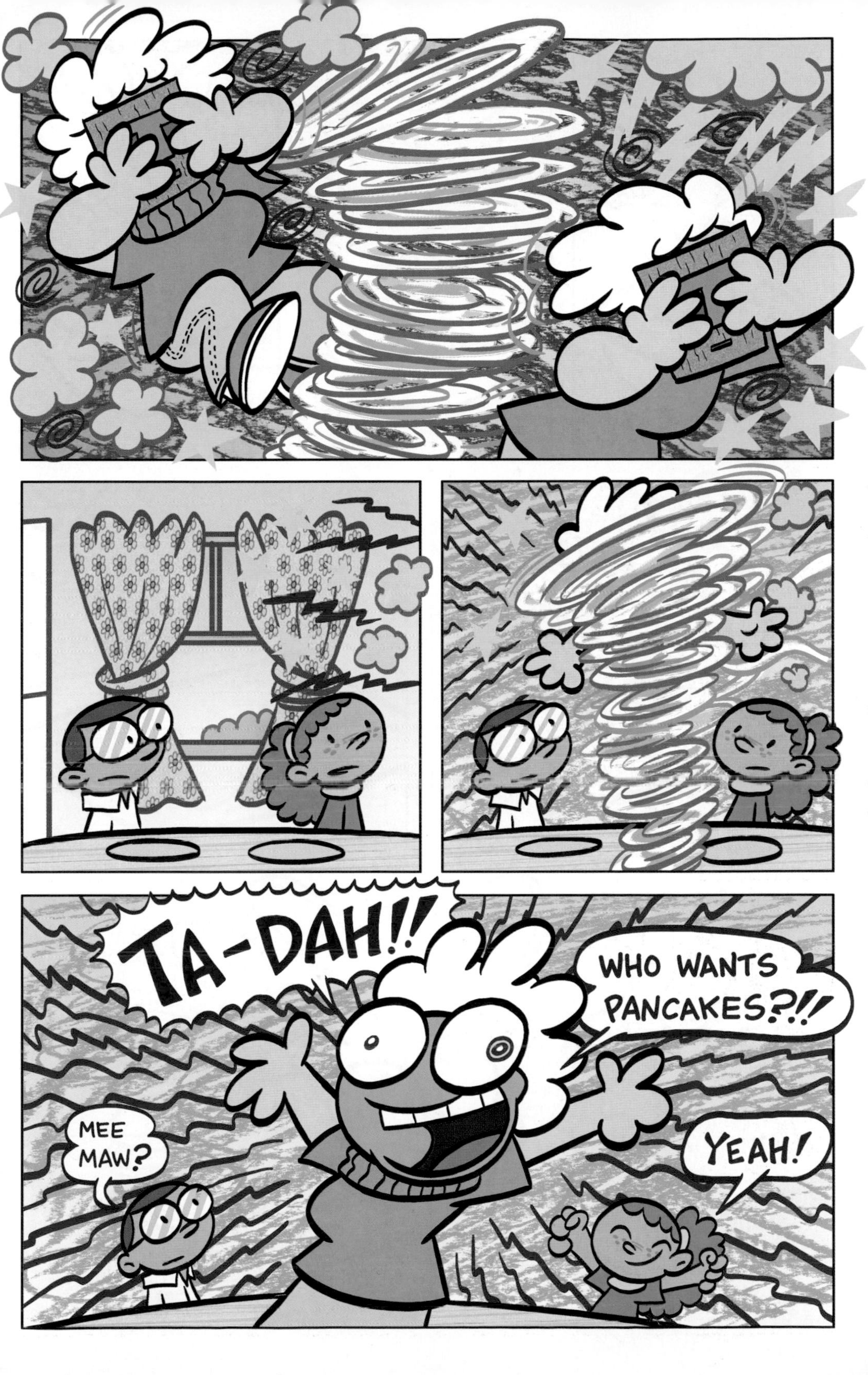
TA-DAH!!
WHO WANTS PANCAKES?!!
MEE MAW?
YEAH!

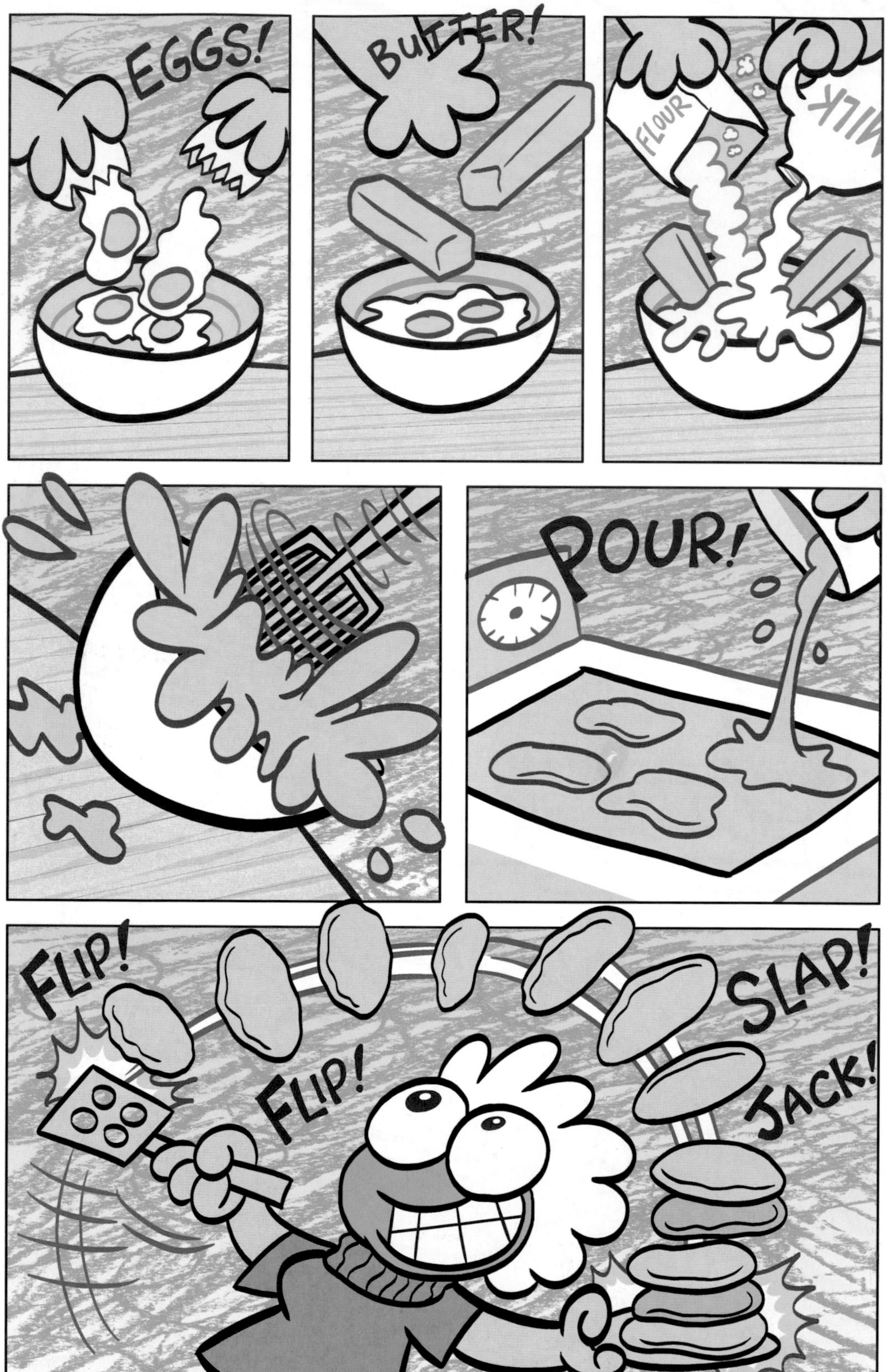
EGGS!
BUTTER!
FLOUR
MILK
POUR!
FLIP!
FLIP!
SLAP!
JACK!

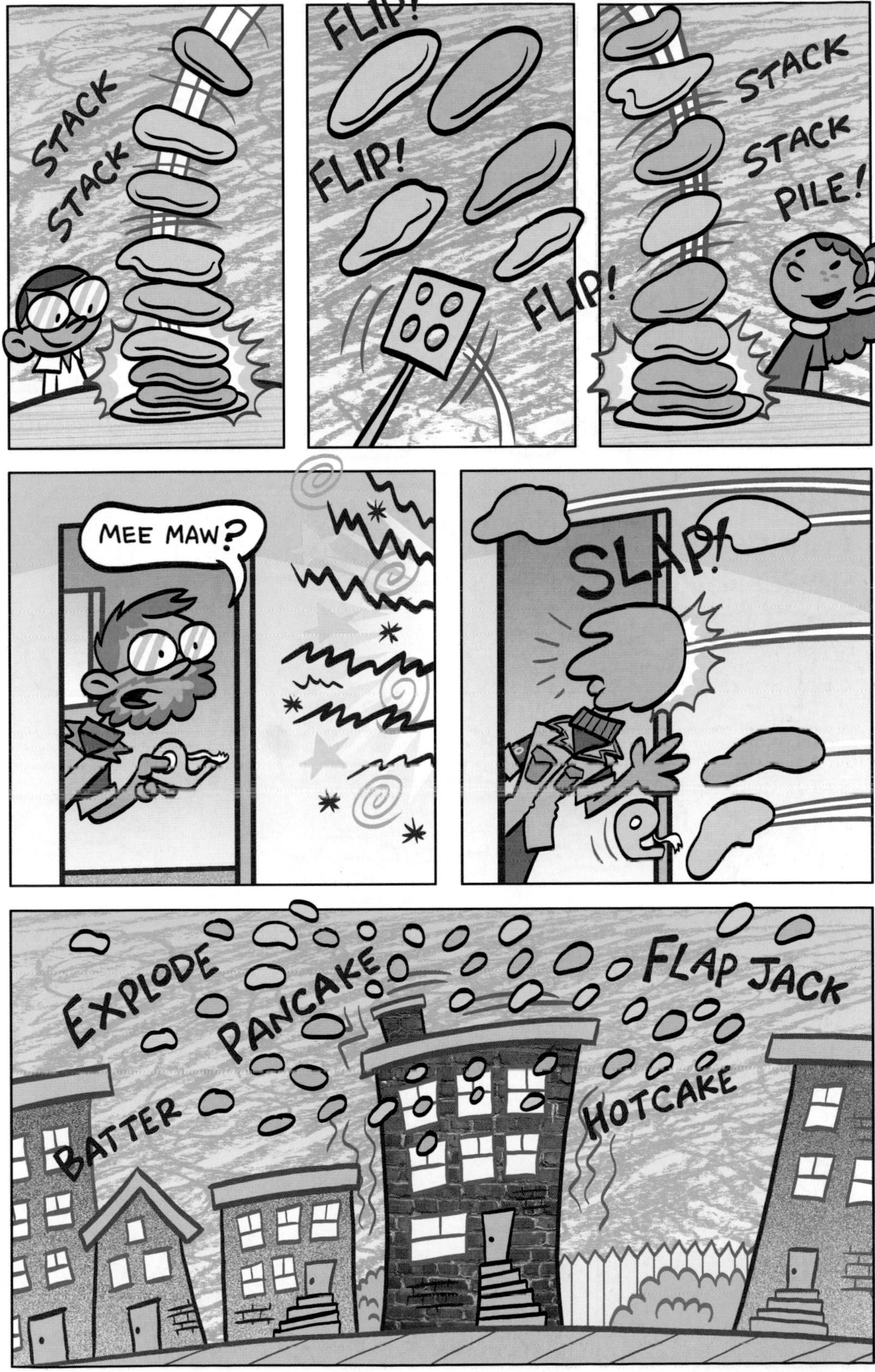
STACK
STACK
FLIP!
FLIP!
FLIP!
STACK
STACK
PILE!
MEE MAW?
SLAP!
EXPLODE
PANCAKE
FLAP JACK
BATTER
HOTCAKE

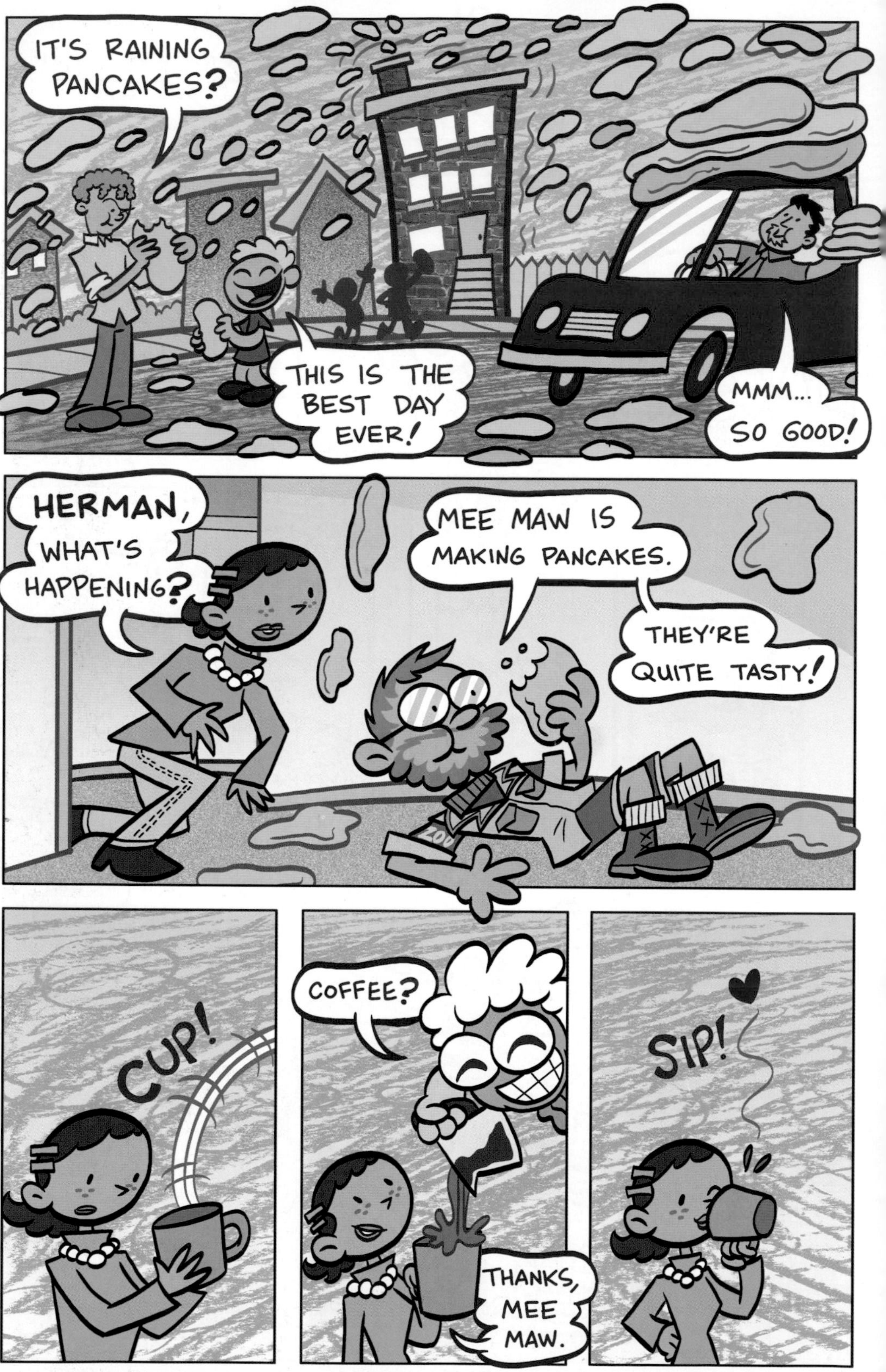
IT'S RAINING PANCAKES?
THIS IS THE BEST DAY EVER!
MMM... SO GOOD!
HERMAN, WHAT'S HAPPENING?
MEE MAW IS MAKING PANCAKES.
THEY'RE QUITE TASTY!
ZOU
CUP!
COFFEE?
THANKS, MEE MAW.
SIP!

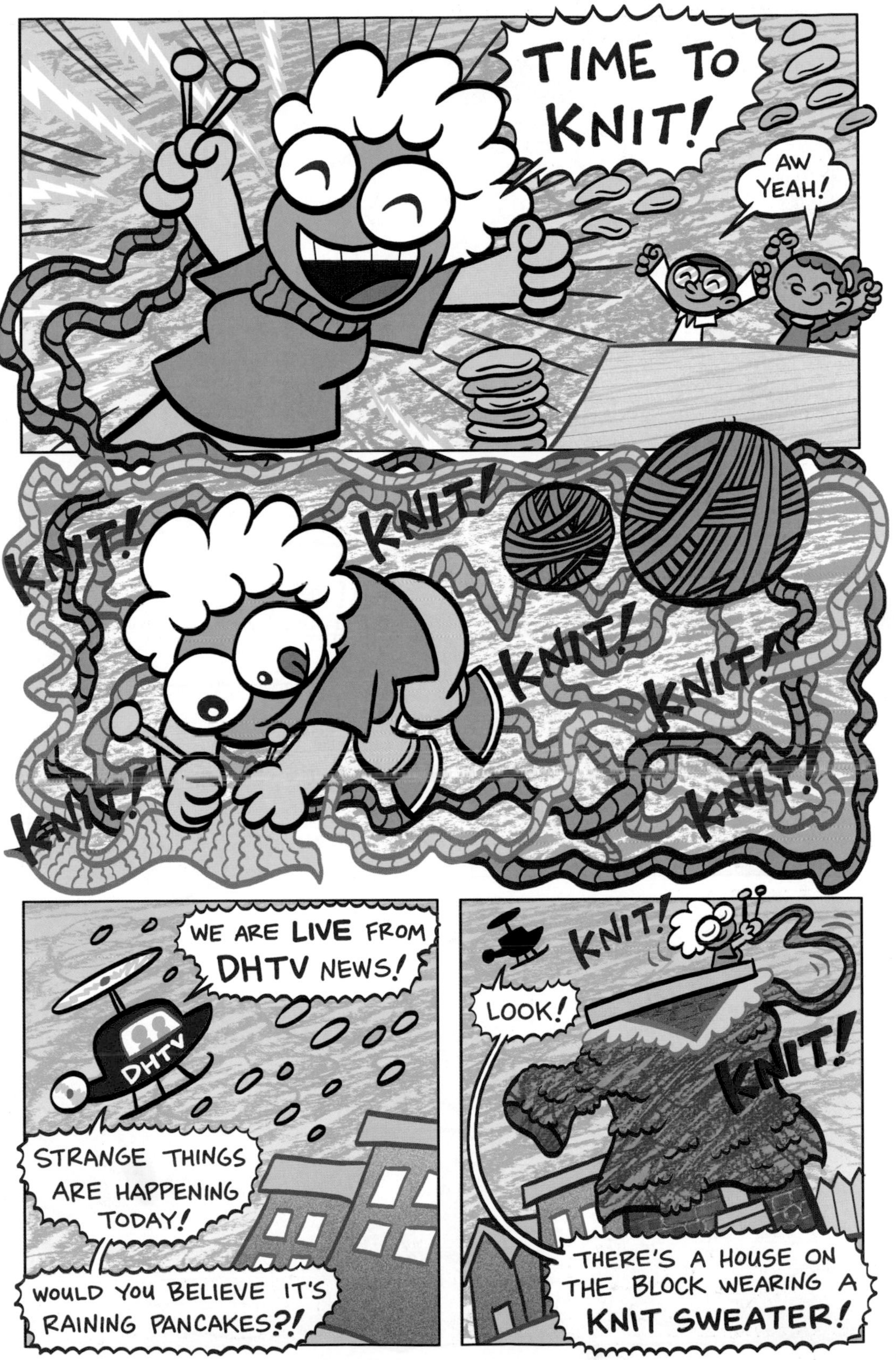

TIME TO KNIT!
AW YEAH!
KNIT!
KNIT!
KNIT!
KNIT!
KNIT!
KNIT!
WE ARE LIVE FROM DHTV NEWS!
DHTV
STRANGE THINGS ARE HAPPENING TODAY!
WOULD YOU BELIEVE IT'S RAINING PANCAKES?!
KNIT!
LOOK!
KNIT!
THERE'S A HOUSE ON THE BLOCK WEARING A KNIT SWEATER!

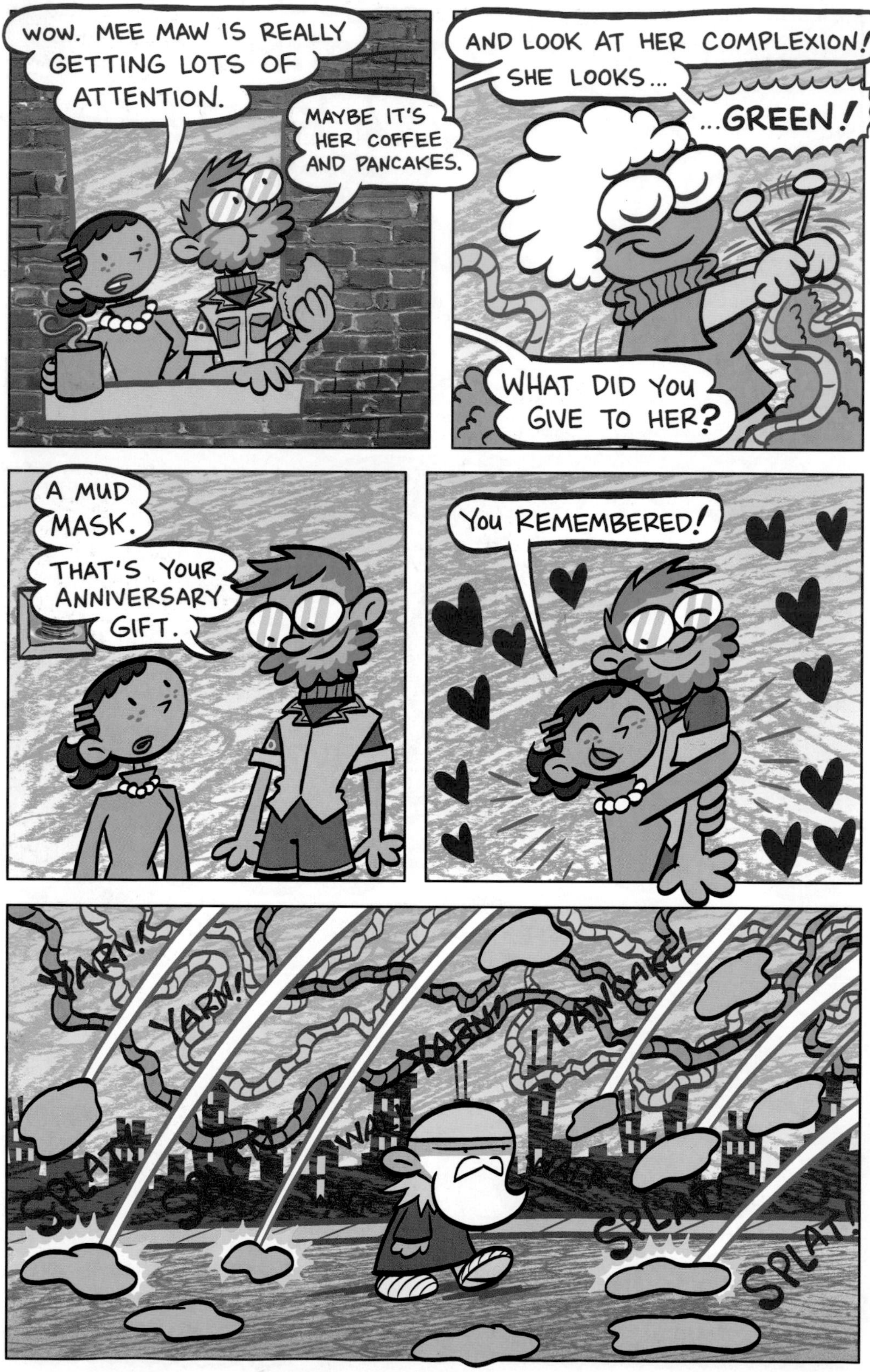
WOW. MEE MAW IS REALLY GETTING LOTS OF ATTENTION.
MAYBE IT'S HER COFFEE AND PANCAKES.
AND LOOK AT HER COMPLEXION!
SHE LOOKS...
...GREEN!
WHAT DID YOU GIVE TO HER?
A MUD MASK.
THAT'S YOUR ANNIVERSARY GIFT.
YOU REMEMBERED!
YARN!
YARN!
PANCAKE!
SPLAT!
SPLAT!

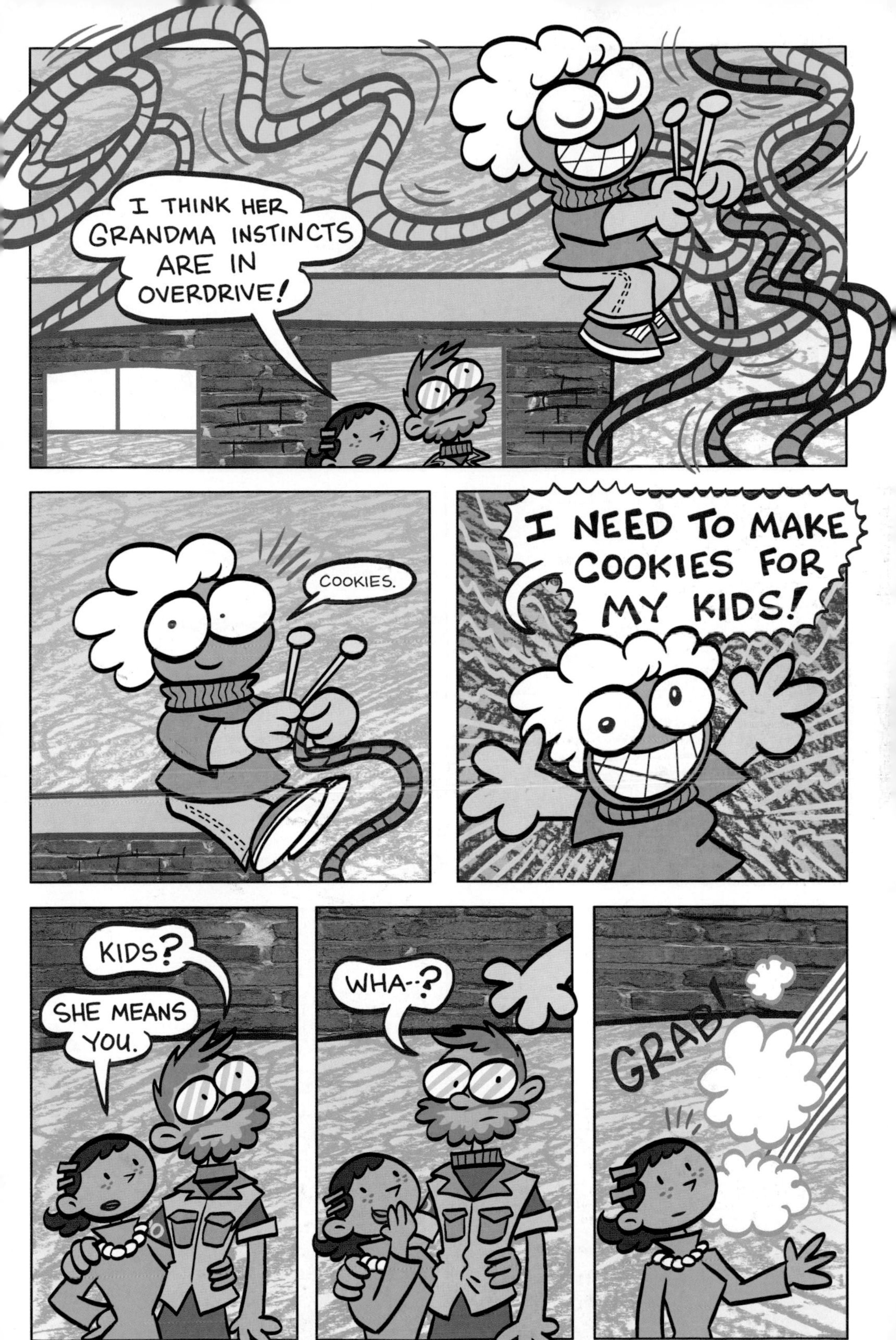
I THINK HER GRANDMA INSTINCTS ARE IN OVERDRIVE!
COOKIES.
I NEED TO MAKE COOKIES FOR MY KIDS!
KIDS?
SHE MEANS YOU.
WHA--?
GRAB!

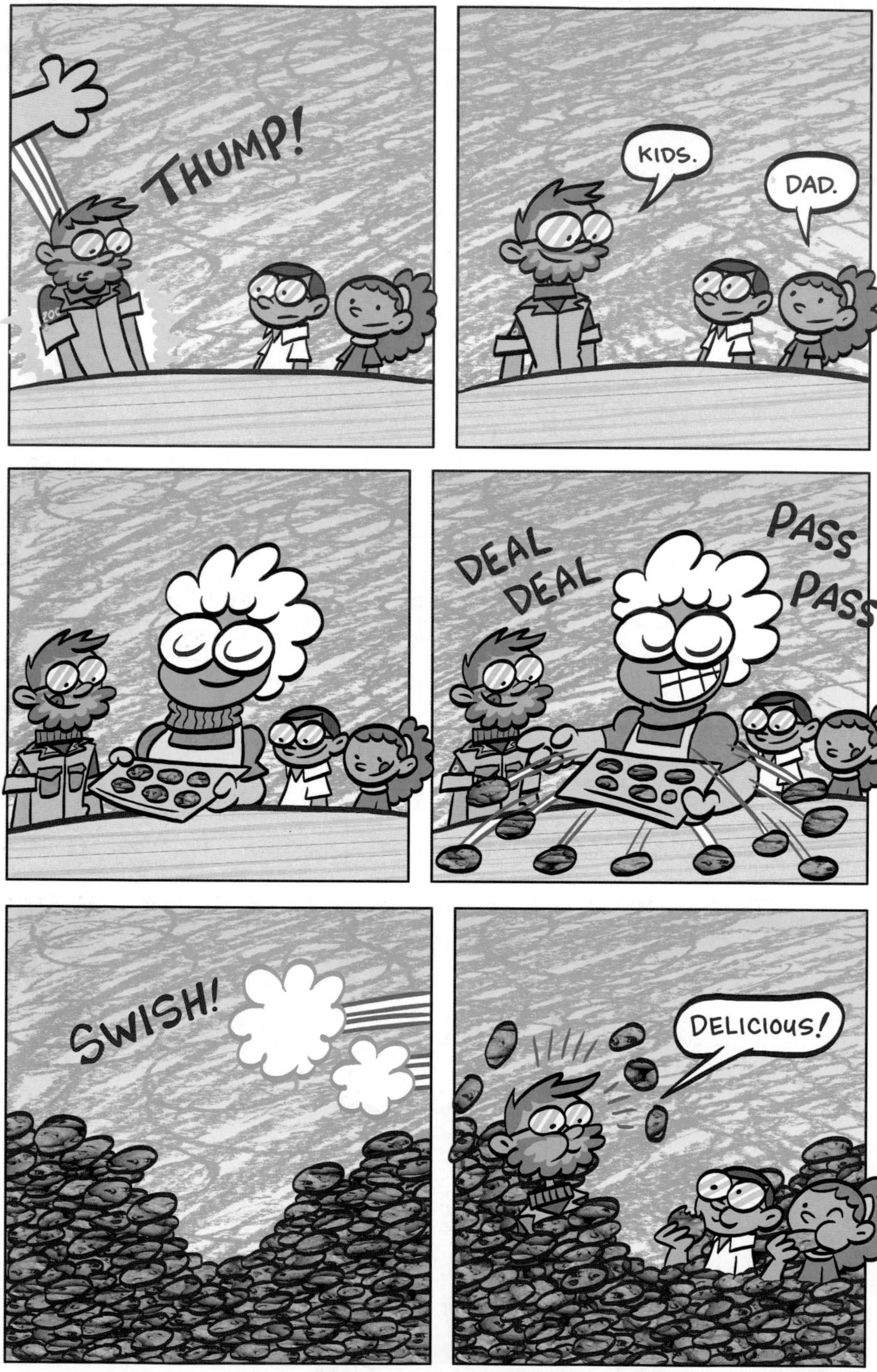
THUMP!
KIDS.
DAD.
DEAL
DEAL
PASS
PASS
SWISH!
DELICIOUS!

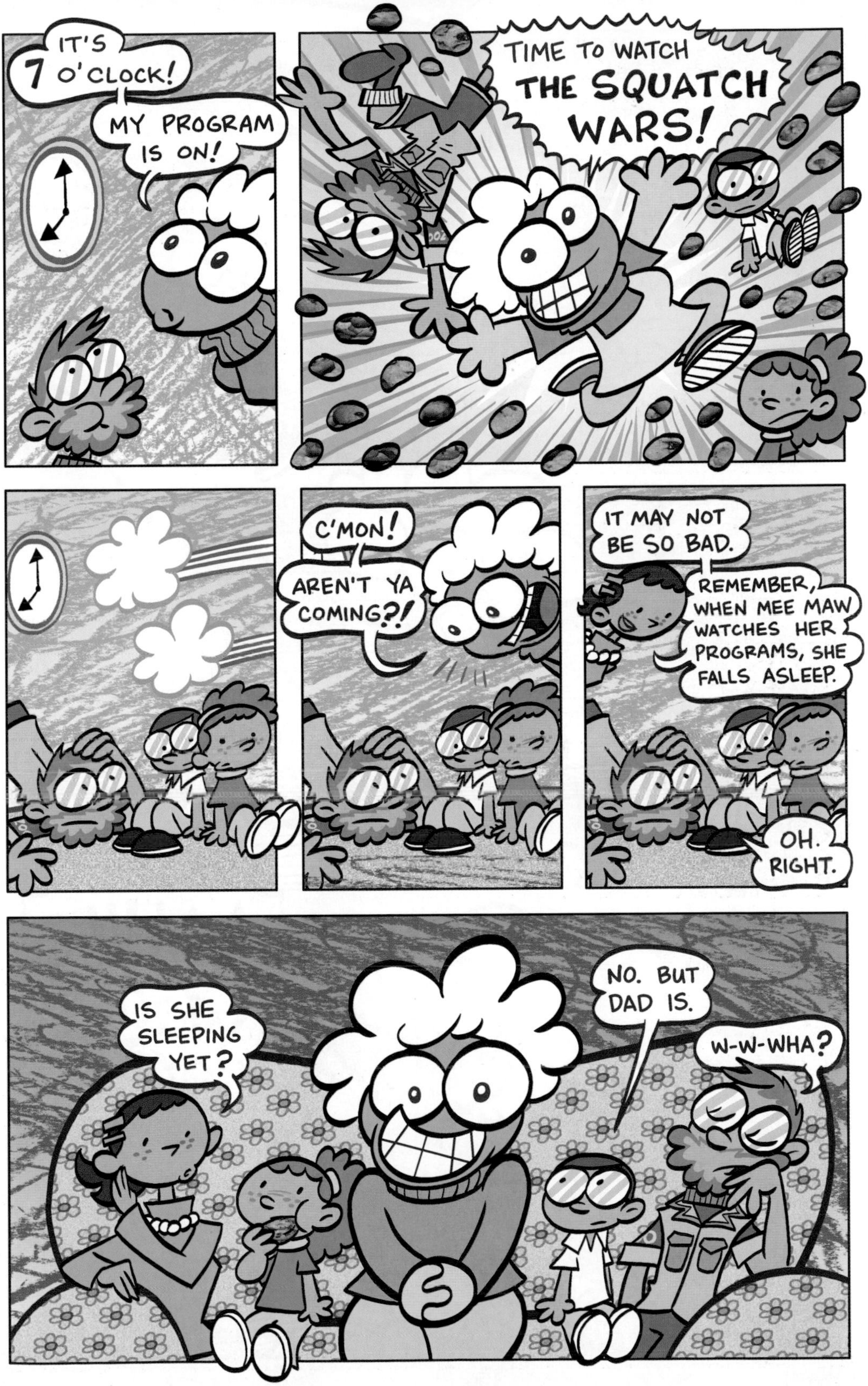
IT'S 7 O'CLOCK!
MY PROGRAM IS ON!
TIME TO WATCH THE SQUATCH WARS!
C'MON!
AREN'T YA COMING?!
IT MAY NOT BE SO BAD.
REMEMBER, WHEN MEE MAW WATCHES HER PROGRAMS, SHE FALLS ASLEEP.
OH. RIGHT.
IS SHE SLEEPING YET?
NO. BUT DAD IS.
W-W-WHA?

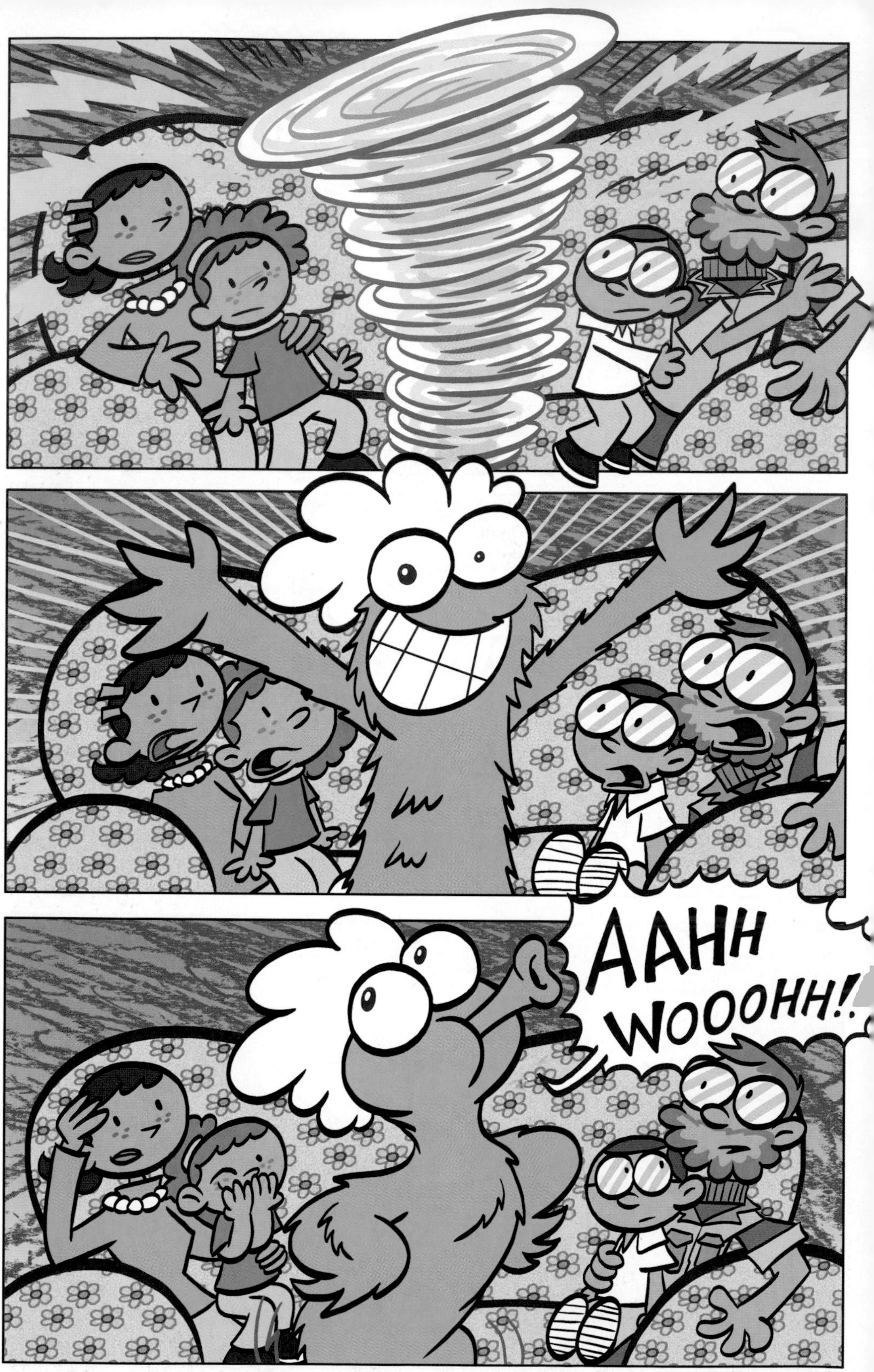
AAHH WOOOHH!!

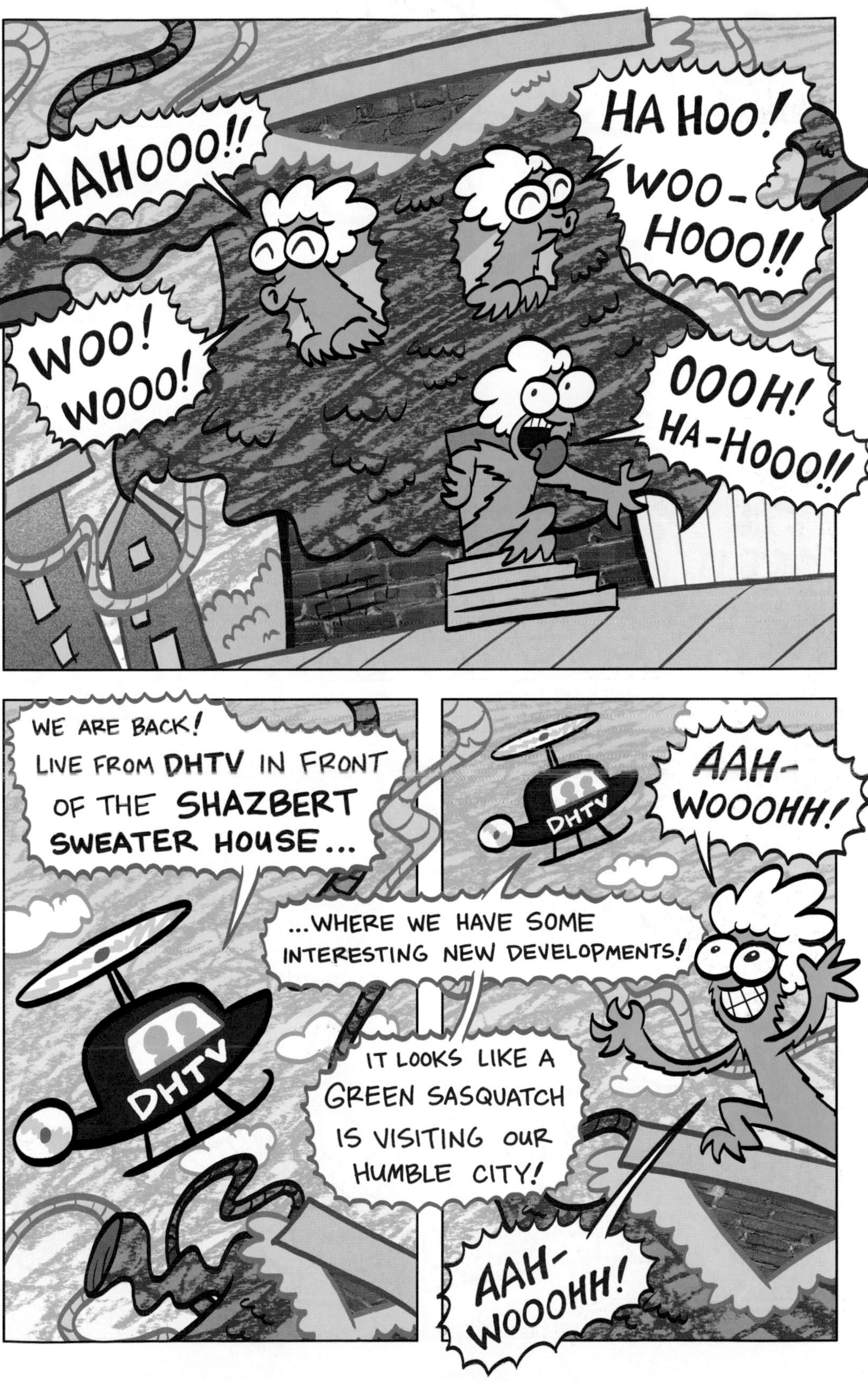
AAHOOO!!
HA HOO! WOO-HOOO!!
WOO! WOOO!
OOOH! HA-HOOO!!
WE ARE BACK! LIVE FROM DHTV IN FRONT OF THE SHAZBERT SWEATER HOUSE...
DHTV
AAH-WOOOHH!
DHTV
...WHERE WE HAVE SOME INTERESTING NEW DEVELOPMENTS!
IT LOOKS LIKE A GREEN SASQUATCH IS VISITING OUR HUMBLE CITY!
AAH-WOOOHH!

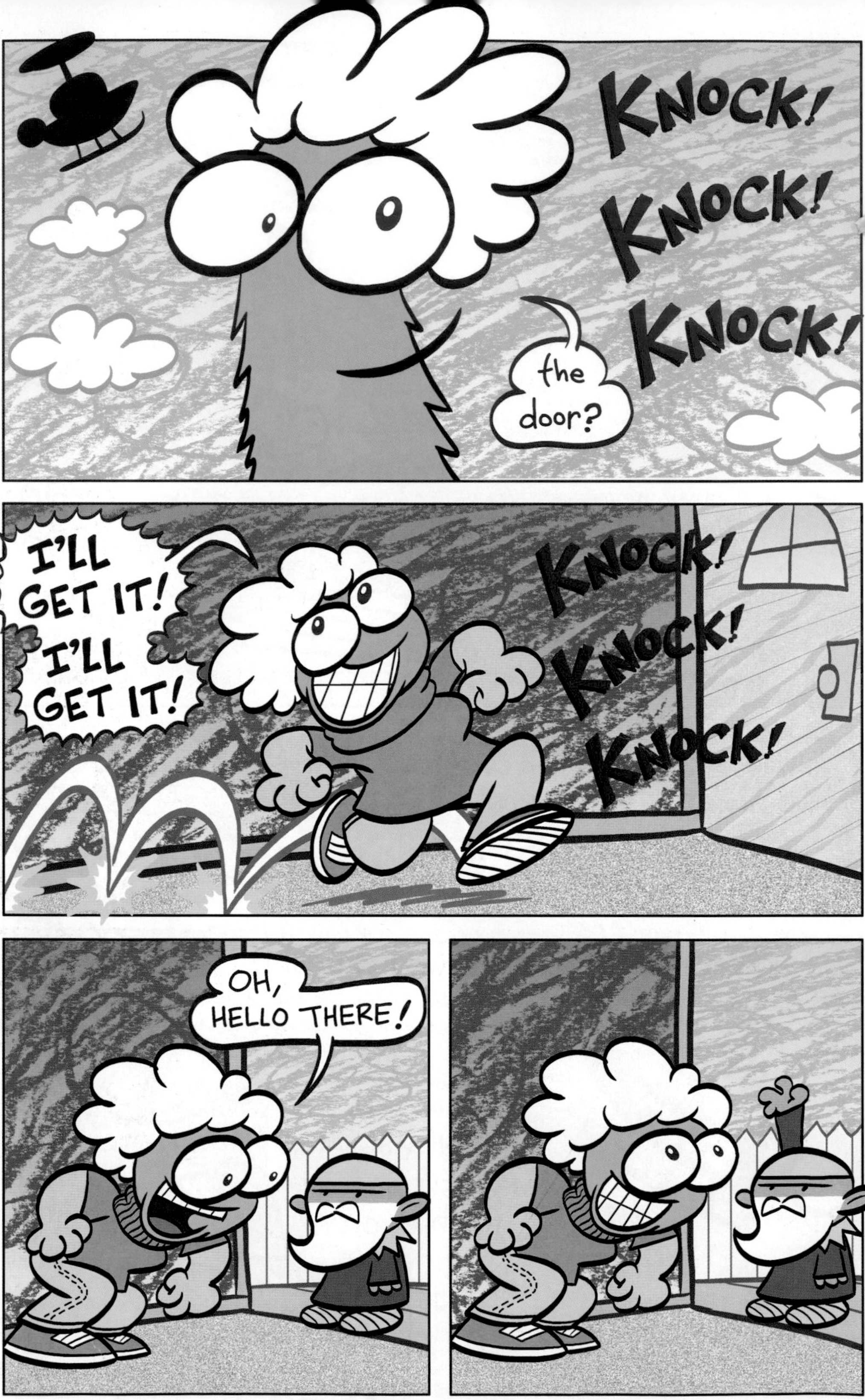
KNOCK! KNOCK! KNOCK!
the door?
I'LL GET IT! I'LL GET IT!
KNOCK! KNOCK! KNOCK!
OH, HELLO THERE!

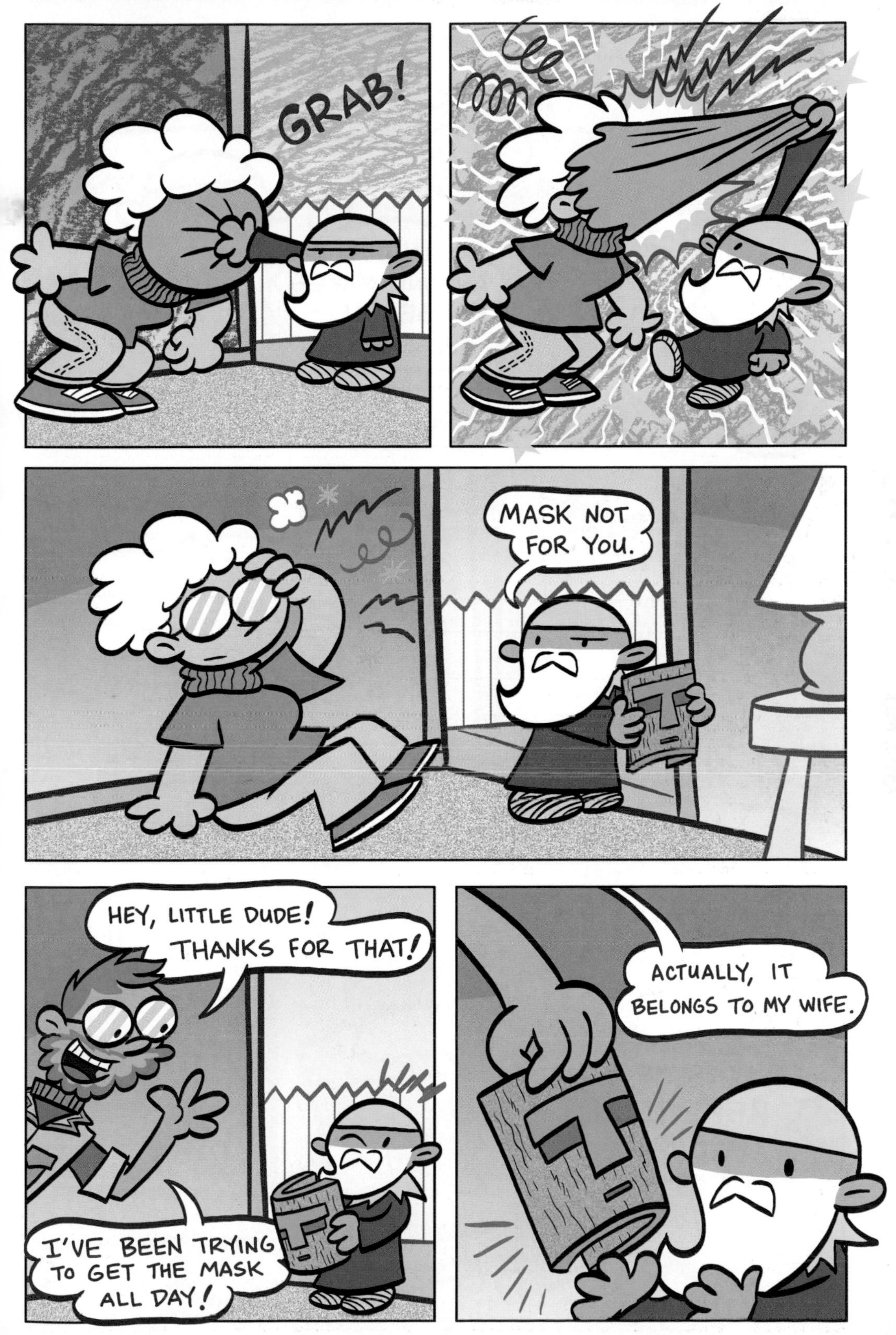
GRAB!
MASK NOT FOR YOU.
HEY, LITTLE DUDE! THANKS FOR THAT!
I'VE BEEN TRYING TO GET THE MASK ALL DAY!
ACTUALLY, IT BELONGS TO MY WIFE.

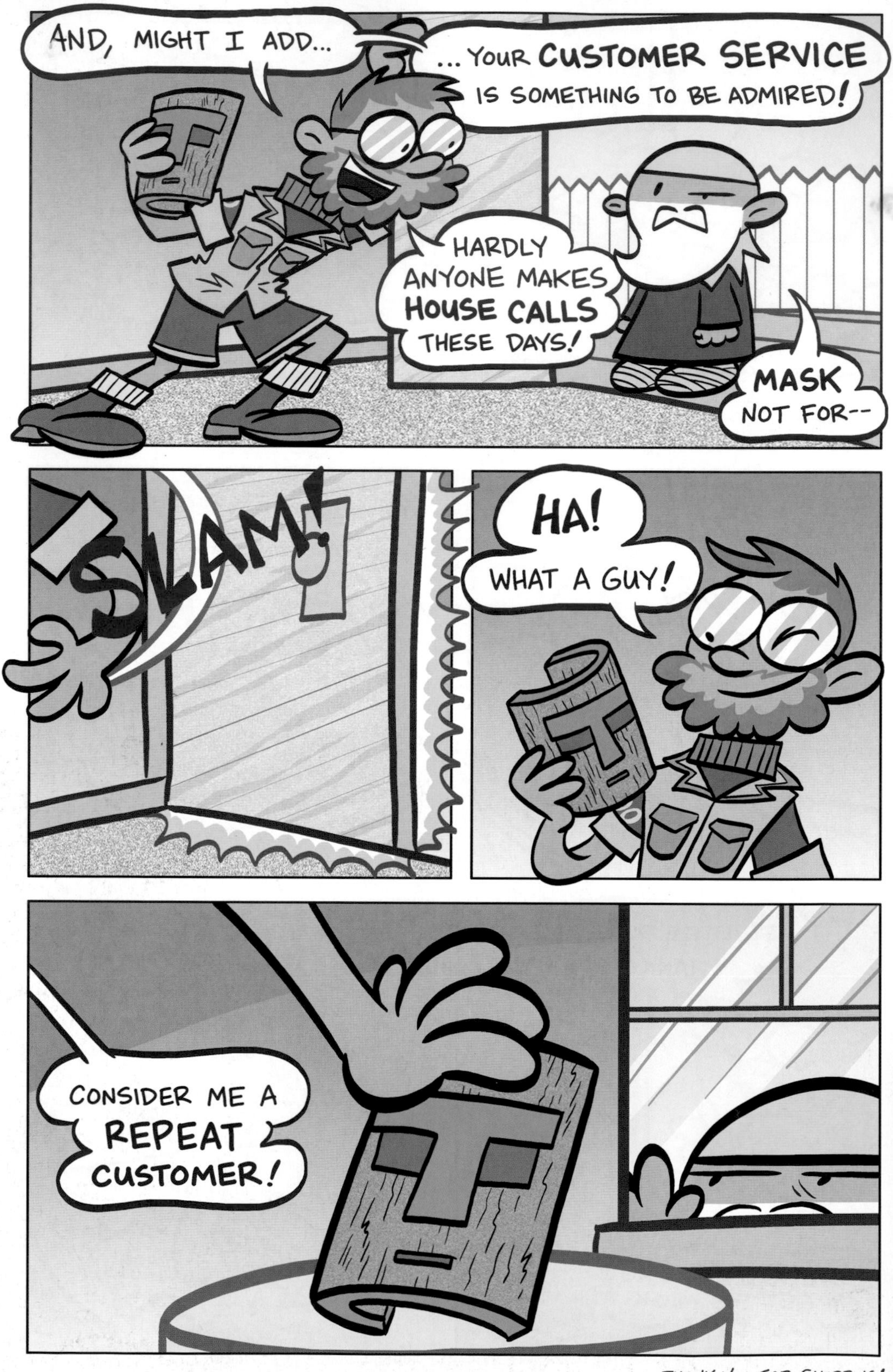
AND, MIGHT I ADD...
... YOUR CUSTOMER SERVICE IS SOMETHING TO BE ADMIRED!
HARDLY ANYONE MAKES HOUSE CALLS THESE DAYS!
MASK NOT FOR--
SLAM!
HA! WHAT A GUY!
CONSIDER ME A REPEAT CUSTOMER!

-THANK YOU FOR SHOPPING!

CHAPTER TWO

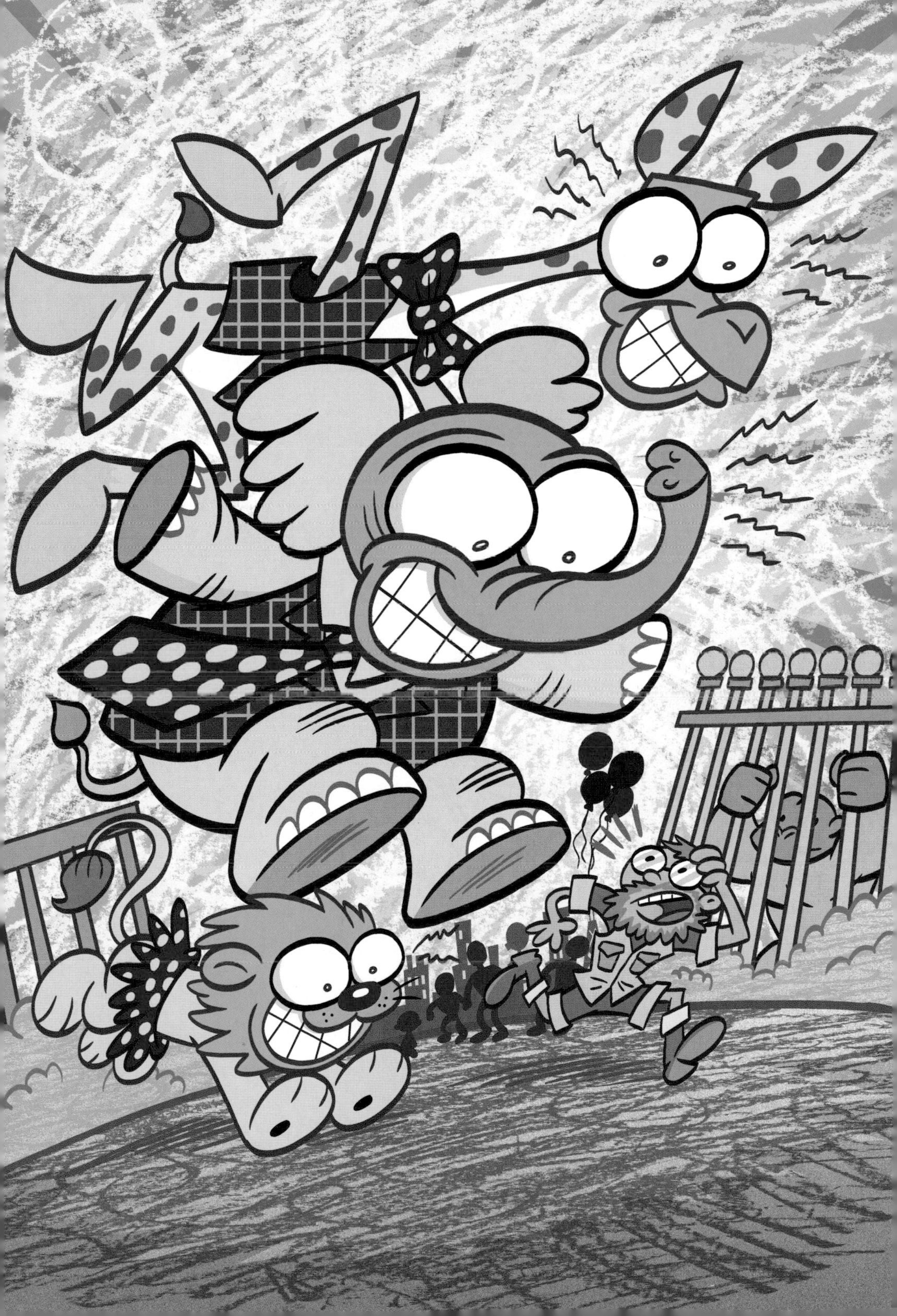

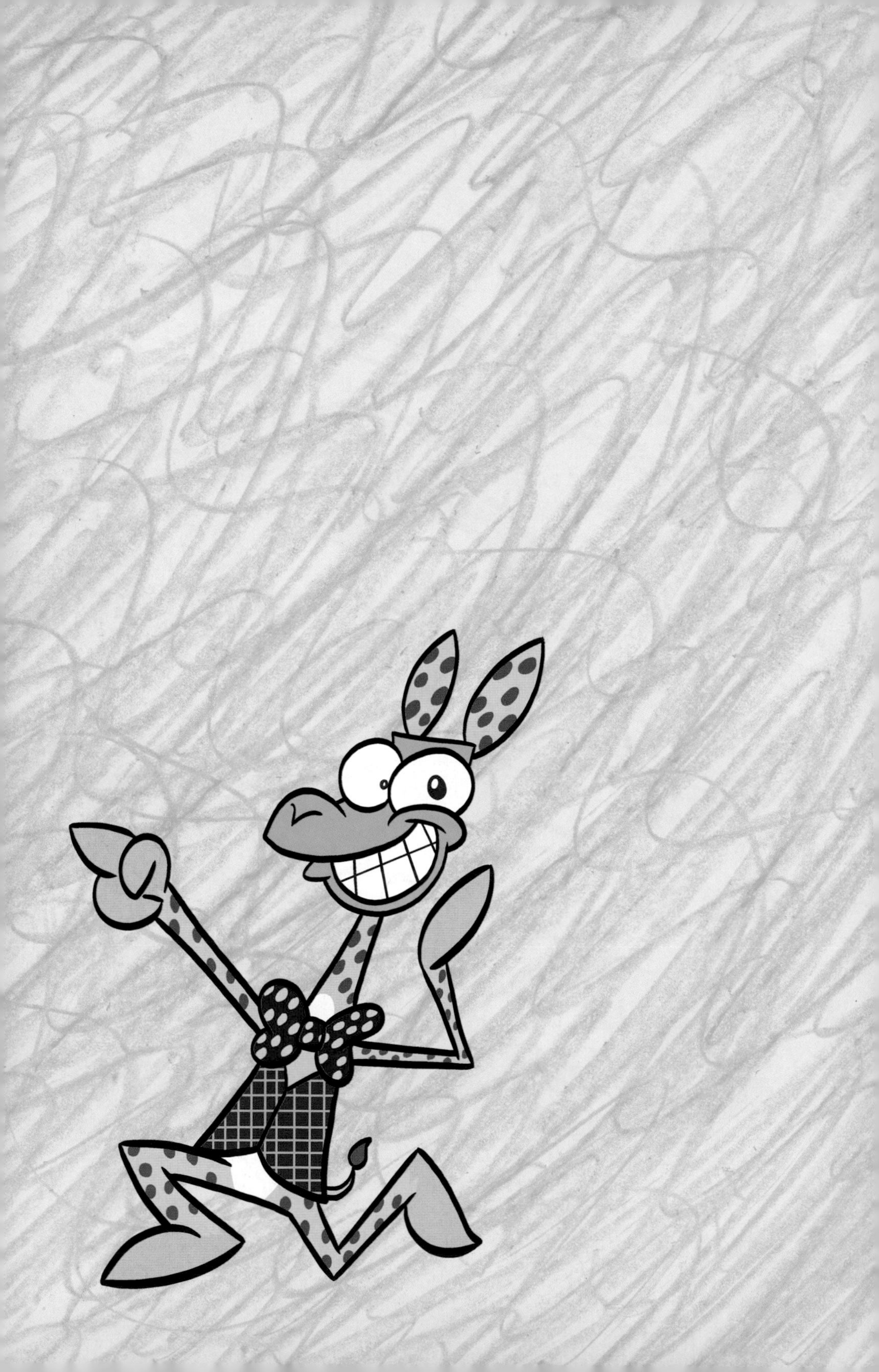

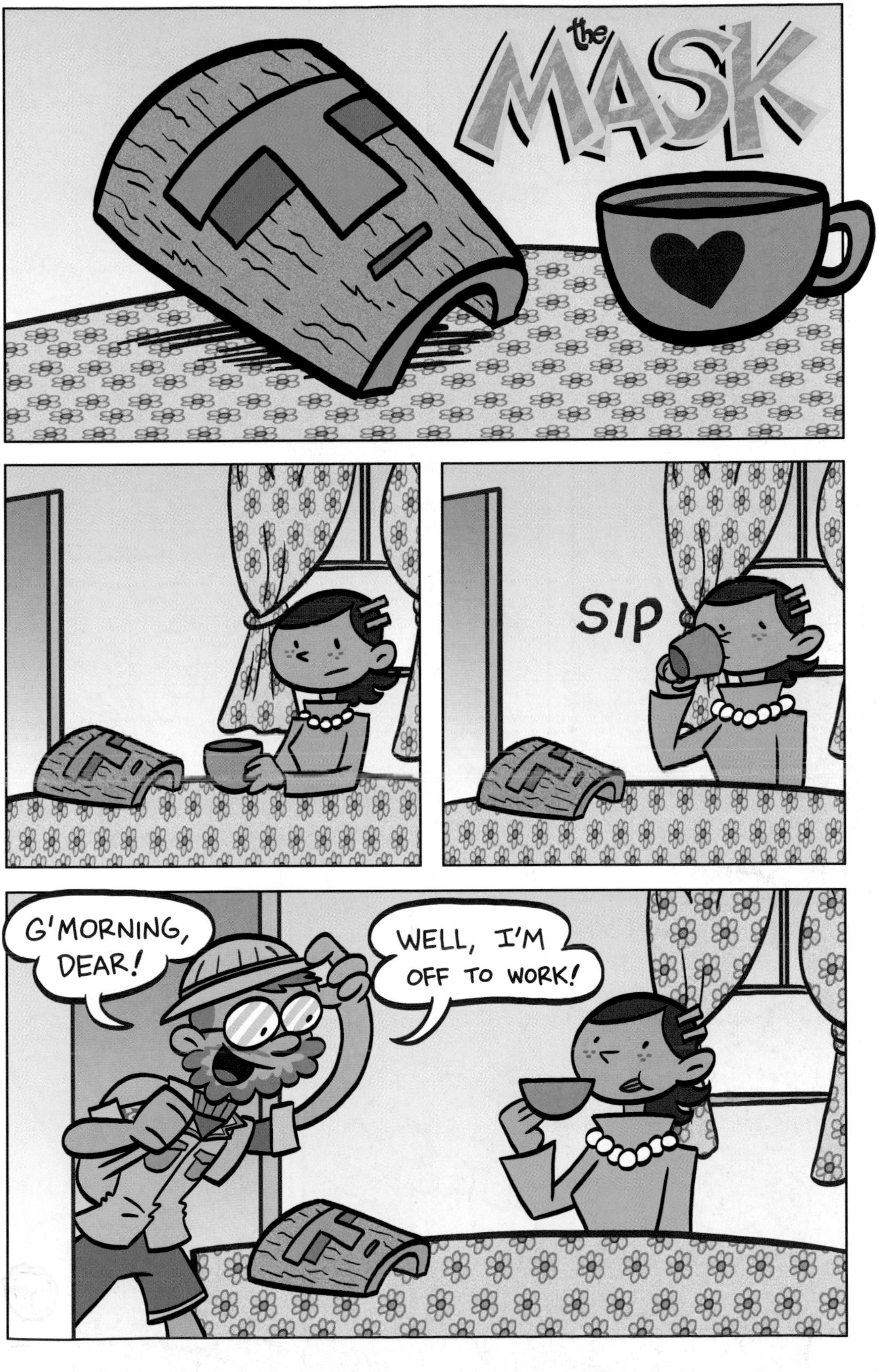
the MASK
SIP
G'MORNING, DEAR!
WELL, I'M OFF TO WORK!

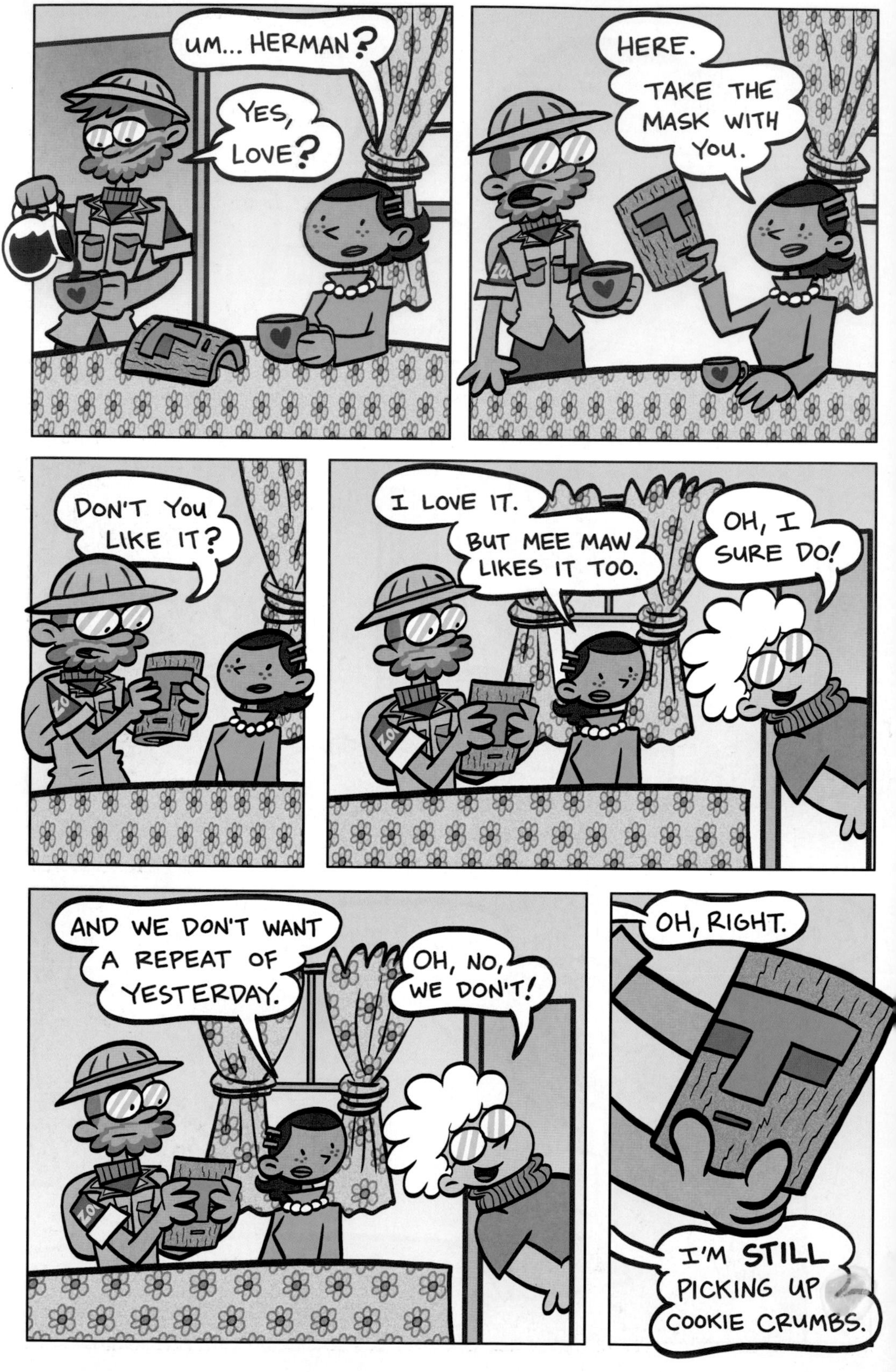
UM... HERMAN?
YES, LOVE?
HERE.
TAKE THE MASK WITH YOU.
DON'T YOU LIKE IT?
I LOVE IT.
BUT MEE MAW LIKES IT TOO.
OH, I SURE DO!
AND WE DON'T WANT A REPEAT OF YESTERDAY.
OH, NO, WE DON'T!
OH, RIGHT.
I'M **STILL** PICKING UP COOKIE CRUMBS.

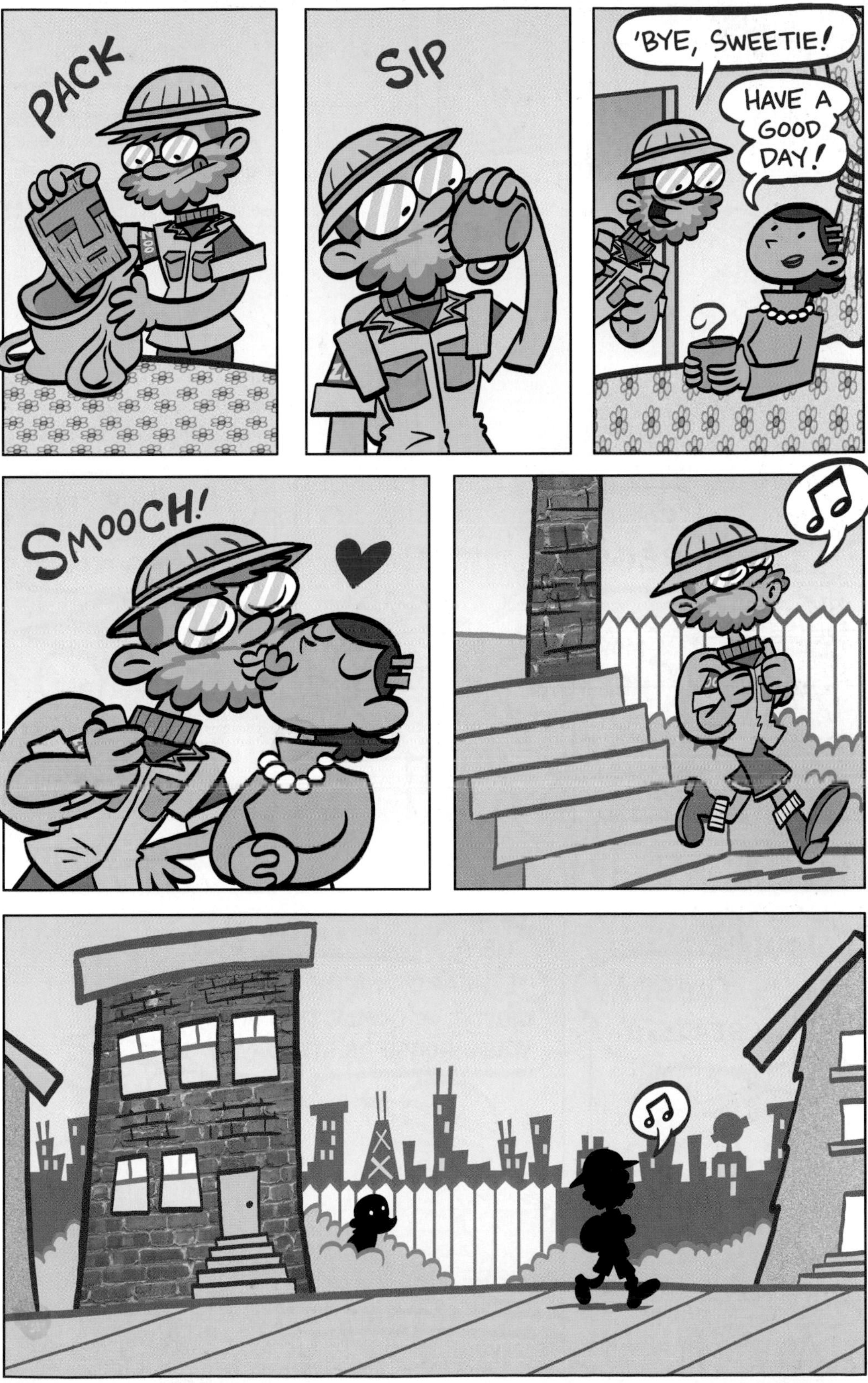
PACK
SIP
'BYE, SWEETIE!
HAVE A GOOD DAY!
SMOOCH!

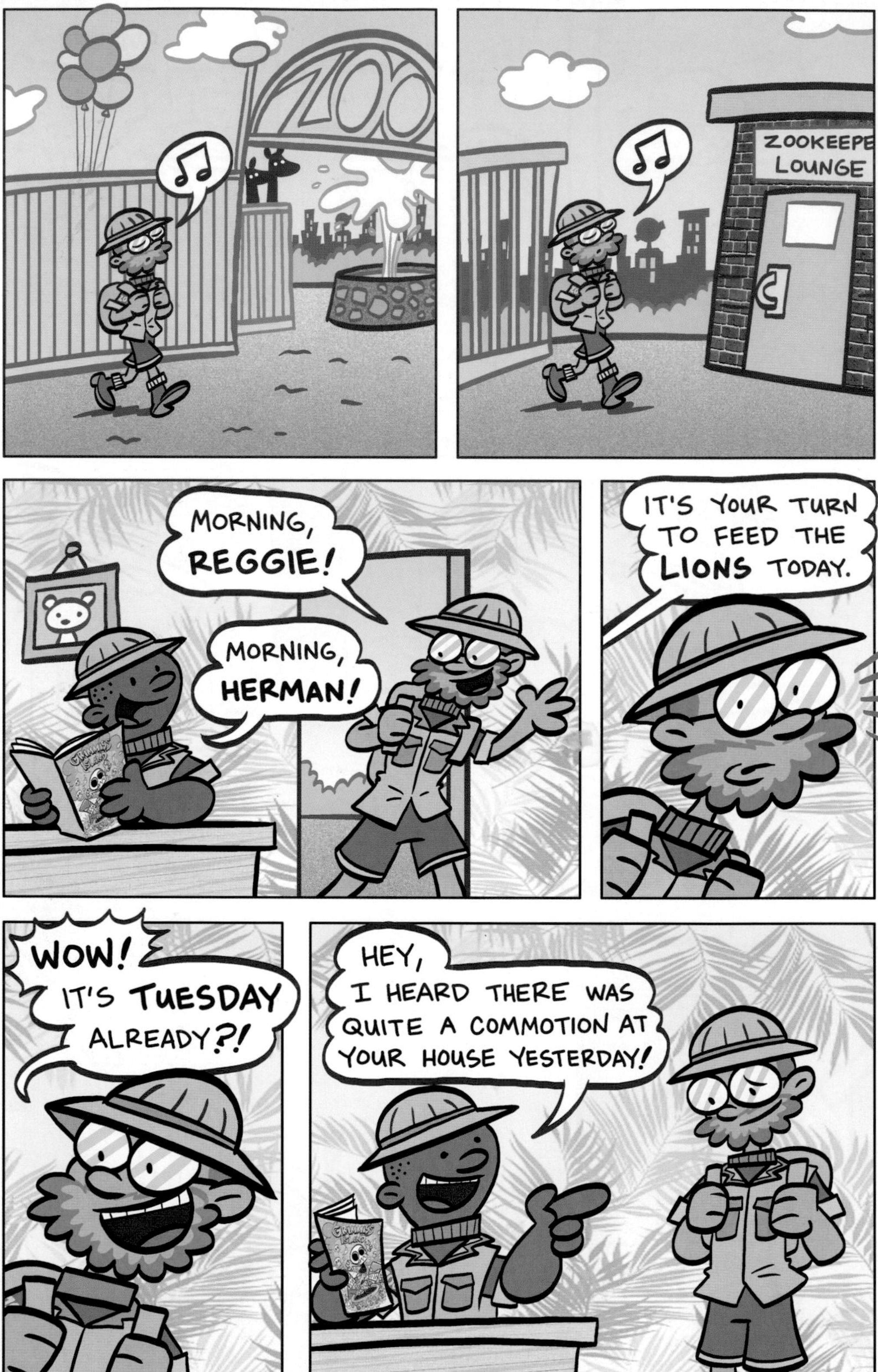
ZOO
ZOOKEEPE
LOUNGE
MORNING, REGGIE!
MORNING, HERMAN!
IT'S YOUR TURN TO FEED THE LIONS TODAY.
WOW! IT'S TUESDAY ALREADY?!
HEY, I HEARD THERE WAS QUITE A COMMOTION AT YOUR HOUSE YESTERDAY!

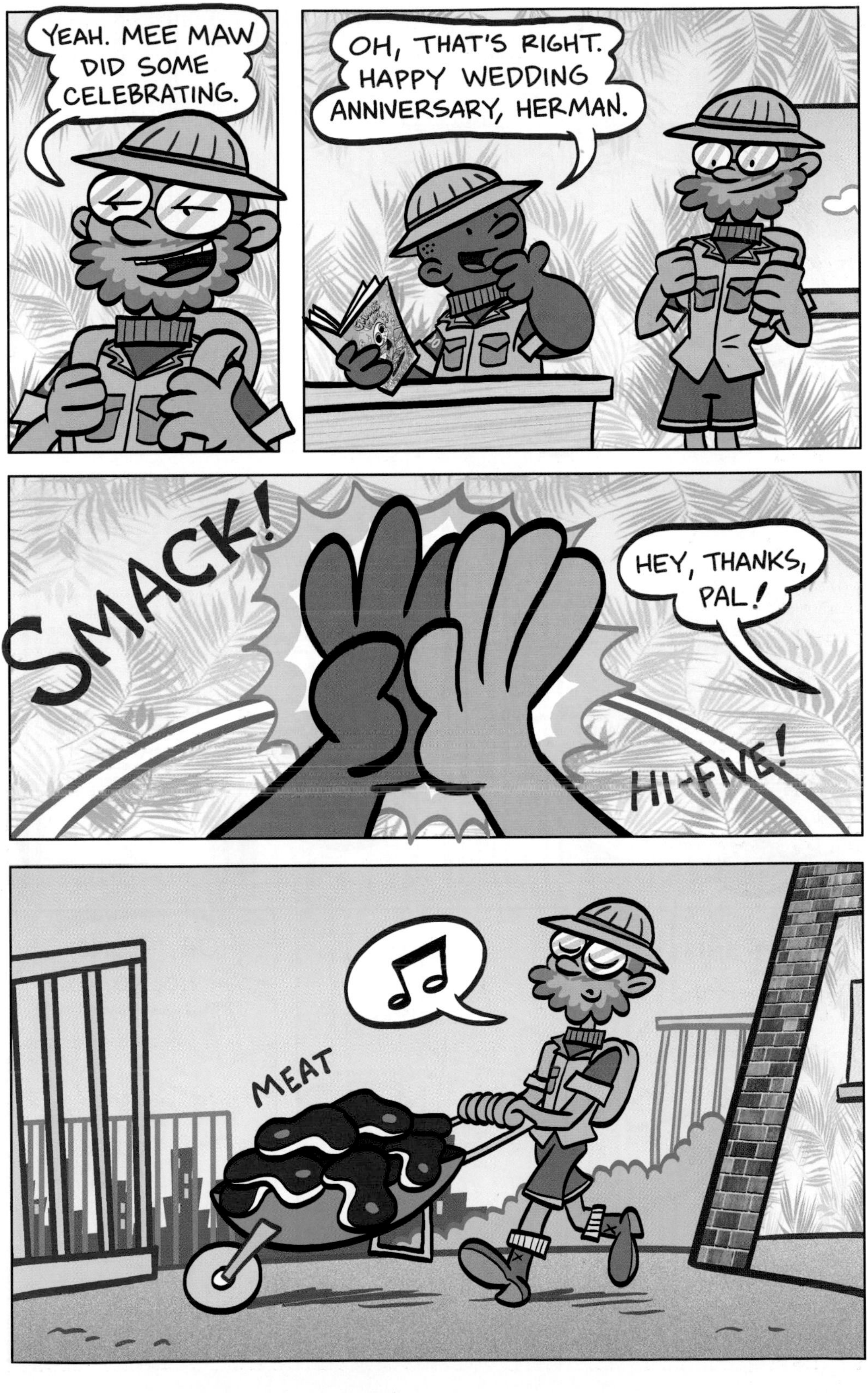
YEAH. MEE MAW DID SOME CELEBRATING.
OH, THAT'S RIGHT. HAPPY WEDDING ANNIVERSARY, HERMAN.
SMACK!
HEY, THANKS, PAL!
HI-FIVE!
MEAT

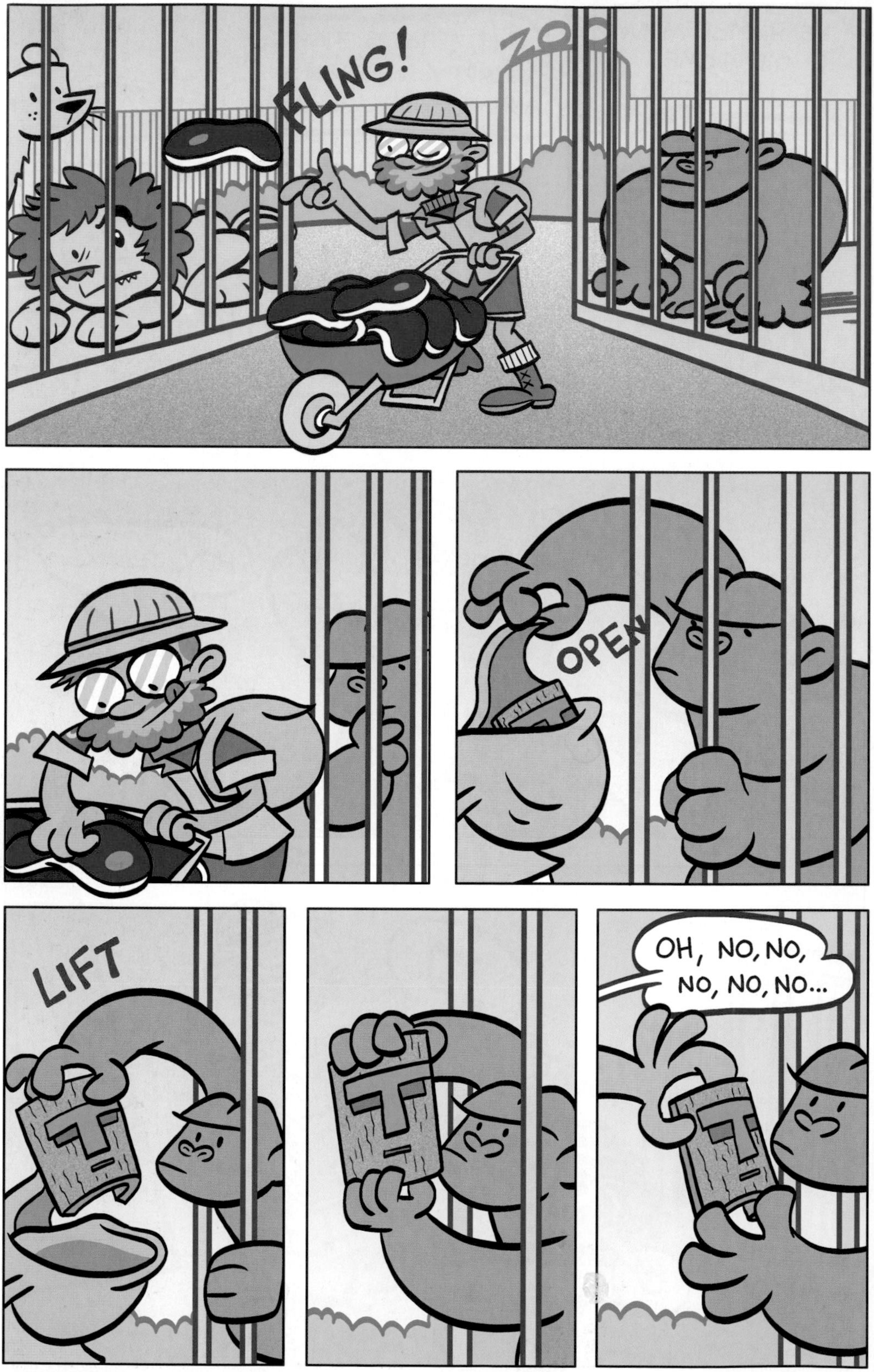
FLING!
ZOO
OPEN
LIFT
OH, NO, NO, NO, NO, NO...

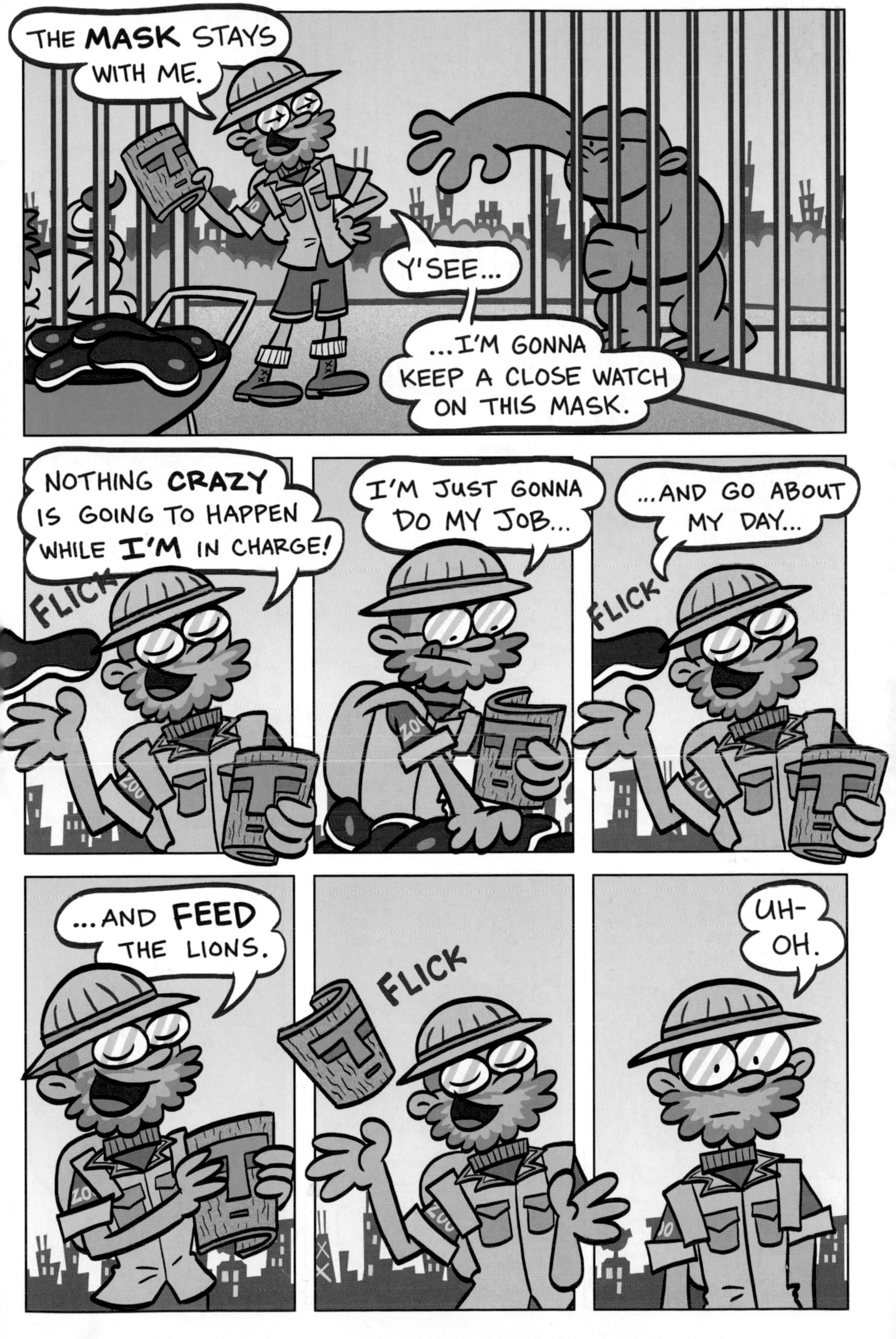
THE MASK STAYS WITH ME.
Y'SEE...
...I'M GONNA KEEP A CLOSE WATCH ON THIS MASK.
NOTHING CRAZY IS GOING TO HAPPEN WHILE I'M IN CHARGE!
FLICK
I'M JUST GONNA DO MY JOB...
...AND GO ABOUT MY DAY...
FLICK
...AND FEED THE LIONS.
FLICK
UH-OH.

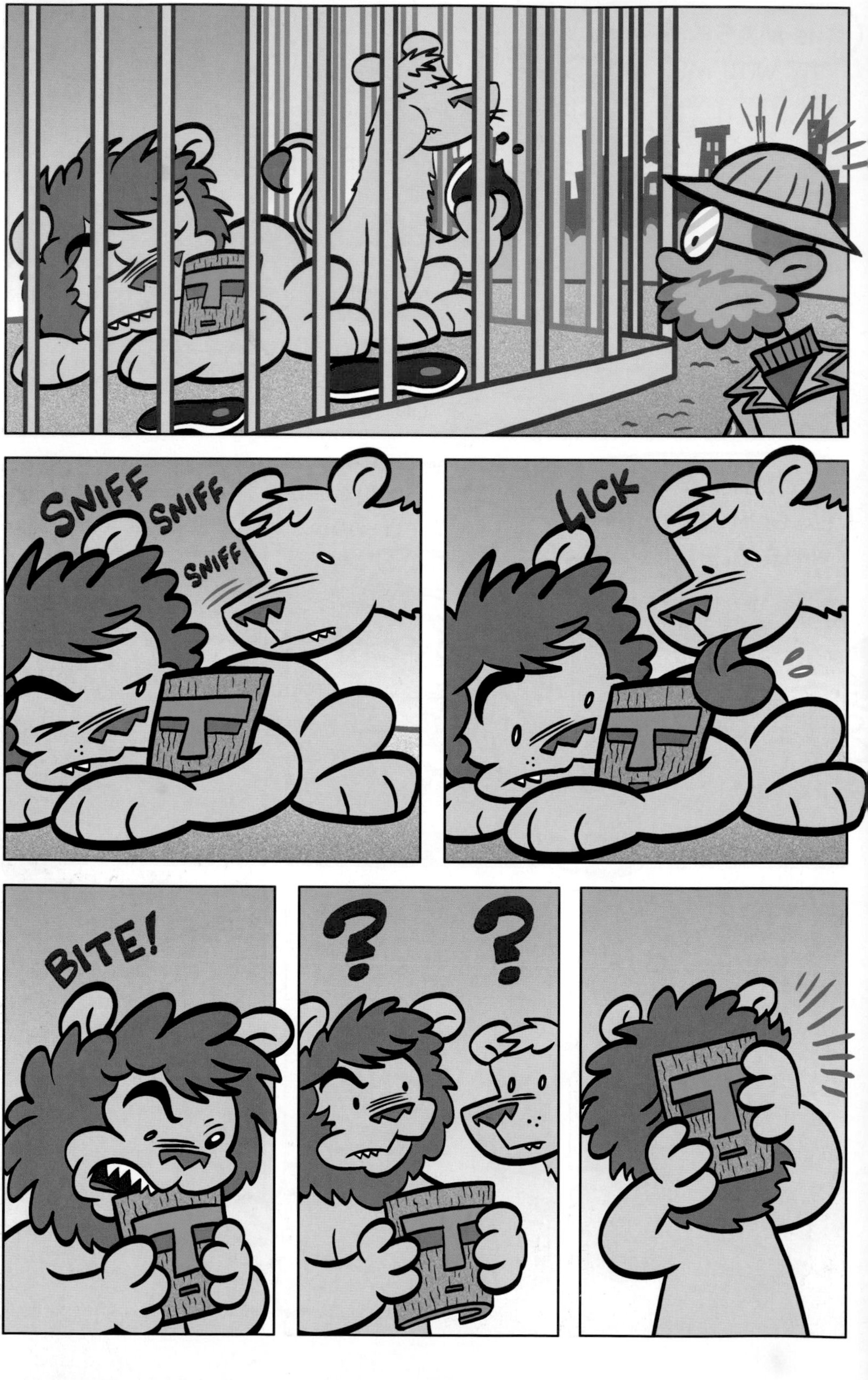
SNIFF
SNIFF
SNIFF
LICK
BITE!
?
?

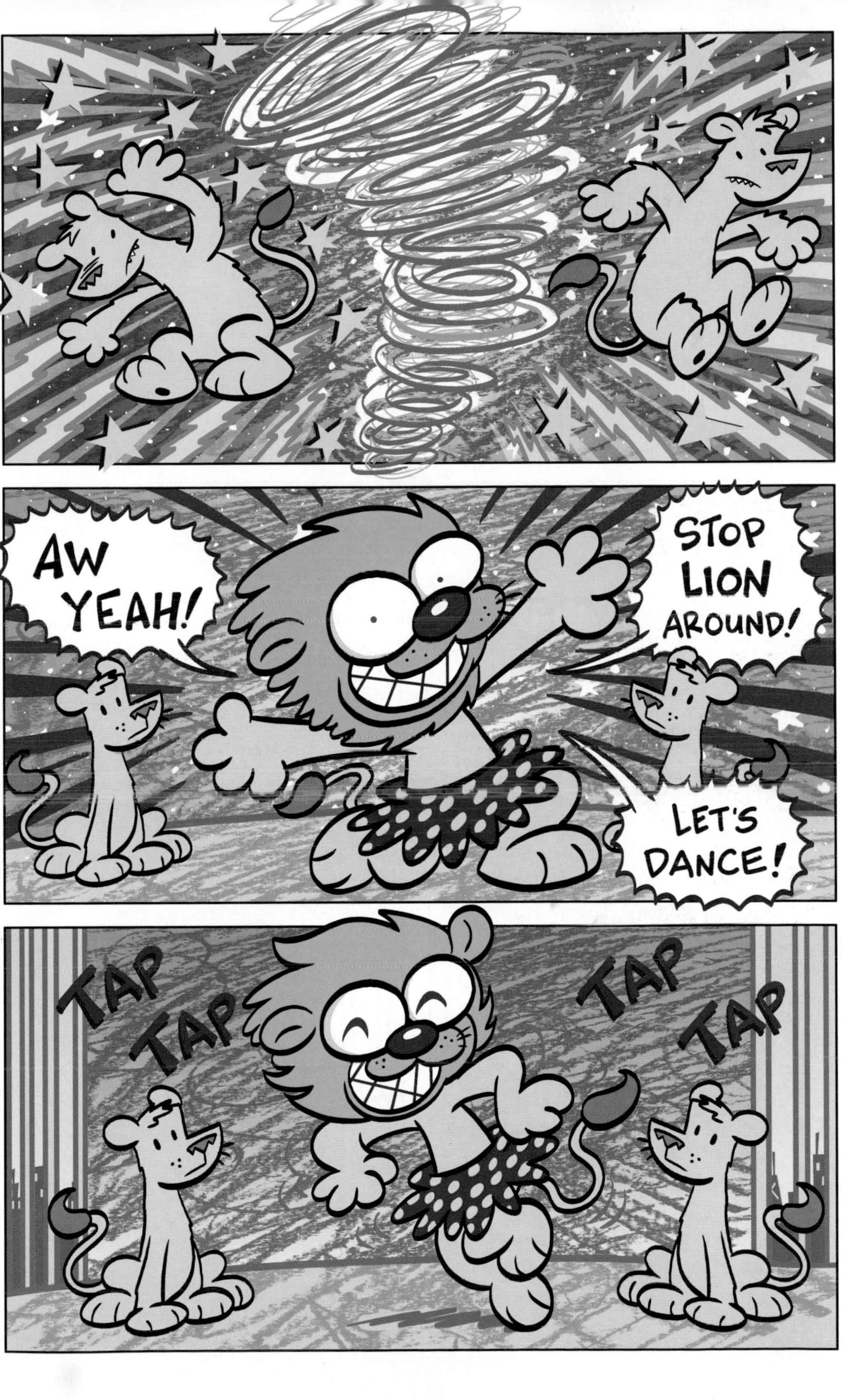
AW YEAH!
STOP LION AROUND!
LET'S DANCE!
TAP TAP
TAP TAP

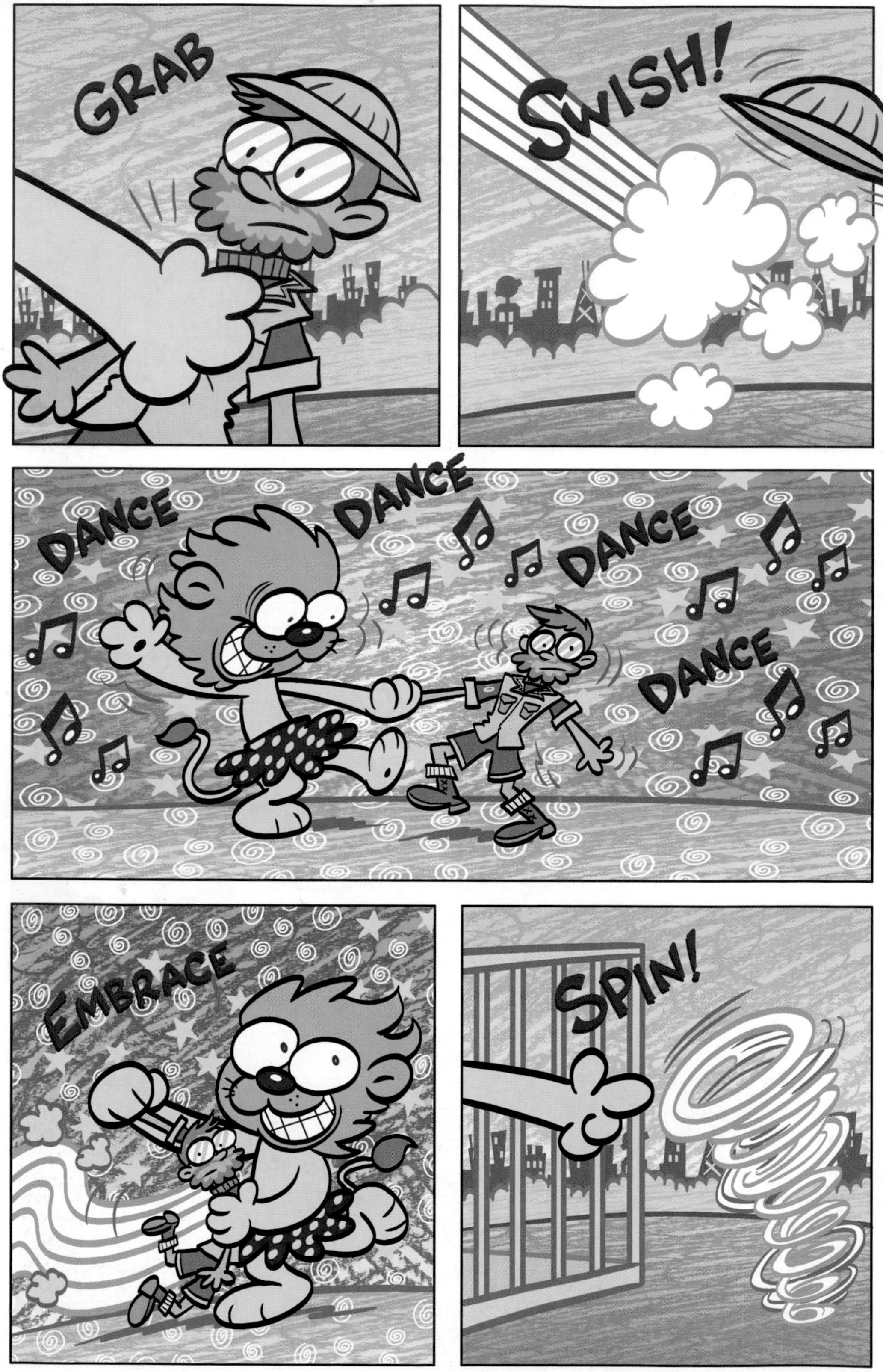
GRAB
SWISH!
DANCE
DANCE
DANCE
DANCE
EMBRACE
SPIN!

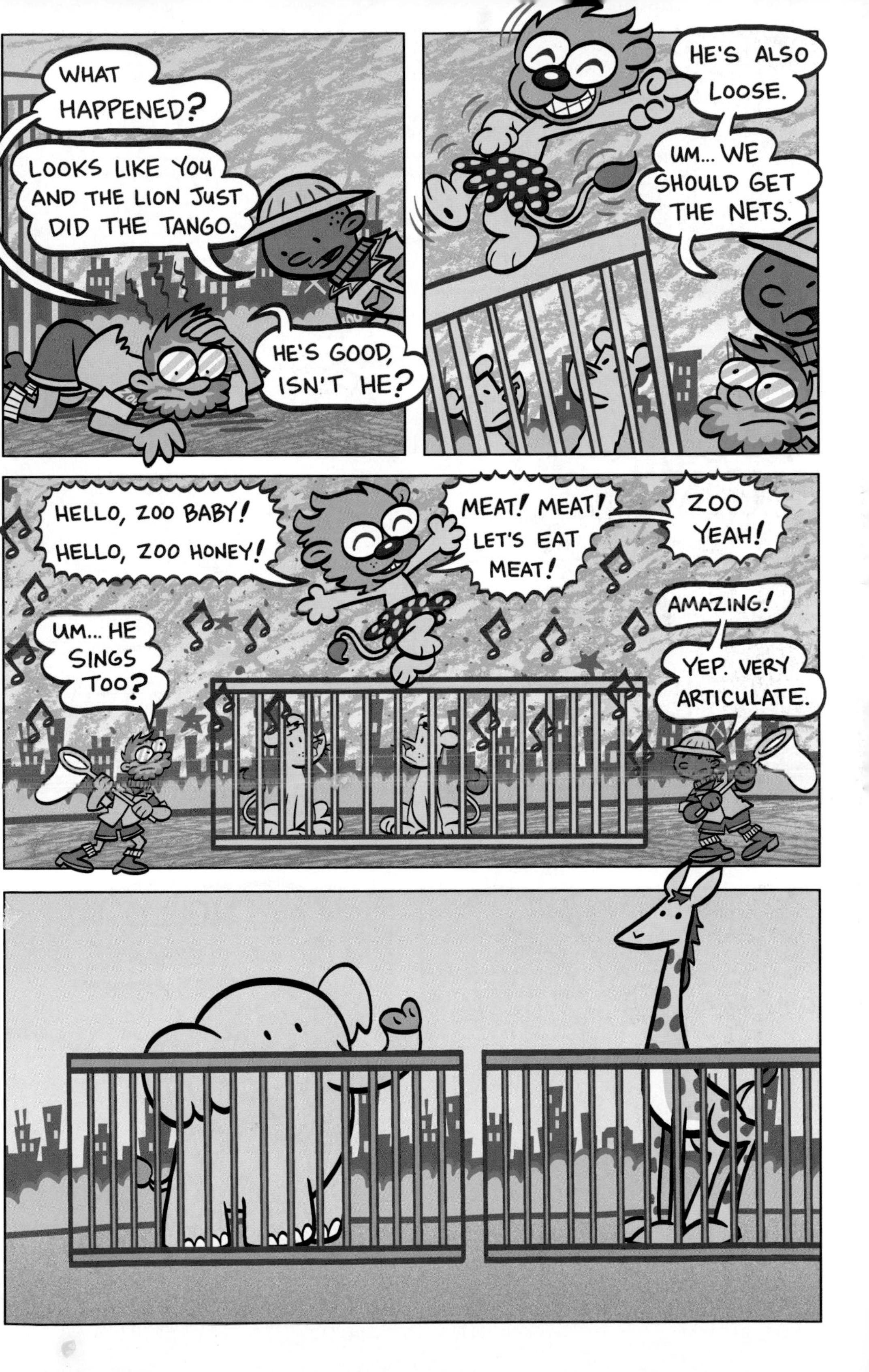
WHAT HAPPENED?
LOOKS LIKE YOU AND THE LION JUST DID THE TANGO.
HE'S GOOD, ISN'T HE?
HE'S ALSO LOOSE.
UM... WE SHOULD GET THE NETS.
HELLO, ZOO BABY!
HELLO, ZOO HONEY!
MEAT! MEAT! LET'S EAT MEAT!
ZOO YEAH!
UM... HE SINGS TOO?
AMAZING!
YEP. VERY ARTICULATE.

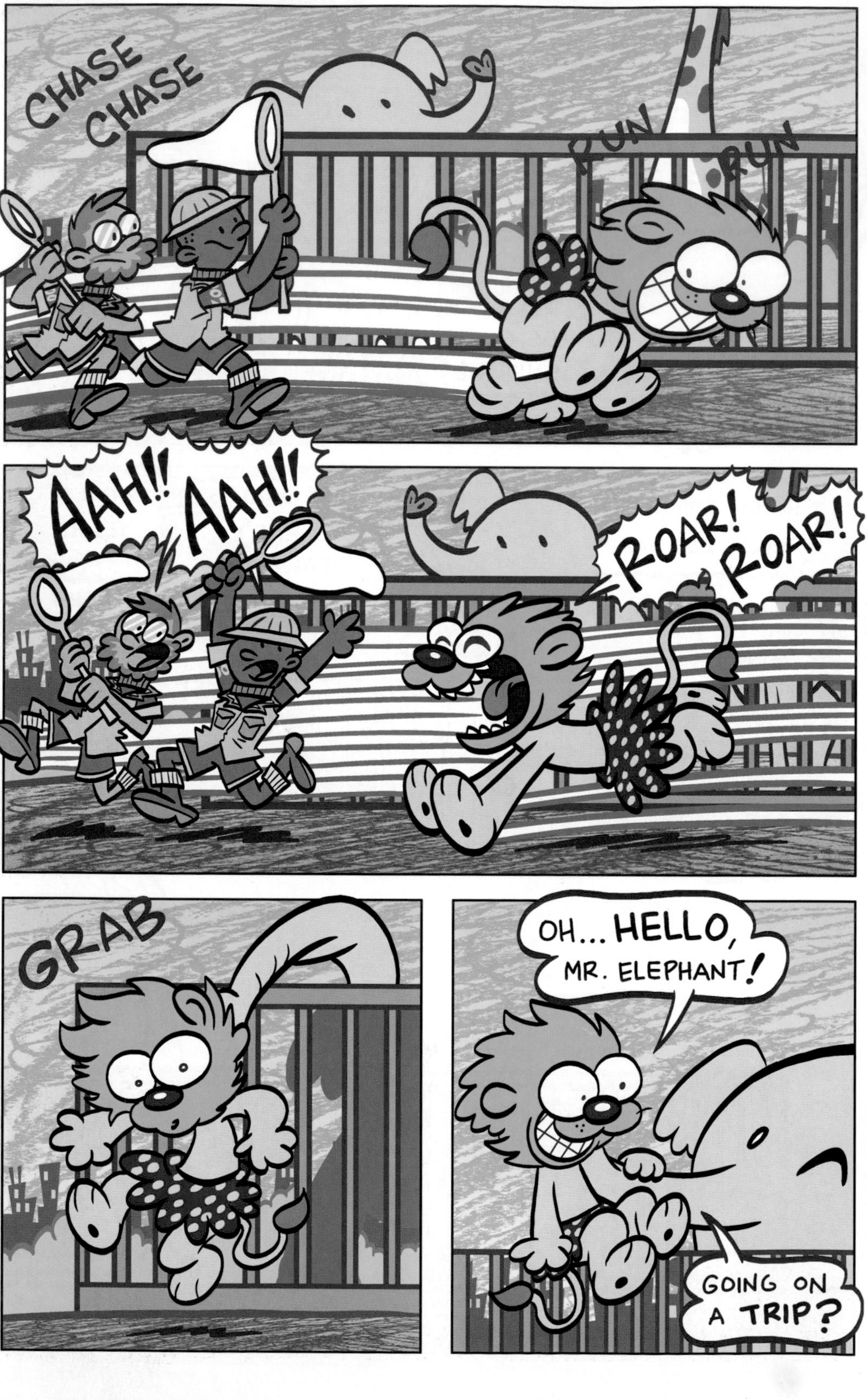
CHASE
CHASE
RUN
RUN
AAH!!
AAH!!
ROAR!
ROAR!
GRAB
OH... HELLO, MR. ELEPHANT!
GOING ON A TRIP?

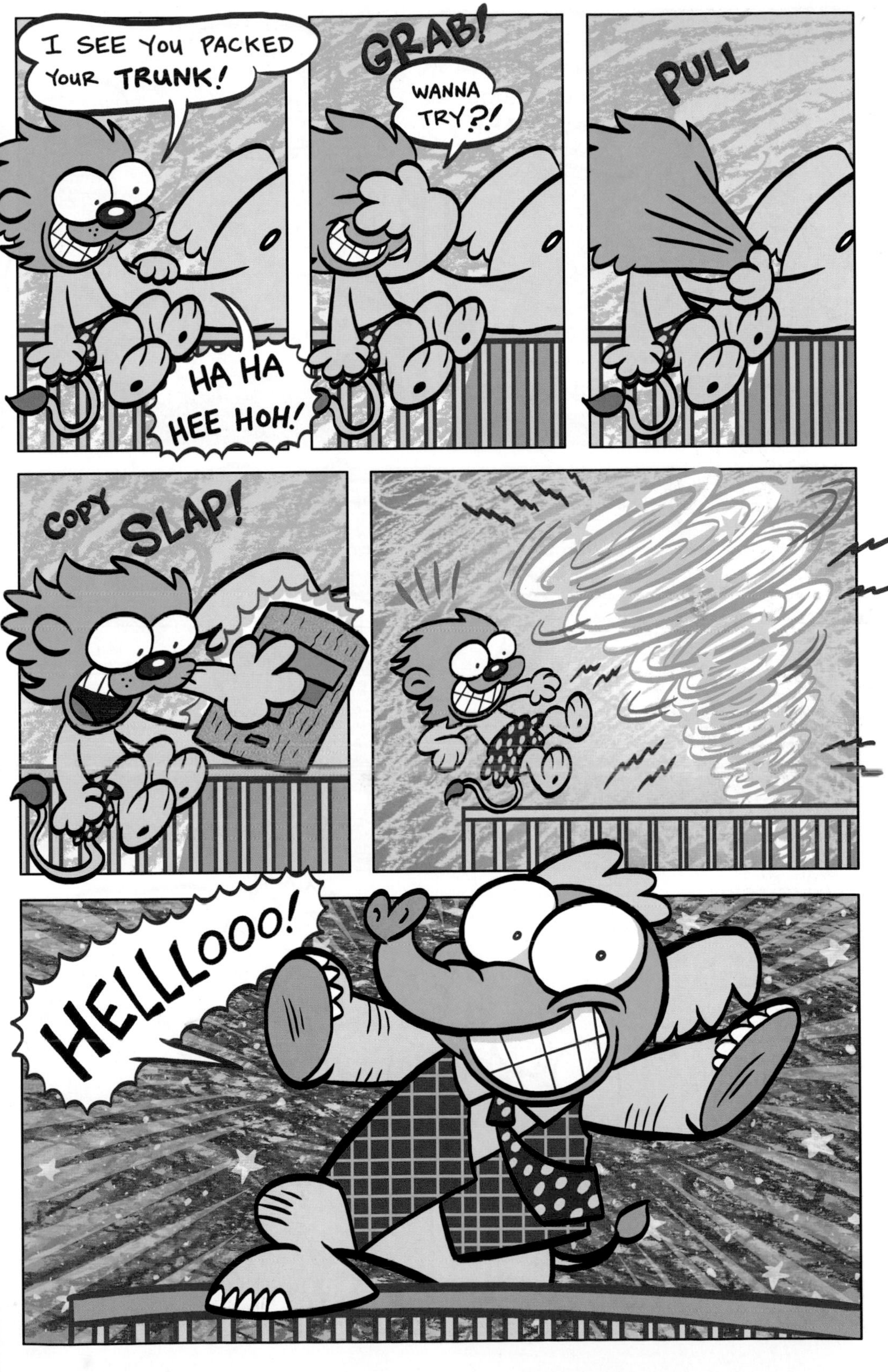
I SEE YOU PACKED YOUR TRUNK!
HA HA HEE HOH!
GRAB!
WANNA TRY?!
PULL
COPY
SLAP!
HELLLOOO!

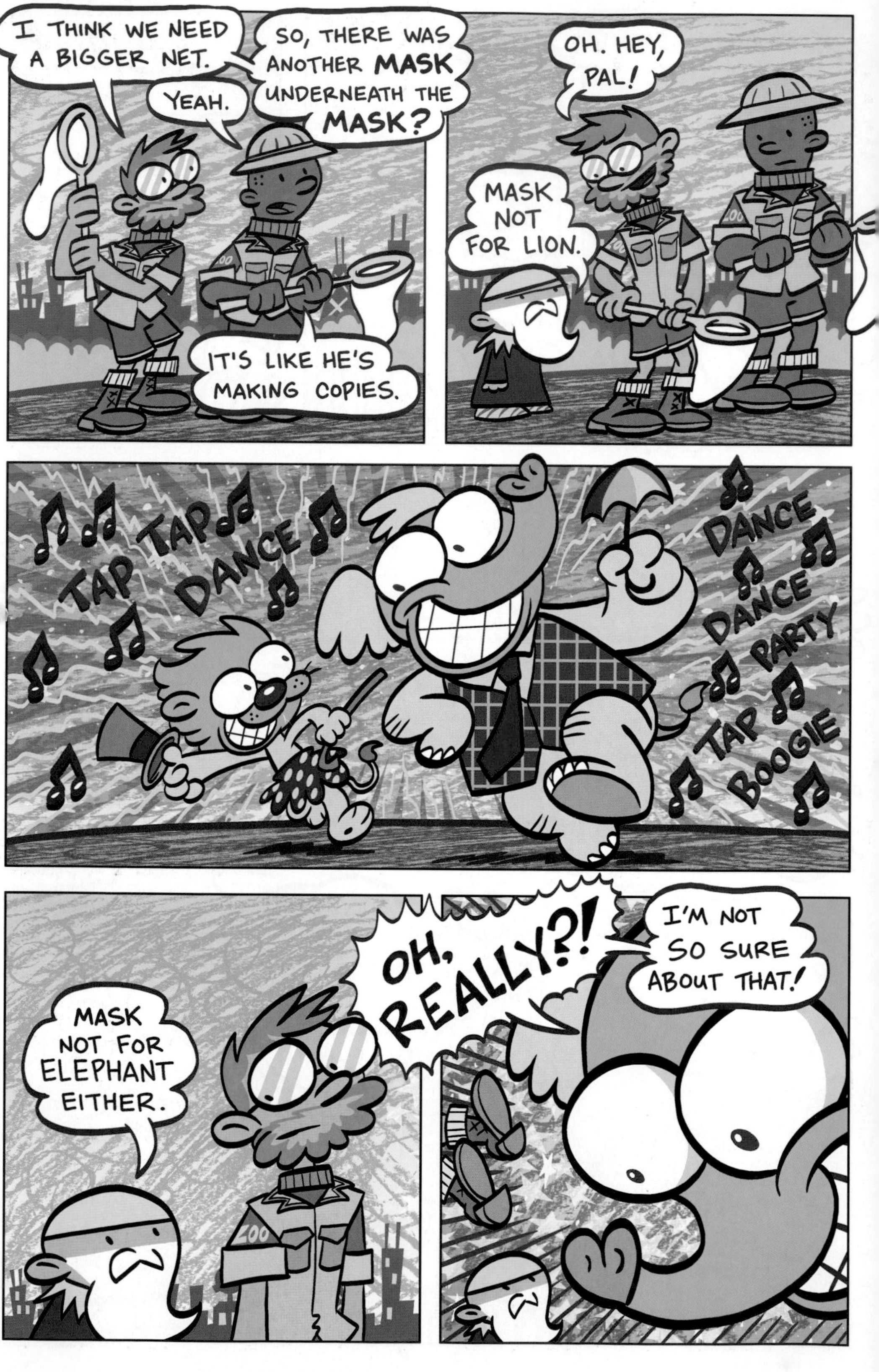
I THINK WE NEED A BIGGER NET.
YEAH.
SO, THERE WAS ANOTHER MASK UNDERNEATH THE MASK?
IT'S LIKE HE'S MAKING COPIES.
OH. HEY, PAL!
MASK NOT FOR LION.
TAP TAP DANCE
DANCE
DANCE
PARTY
TAP
BOOGIE
MASK NOT FOR ELEPHANT EITHER.
OH, REALLY?!
I'M NOT SO SURE ABOUT THAT!

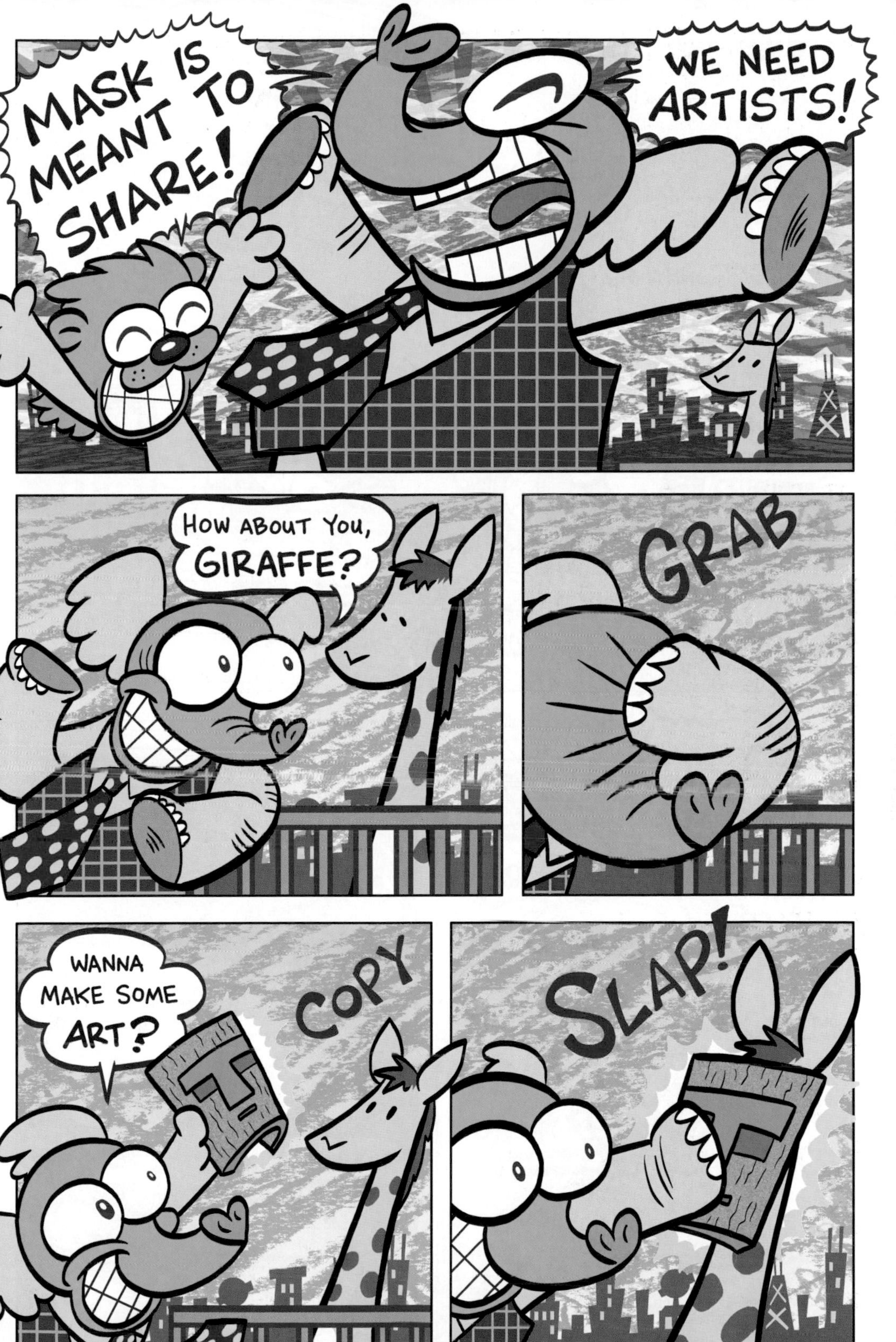
MASK IS MEANT TO SHARE!
WE NEED ARTISTS!
HOW ABOUT YOU, GIRAFFE?
GRAB
WANNA MAKE SOME ART?
COPY
SLAP!

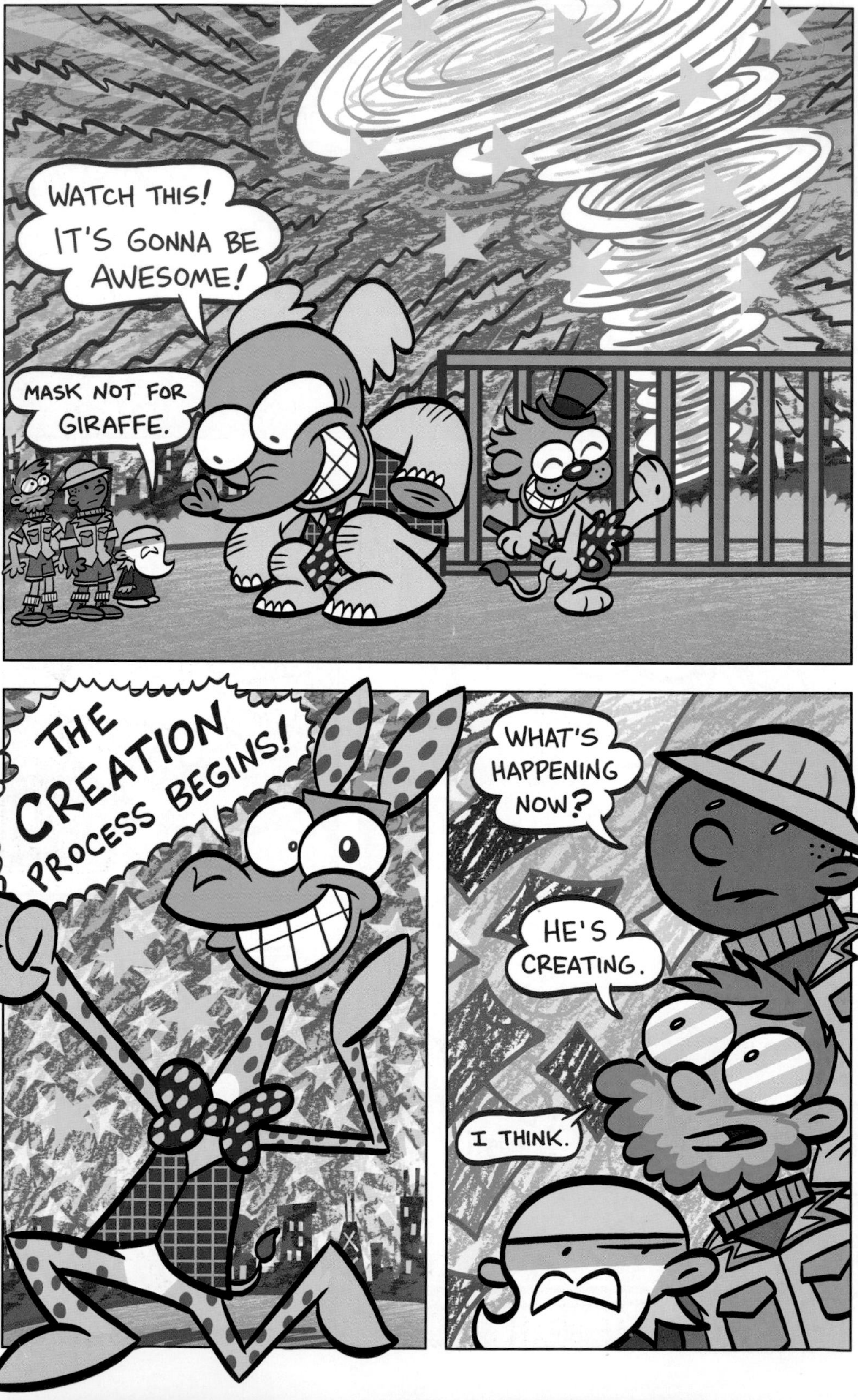
WATCH THIS! IT'S GONNA BE AWESOME!
MASK NOT FOR GIRAFFE.
THE CREATION PROCESS BEGINS!
WHAT'S HAPPENING NOW?
HE'S CREATING.
I THINK.

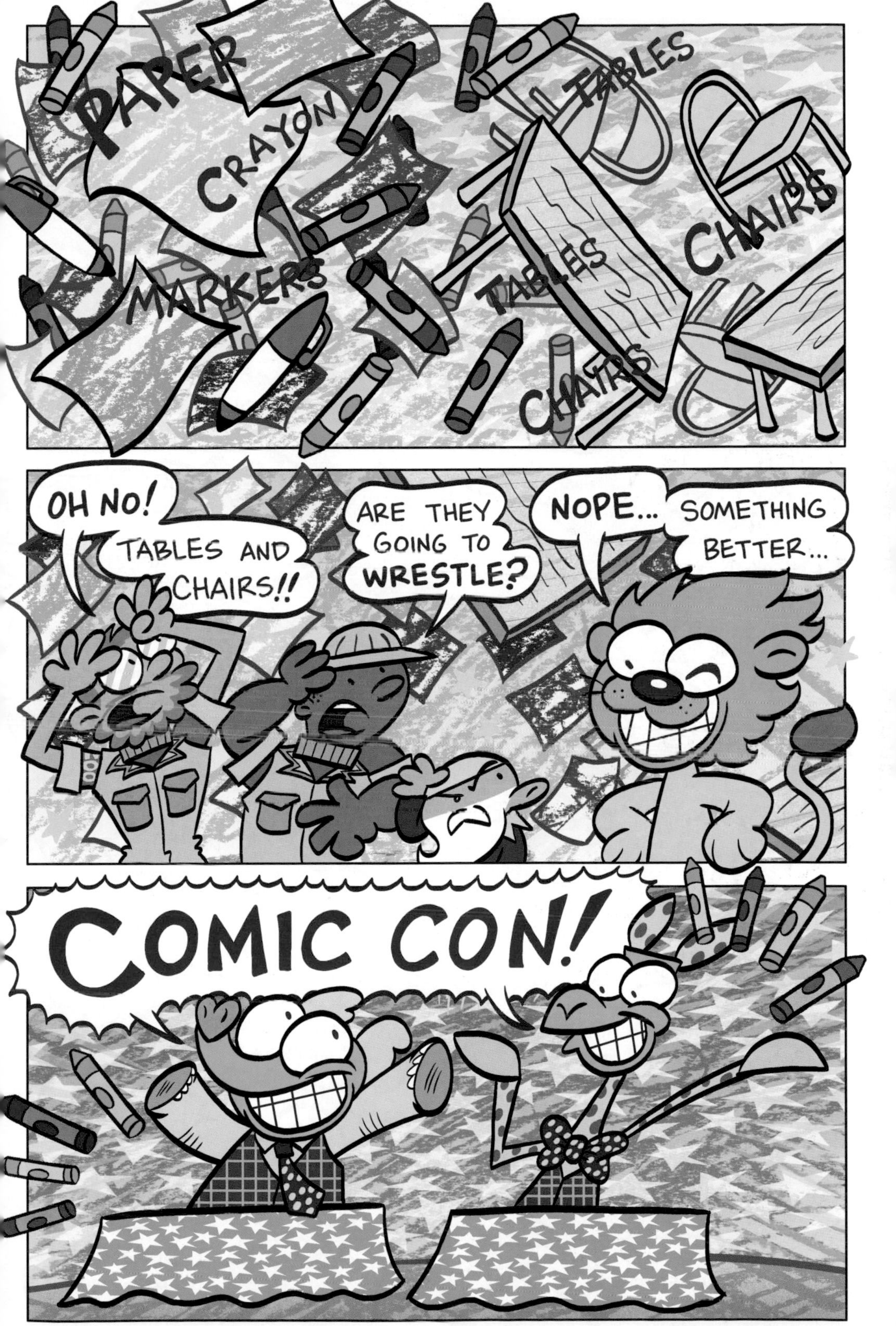
PAPER
CRAYON
MARKERS
TABLES
TABLES
CHAIRS
CHAIRS
OH NO!
TABLES AND CHAIRS!!
ARE THEY GOING TO WRESTLE?
NOPE...
SOMETHING BETTER...
COMIC CON!

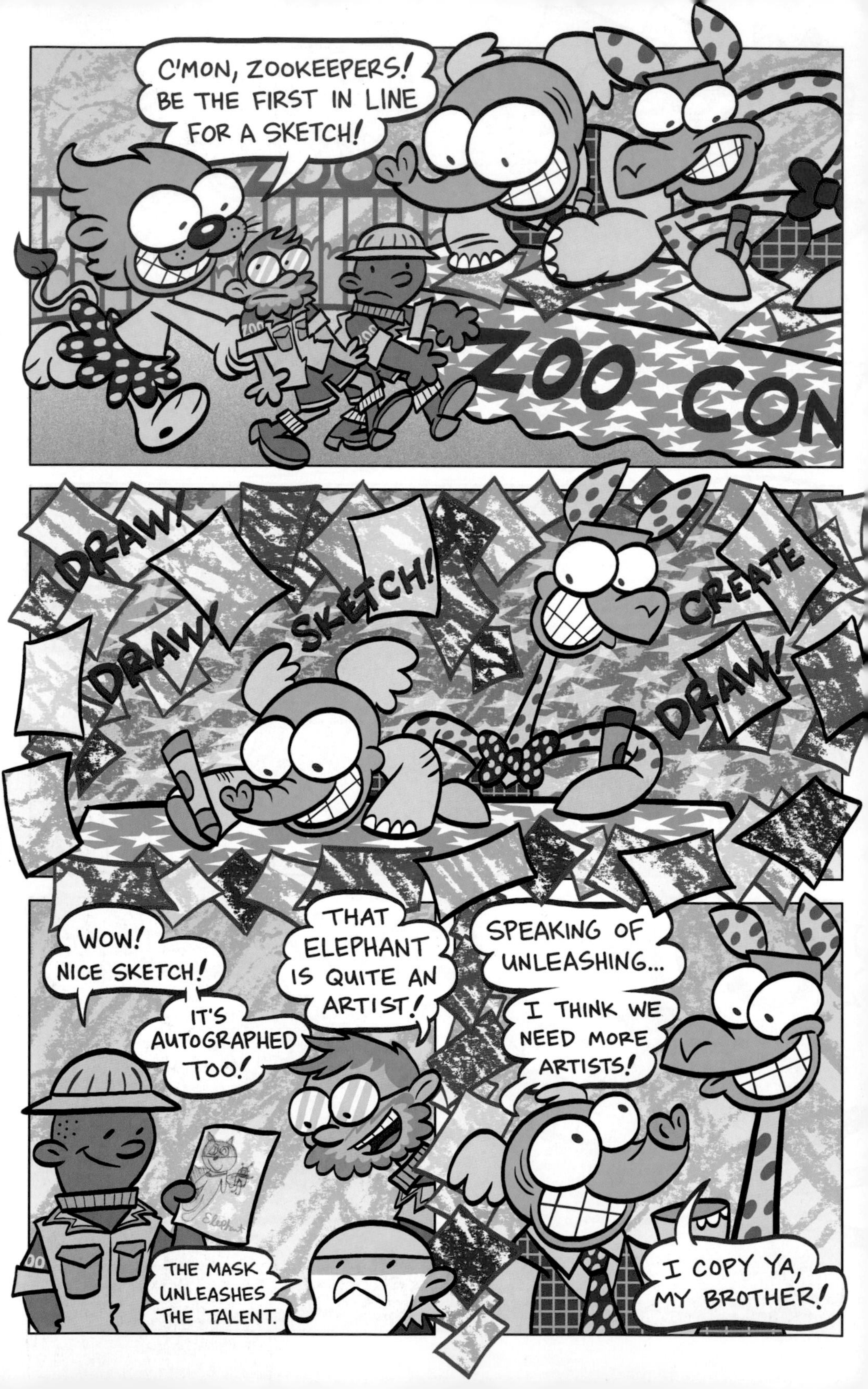
C'MON, ZOOKEEPERS! BE THE FIRST IN LINE FOR A SKETCH!
ZOO CON
DRAW!
DRAW!
SKETCH!
CREATE
DRAW!
WOW! NICE SKETCH!
IT'S AUTOGRAPHED TOO!
THAT ELEPHANT IS QUITE AN ARTIST!
SPEAKING OF UNLEASHING...
I THINK WE NEED MORE ARTISTS!
THE MASK UNLEASHES THE TALENT.
I COPY YA, MY BROTHER!

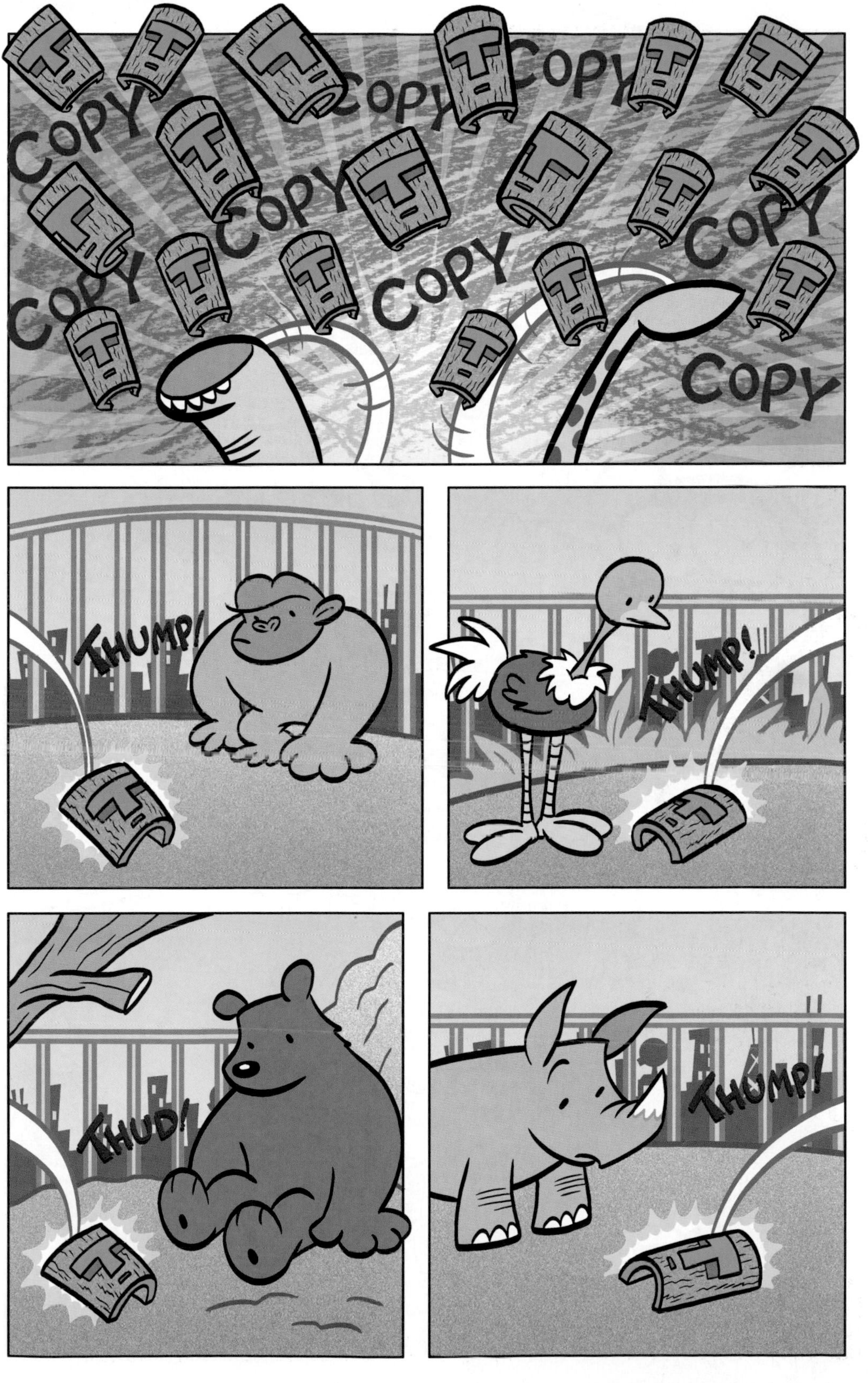
COPY
COPY
COPY
COPY
COPY
COPY
COPY
COPY
THUMP!
THUMP!
THUD!
THUMP!

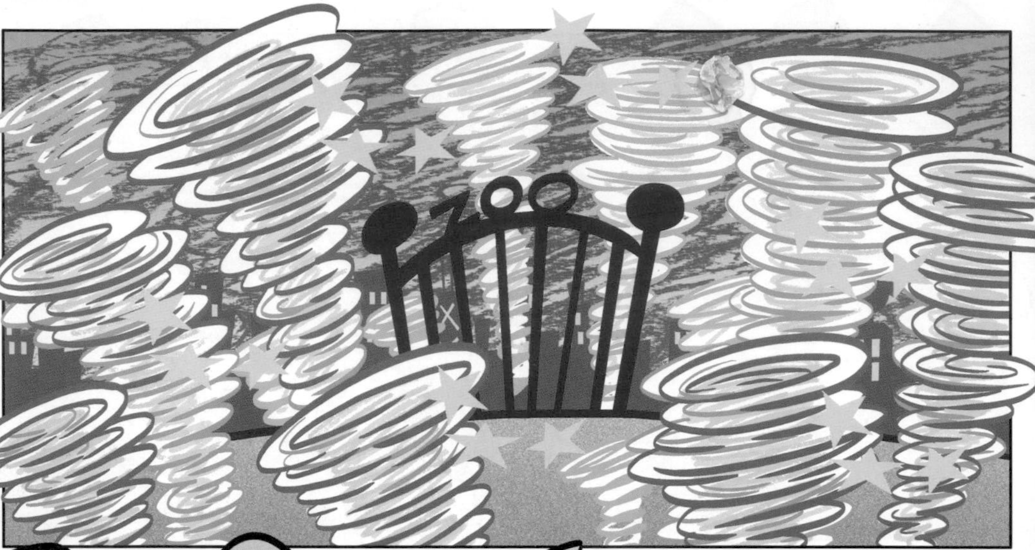
ZOO

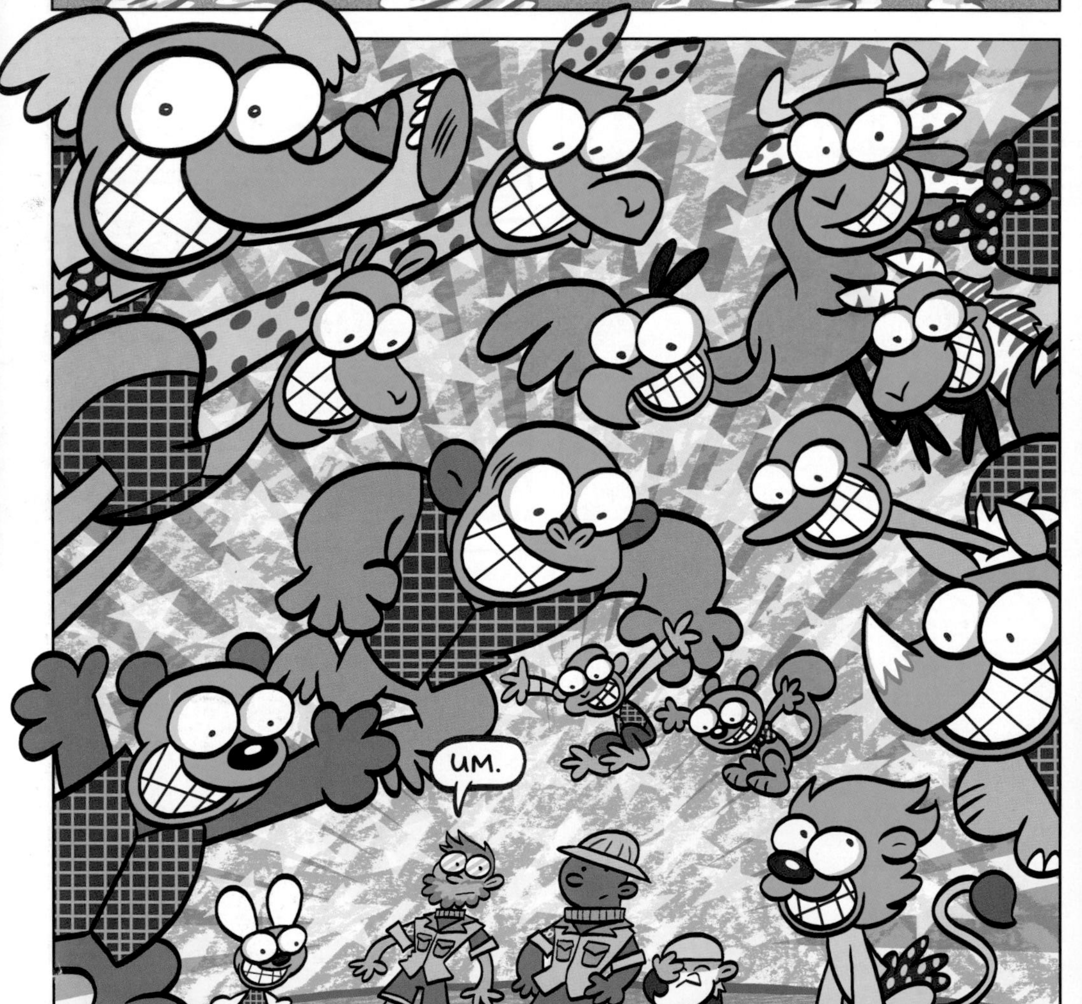
UM.

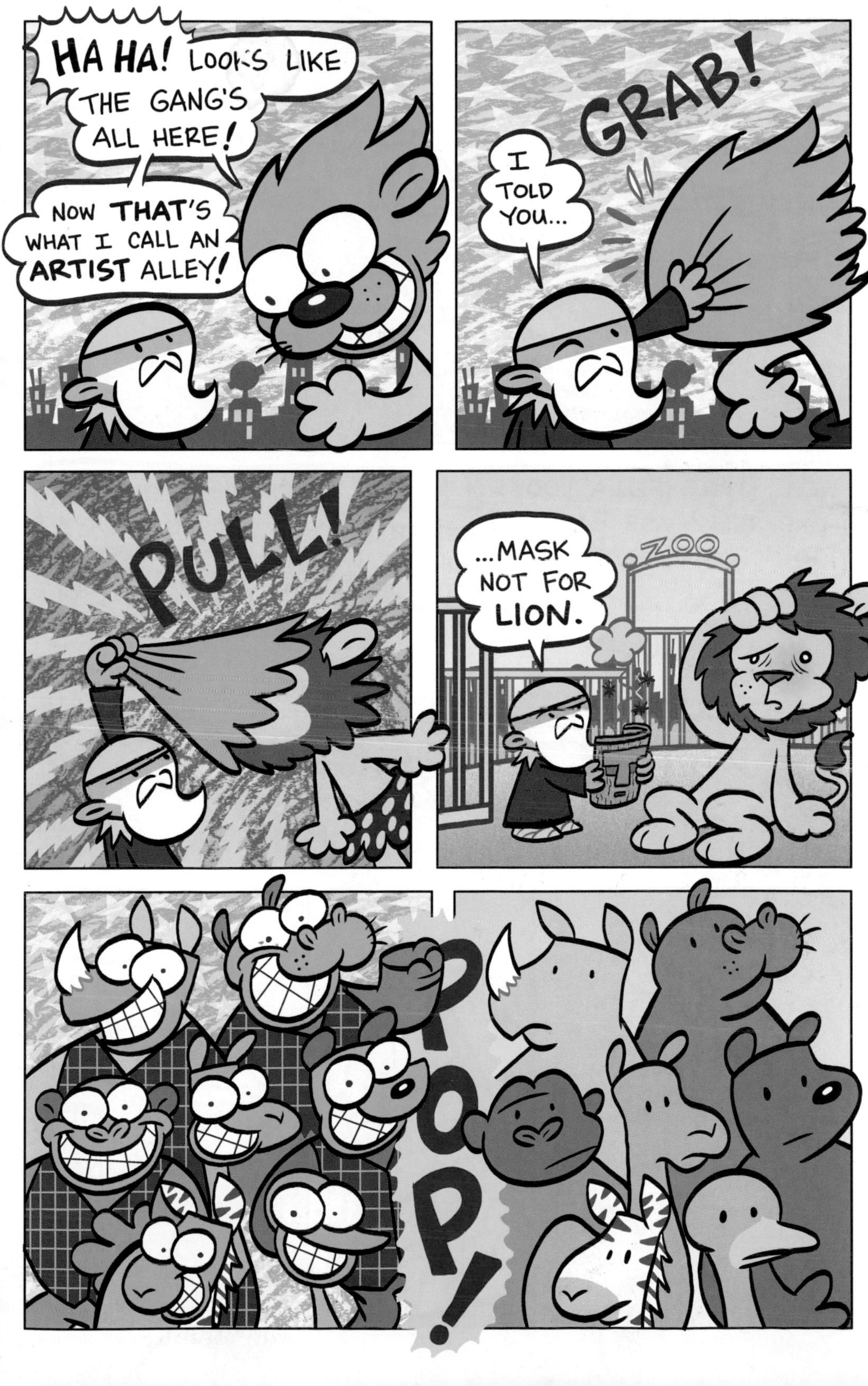
HA HA! LOOKS LIKE THE GANG'S ALL HERE!
NOW THAT'S WHAT I CALL AN ARTIST ALLEY!
GRAB!
I TOLD YOU...
PULL!
...MASK NOT FOR LION.
ZOO
POP!

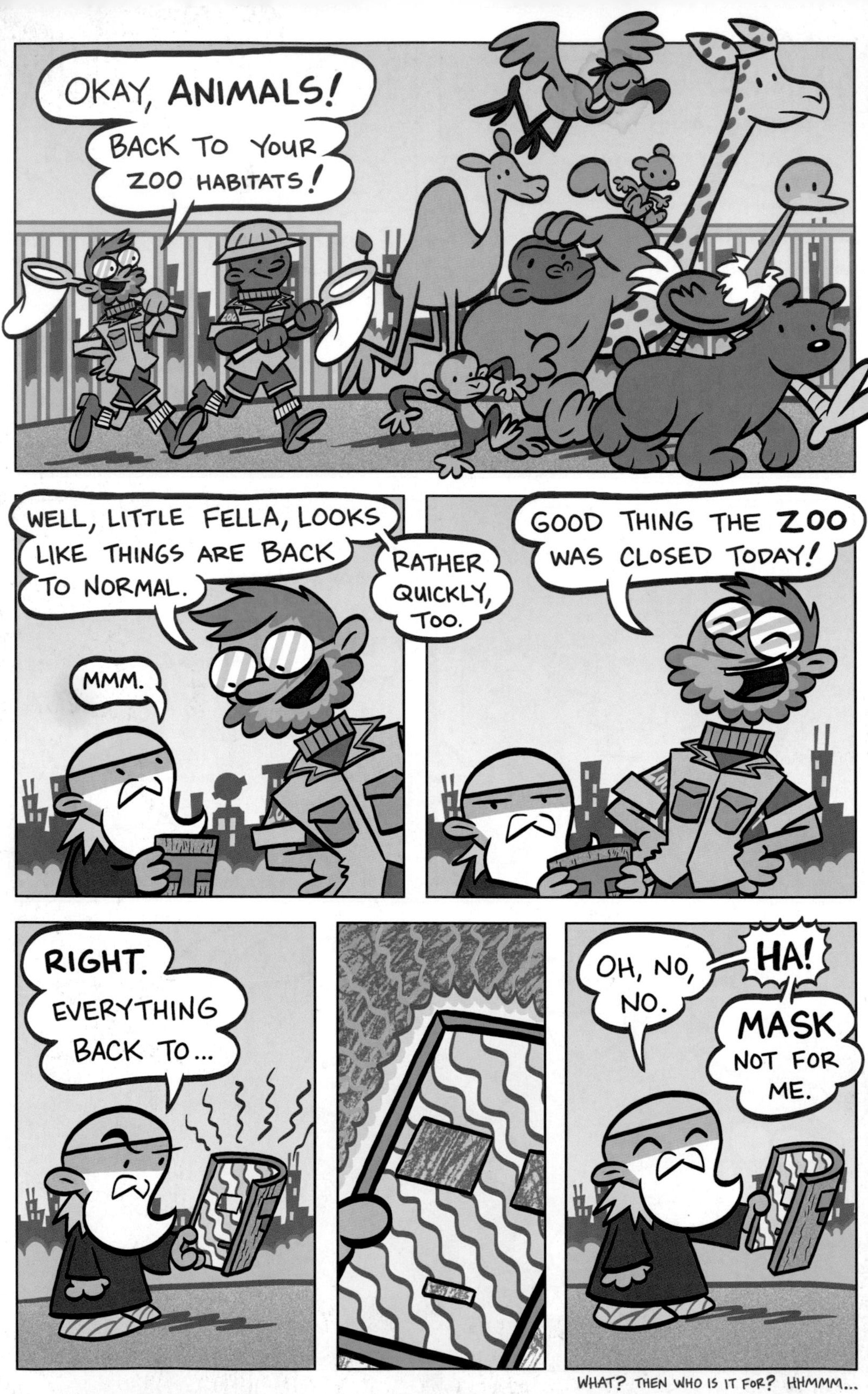
OKAY, ANIMALS!
BACK TO YOUR ZOO HABITATS!
WELL, LITTLE FELLA, LOOKS LIKE THINGS ARE BACK TO NORMAL.
RATHER QUICKLY, TOO.
MMM.
GOOD THING THE ZOO WAS CLOSED TODAY!
RIGHT.
EVERYTHING BACK TO...
OH, NO, NO.
HA!
MASK NOT FOR ME.

WHAT? THEN WHO IS IT FOR? HHMMM...

CHAPTER THREE

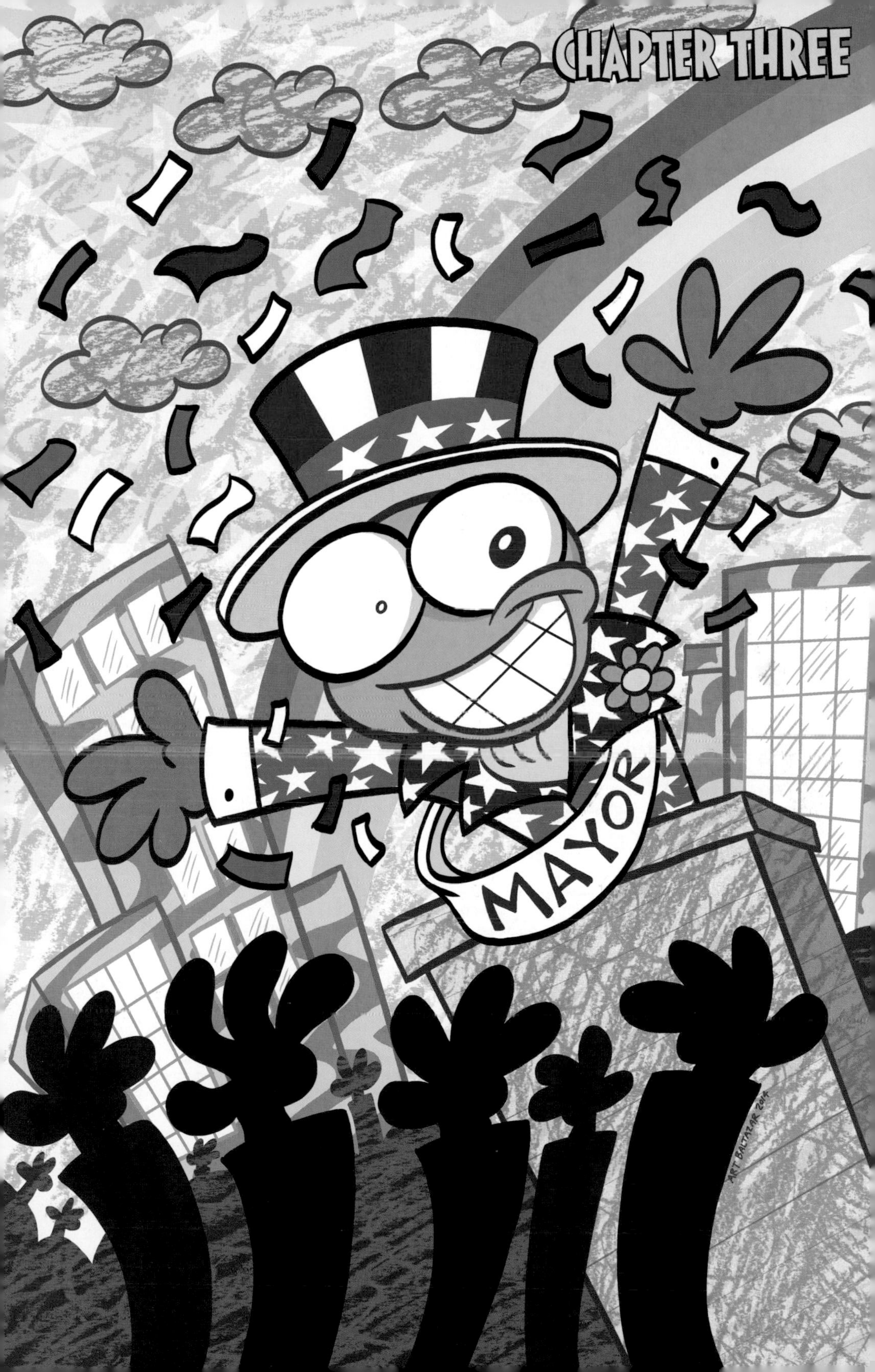
MAYOR
ART BALTAZAR 2014

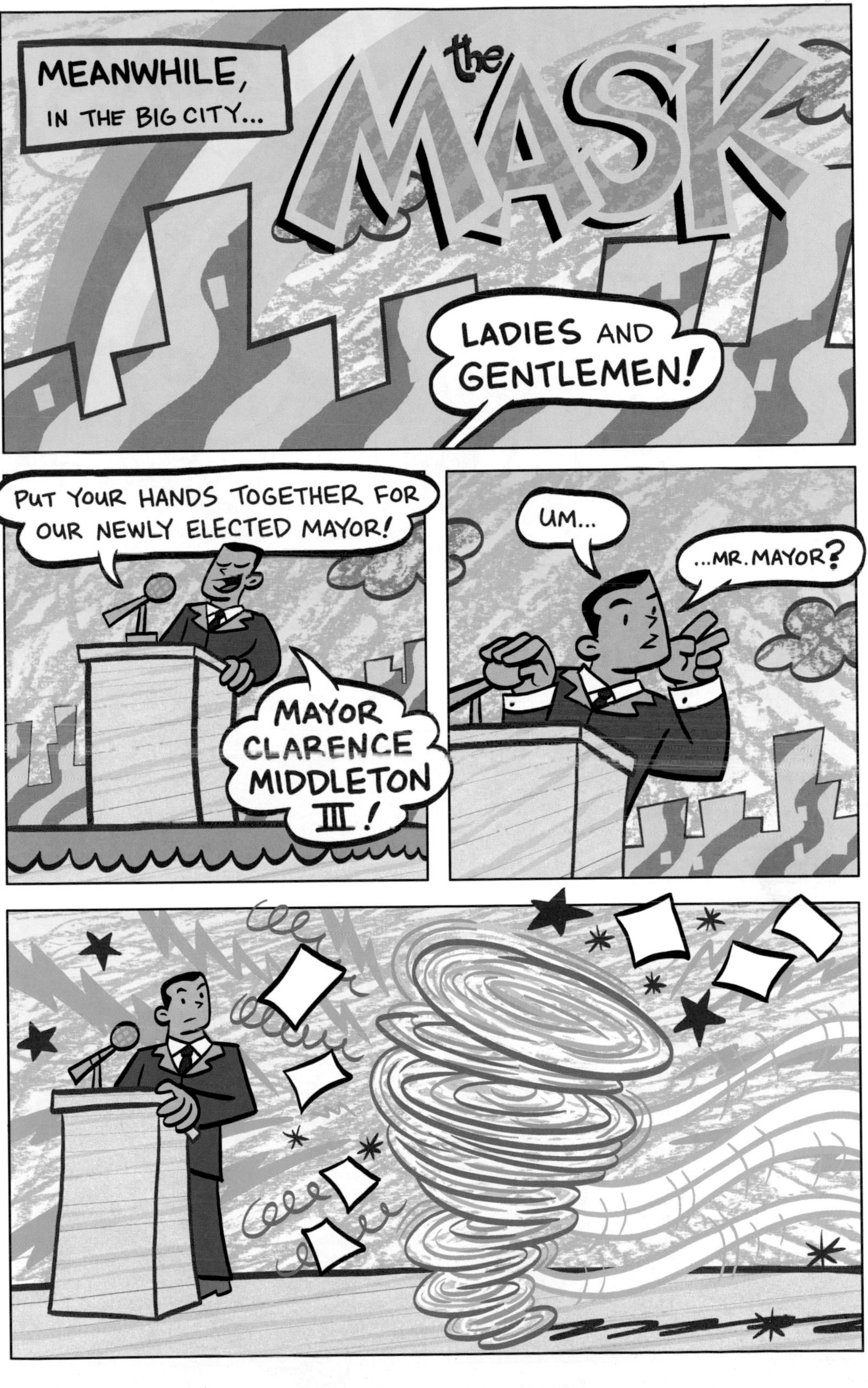
MEANWHILE, IN THE BIG CITY...
the MASK
LADIES AND GENTLEMEN!
PUT YOUR HANDS TOGETHER FOR OUR NEWLY ELECTED MAYOR!
MAYOR CLARENCE MIDDLETON III!
UM...
...MR. MAYOR?

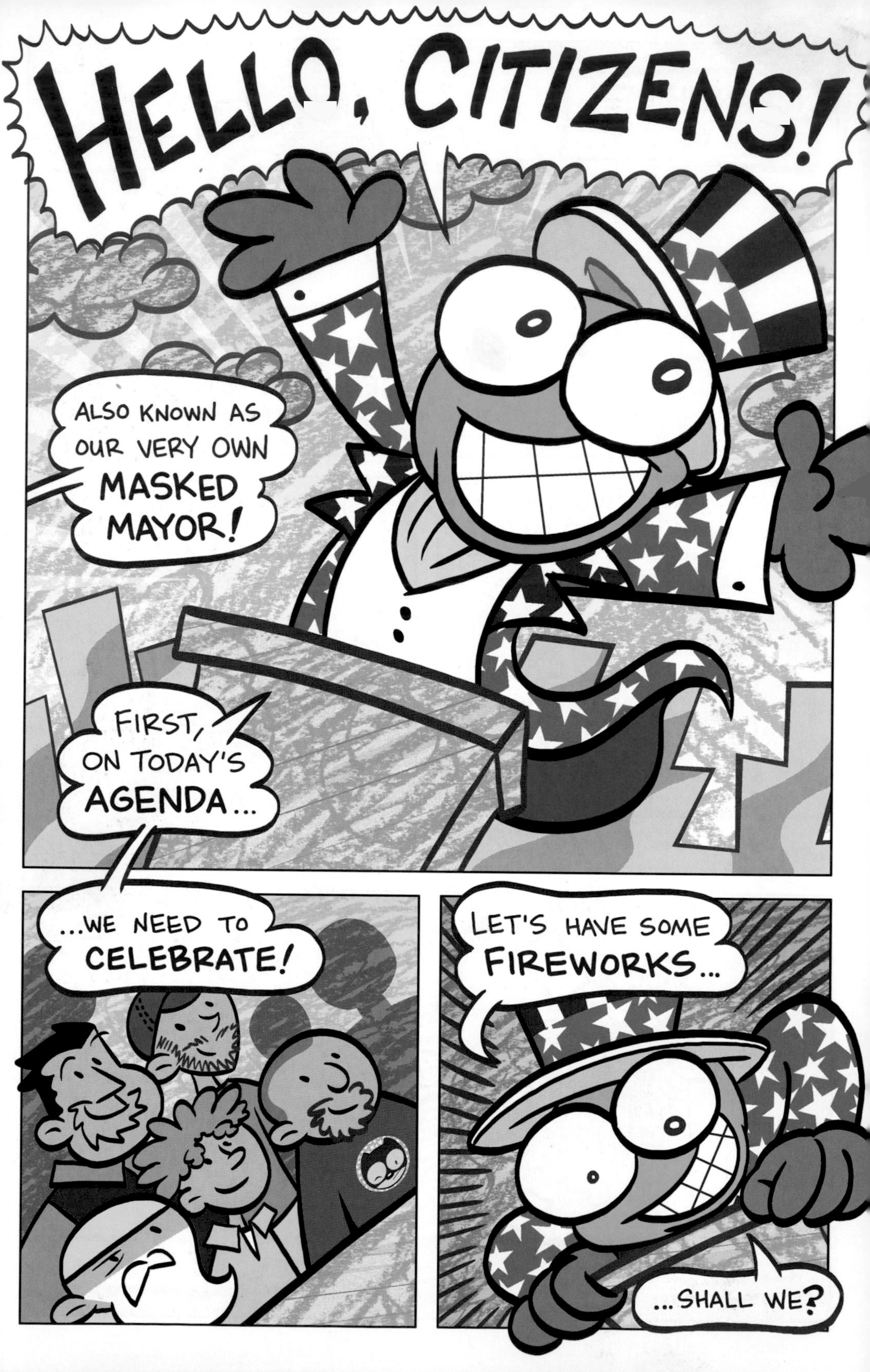
HELLO, CITIZENS!
ALSO KNOWN AS OUR VERY OWN MASKED MAYOR!
FIRST, ON TODAY'S AGENDA...
...WE NEED TO CELEBRATE!
LET'S HAVE SOME FIREWORKS...
...SHALL WE?

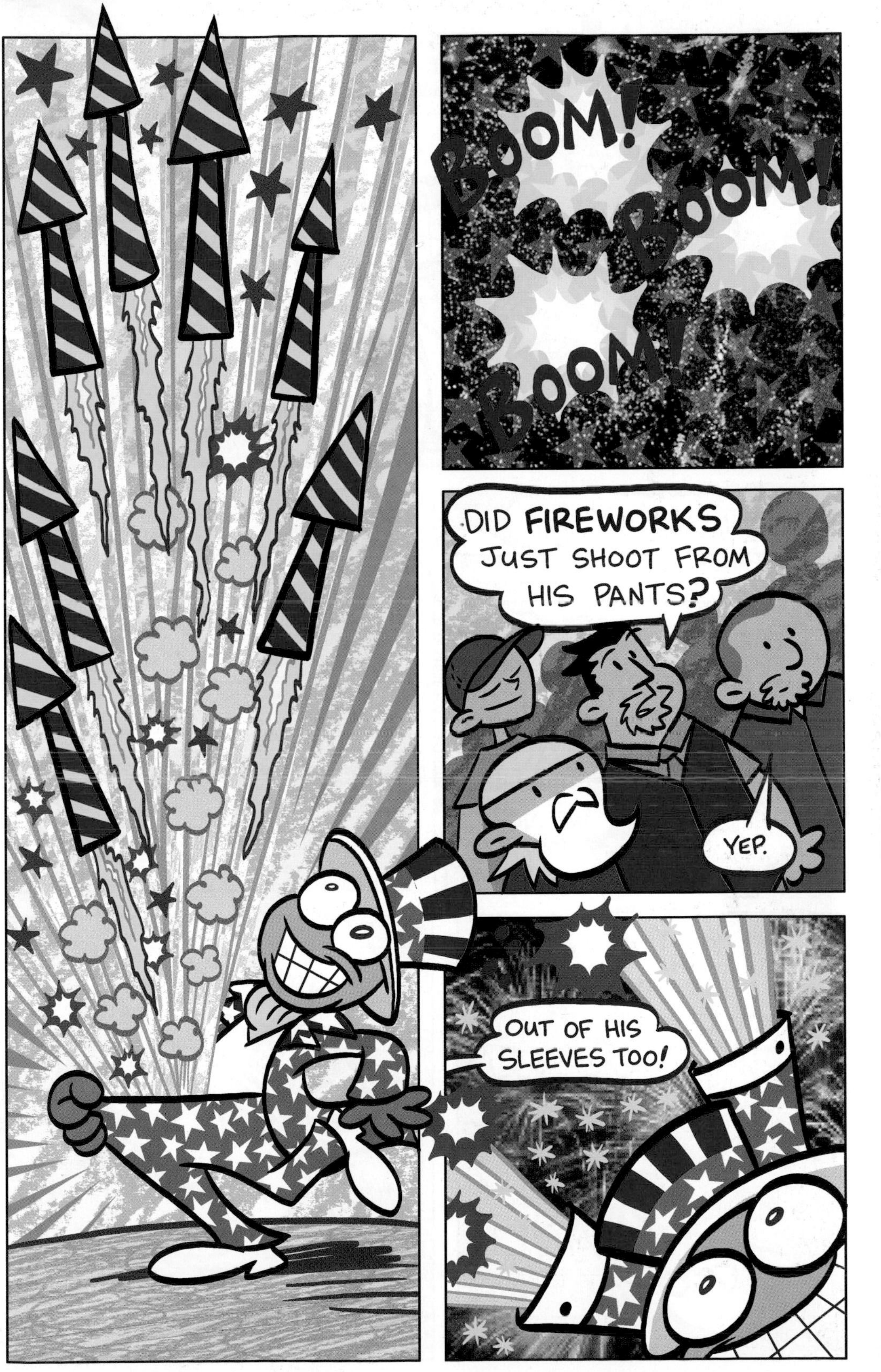
BOOM!
BOOM!
BOOM!
DID FIREWORKS JUST SHOOT FROM HIS PANTS?
YEP.
OUT OF HIS SLEEVES TOO!

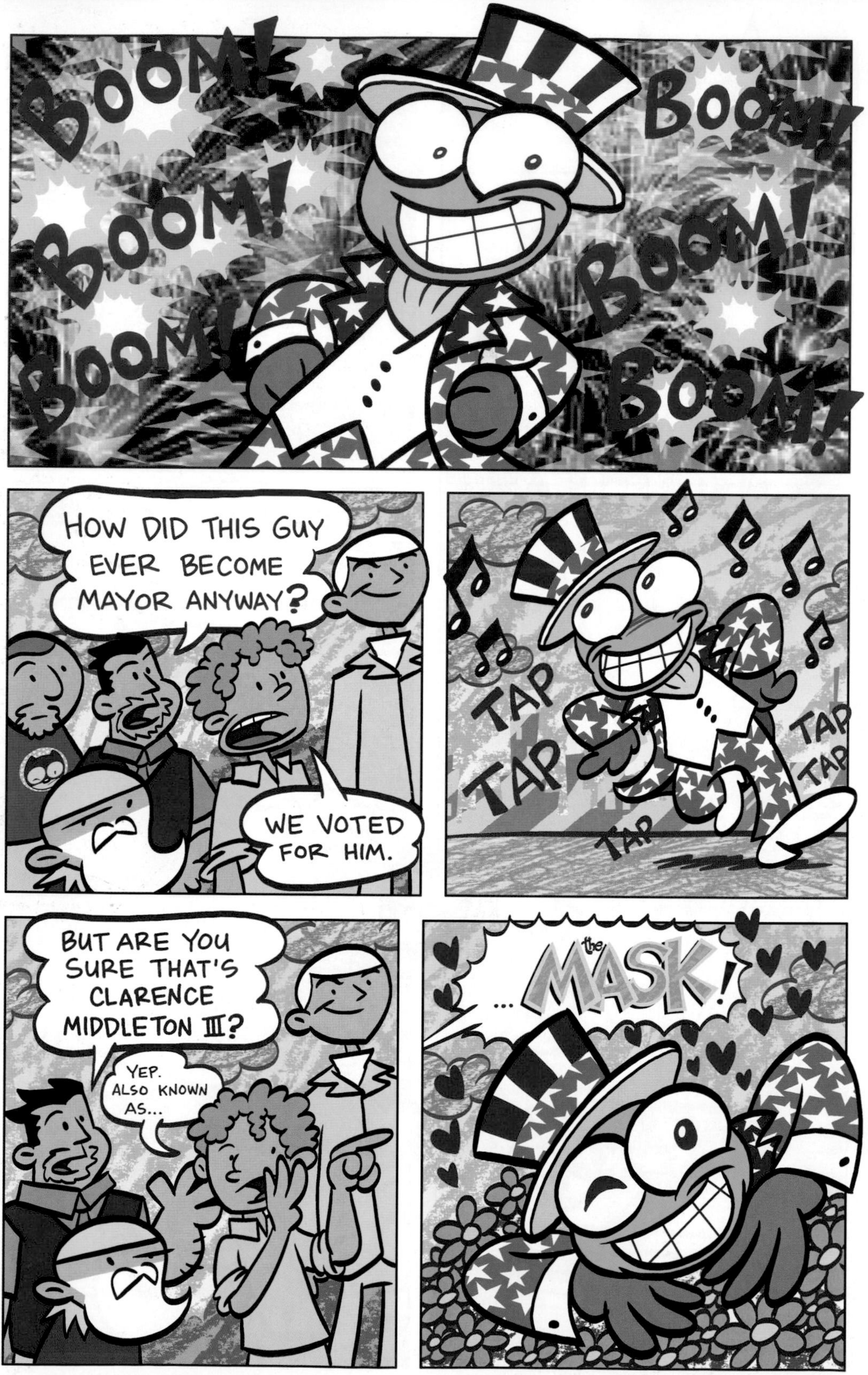
BOOM!
BOOM!
BOOM!
BOOM!
BOOM!
BOOM!
HOW DID THIS GUY EVER BECOME MAYOR ANYWAY?
WE VOTED FOR HIM.
TAP
TAP
TAP
TAP
TAP
BUT ARE YOU SURE THAT'S CLARENCE MIDDLETON III?
YEP. ALSO KNOWN AS...
...the MASK!

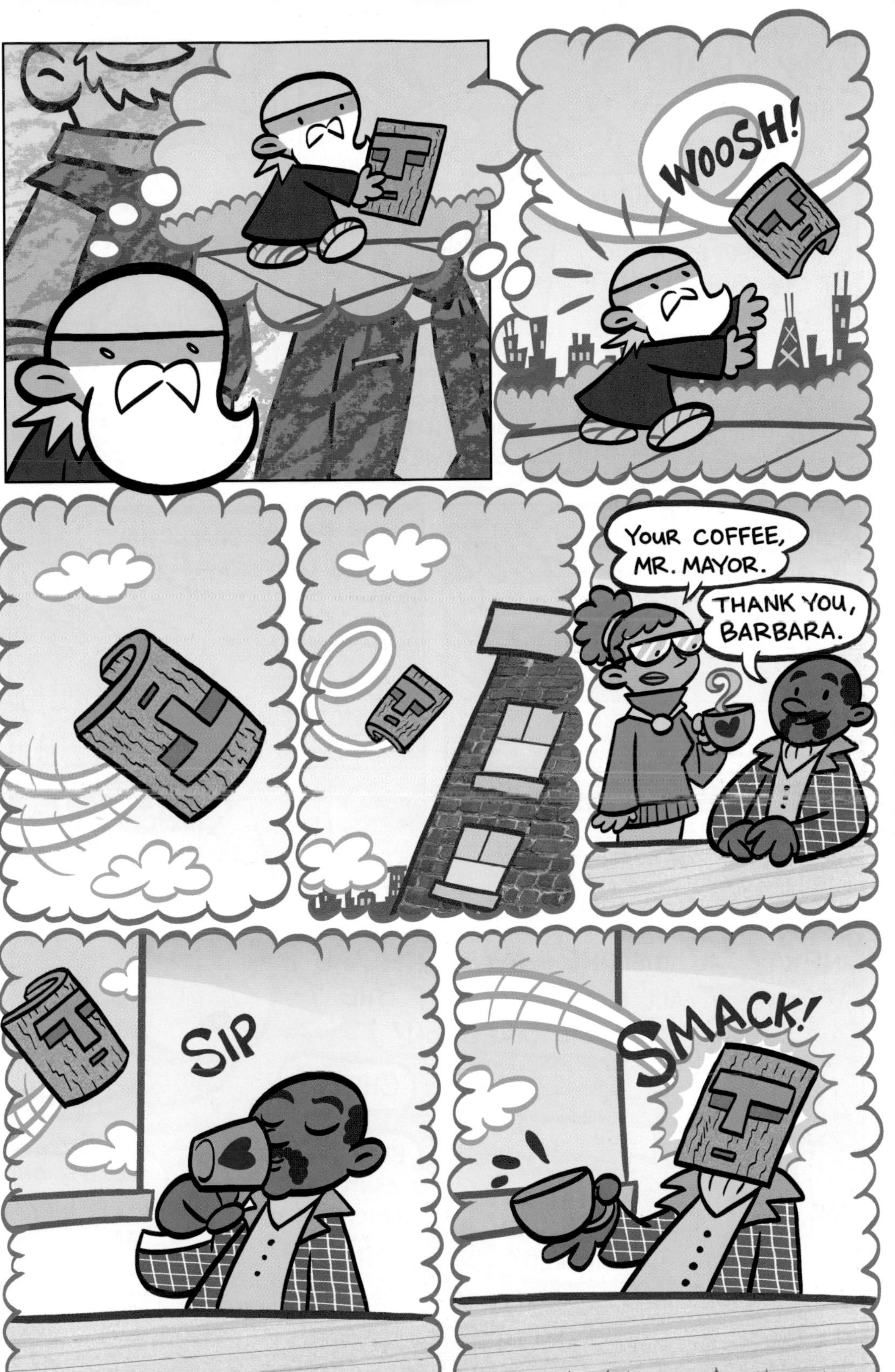
WOOSH!
YOUR COFFEE, MR. MAYOR.
THANK YOU, BARBARA.
SIP
SMACK!

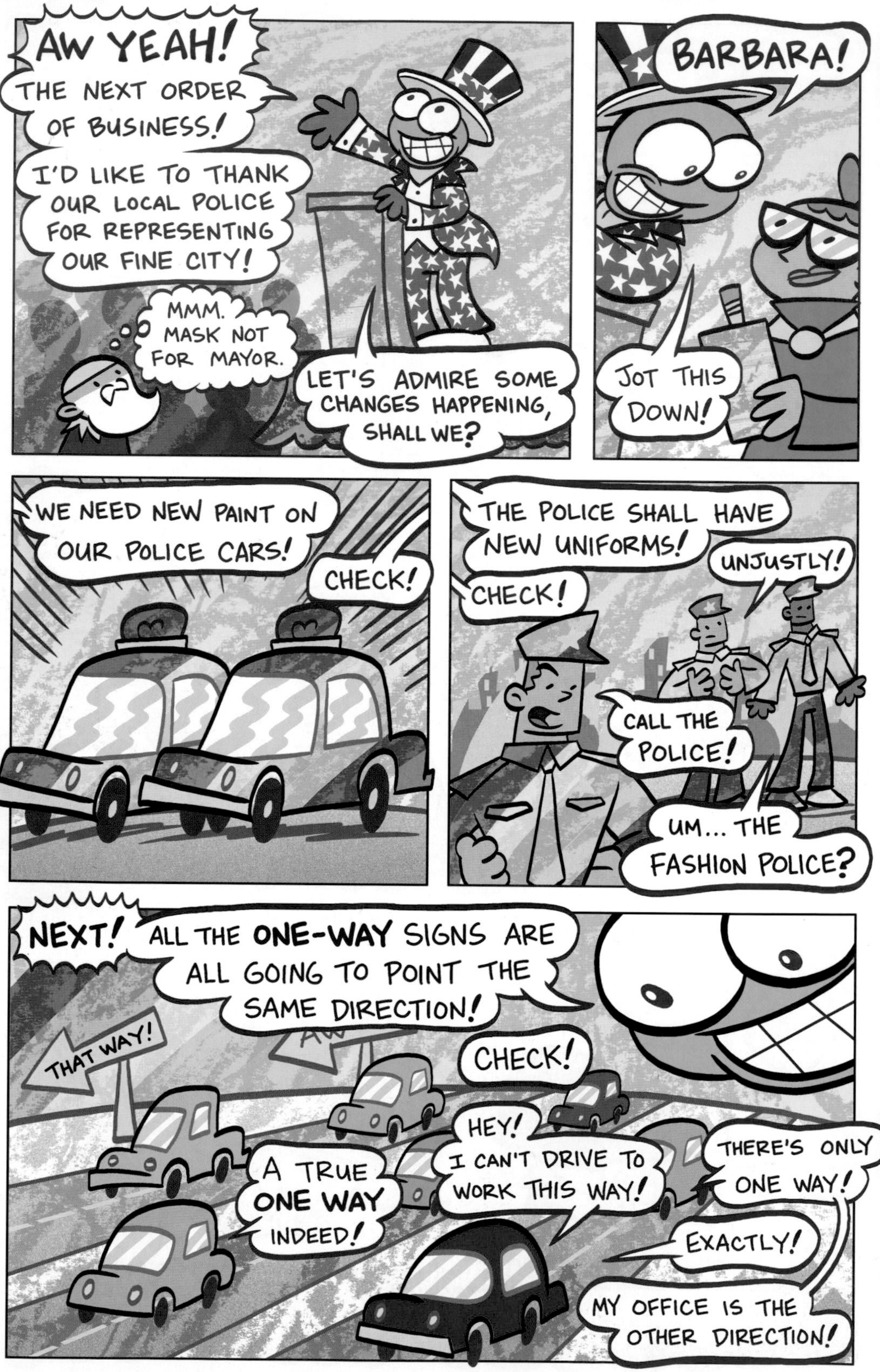
AW YEAH!
THE NEXT ORDER OF BUSINESS!
I'D LIKE TO THANK OUR LOCAL POLICE FOR REPRESENTING OUR FINE CITY!
MMM. MASK NOT FOR MAYOR.
LET'S ADMIRE SOME CHANGES HAPPENING, SHALL WE?
BARBARA!
JOT THIS DOWN!
WE NEED NEW PAINT ON OUR POLICE CARS!
CHECK!
THE POLICE SHALL HAVE NEW UNIFORMS!
CHECK!
UNJUSTLY!
CALL THE POLICE!
UM... THE FASHION POLICE?
NEXT!
ALL THE ONE-WAY SIGNS ARE ALL GOING TO POINT THE SAME DIRECTION!
THAT WAY!
CHECK!
HEY! I CAN'T DRIVE TO WORK THIS WAY!
A TRUE ONE WAY INDEED!
THERE'S ONLY ONE WAY!
EXACTLY!
MY OFFICE IS THE OTHER DIRECTION!

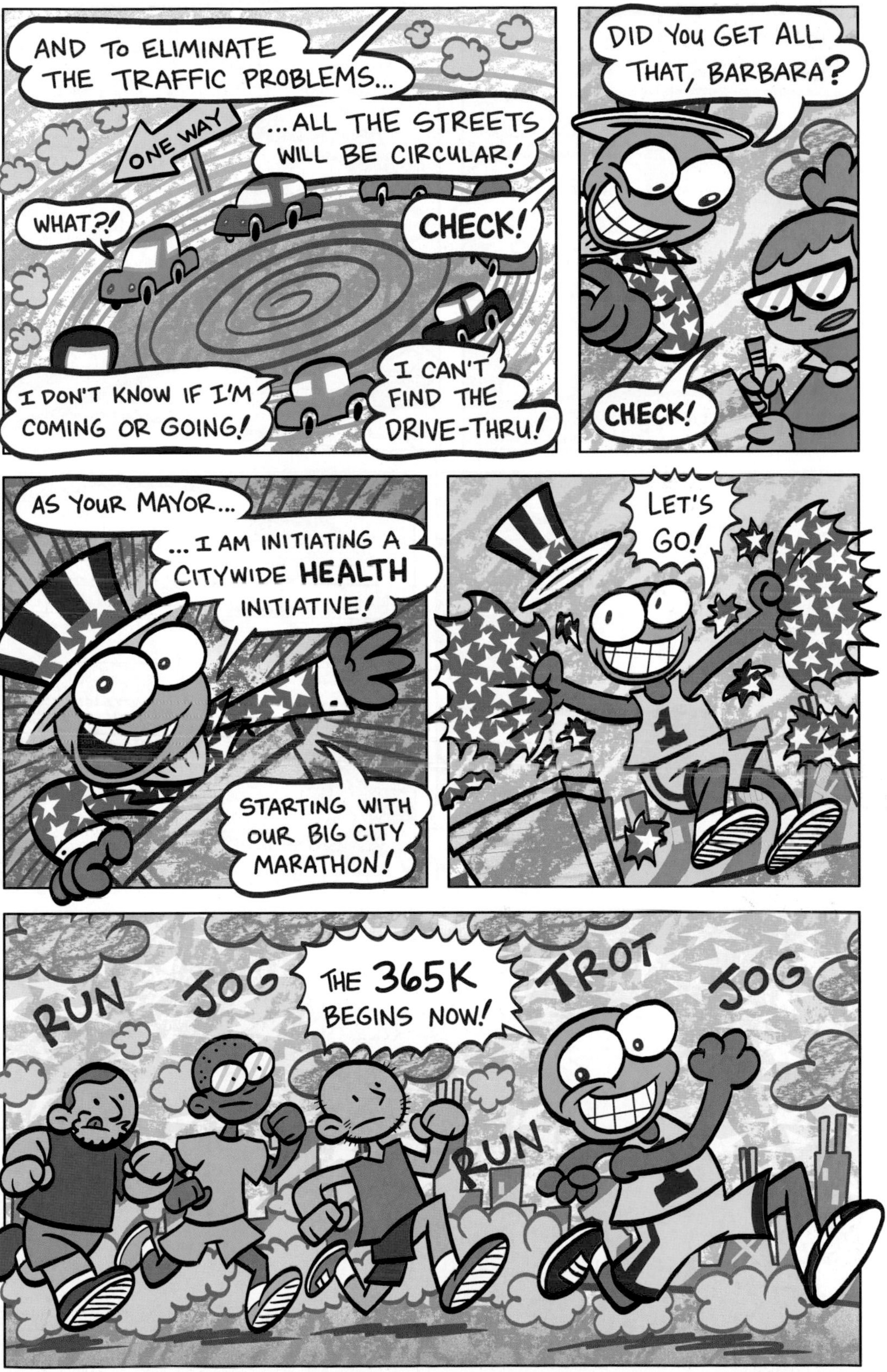
AND TO ELIMINATE THE TRAFFIC PROBLEMS...
ONE WAY
...ALL THE STREETS WILL BE CIRCULAR!
WHAT?!
CHECK!
I DON'T KNOW IF I'M COMING OR GOING!
I CAN'T FIND THE DRIVE-THRU!
DID YOU GET ALL THAT, BARBARA?
CHECK!
AS YOUR MAYOR...
...I AM INITIATING A CITYWIDE HEALTH INITIATIVE!
STARTING WITH OUR BIG CITY MARATHON!
LET'S GO!
RUN
JOG
THE 365K BEGINS NOW!
TROT
JOG
RUN

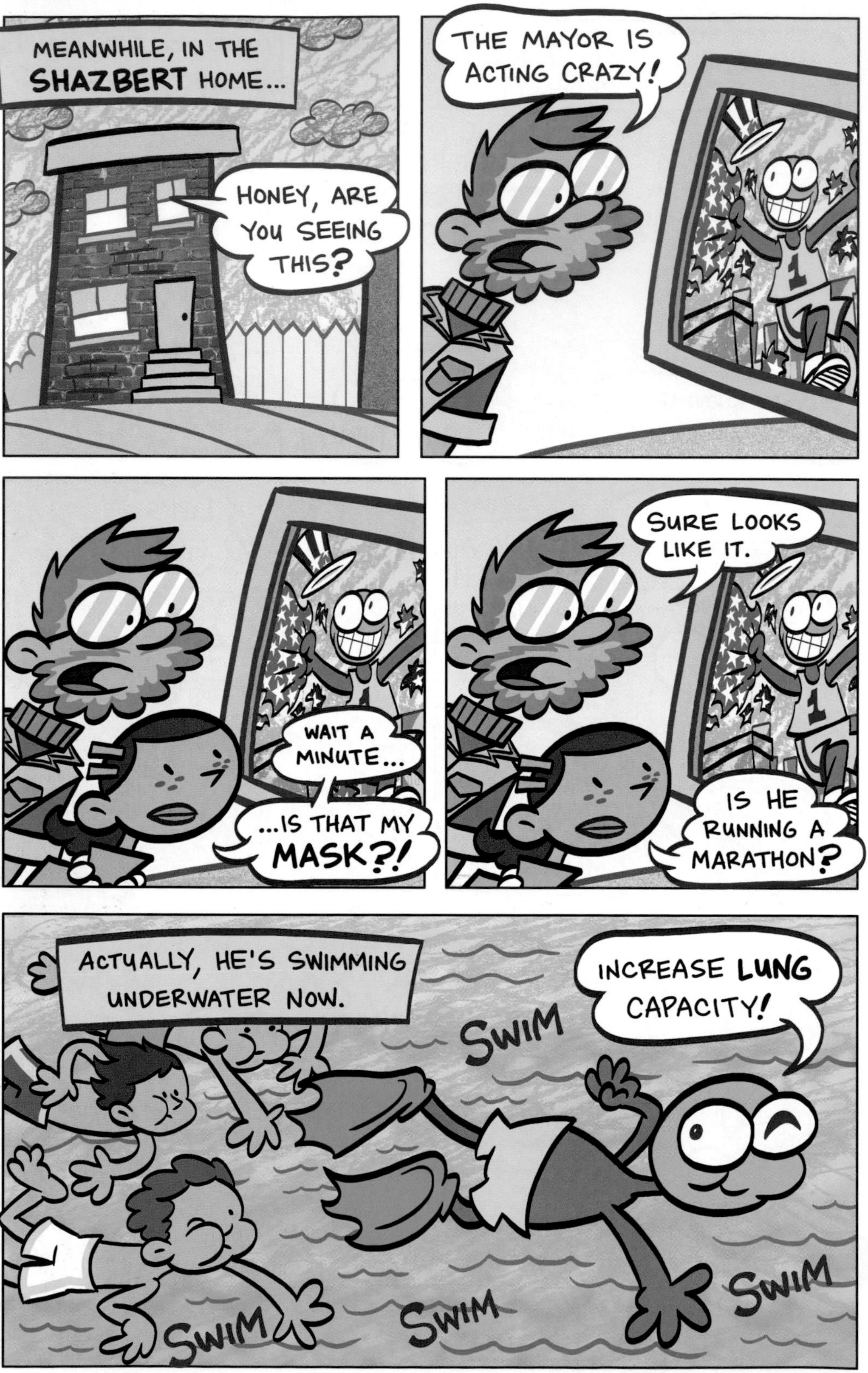
MEANWHILE, IN THE SHAZBERT HOME...
HONEY, ARE YOU SEEING THIS?
THE MAYOR IS ACTING CRAZY!
WAIT A MINUTE...
...IS THAT MY MASK?!
SURE LOOKS LIKE IT.
IS HE RUNNING A MARATHON?
ACTUALLY, HE'S SWIMMING UNDERWATER NOW.
INCREASE LUNG CAPACITY!
SWIM
SWIM
SWIM
SWIM

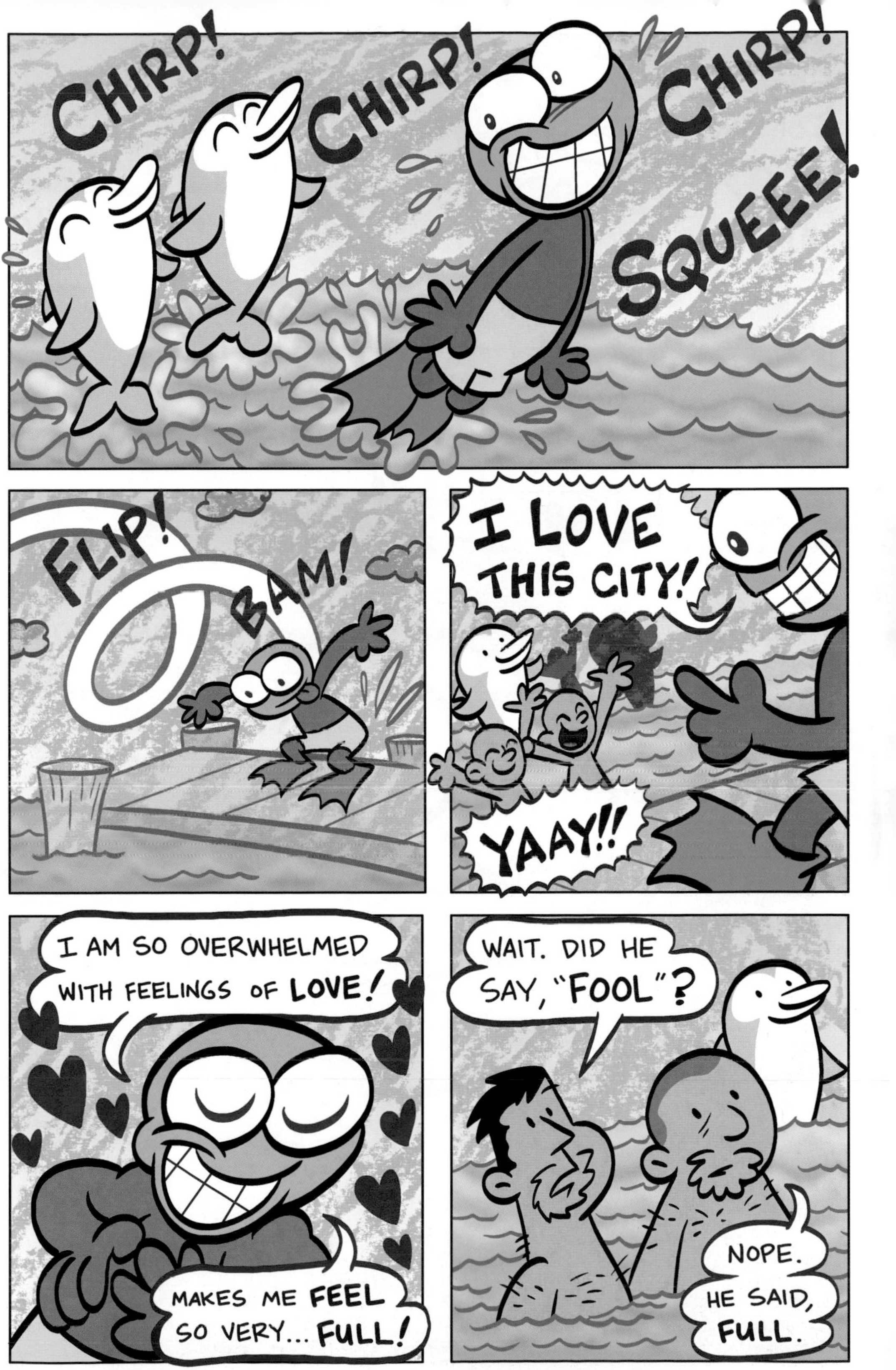
CHIRP!
CHIRP!
CHIRP!
SQUEEE!
FLIP!
BAM!
I LOVE THIS CITY!
YAAY!!
I AM SO OVERWHELMED WITH FEELINGS OF LOVE!
MAKES ME FEEL SO VERY... FULL!
WAIT. DID HE SAY, "FOOL"?
NOPE.
HE SAID, FULL.

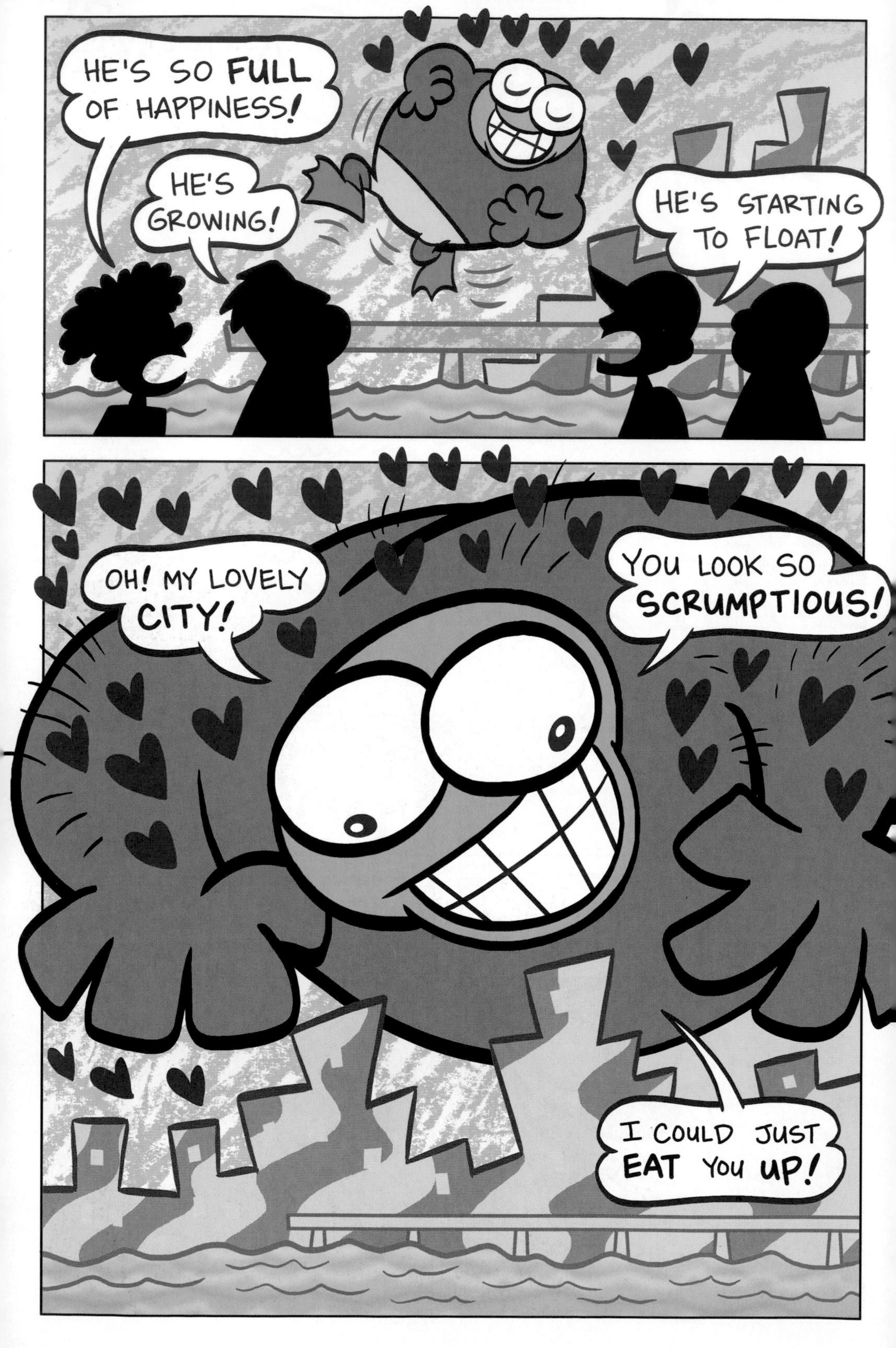
HE'S SO FULL OF HAPPINESS!
HE'S GROWING!
HE'S STARTING TO FLOAT!
OH! MY LOVELY CITY!
YOU LOOK SO SCRUMPTIOUS!
I COULD JUST EAT YOU UP!

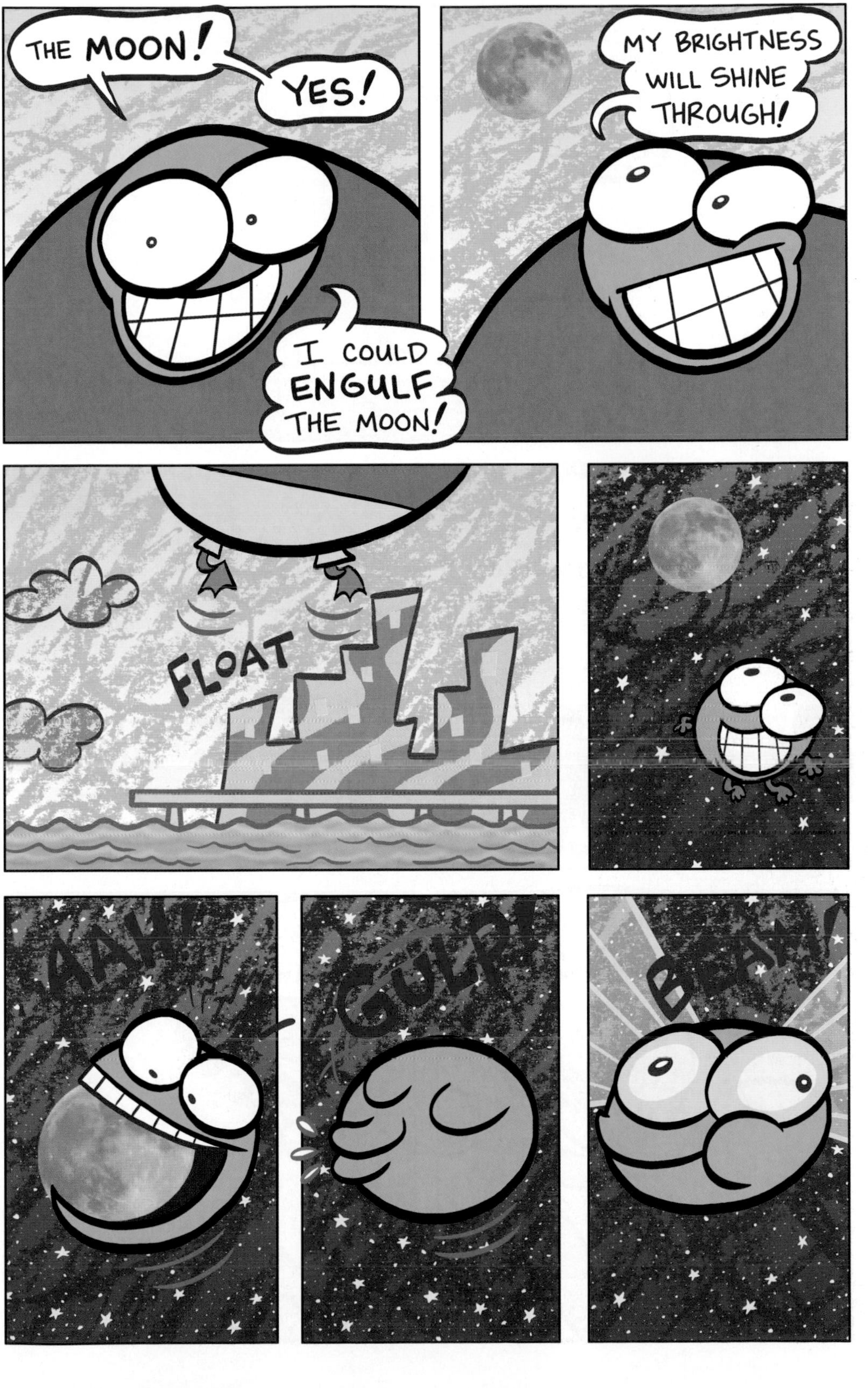
THE MOON!
YES!
I COULD ENGULF THE MOON!
MY BRIGHTNESS WILL SHINE THROUGH!
FLOAT
GULP!

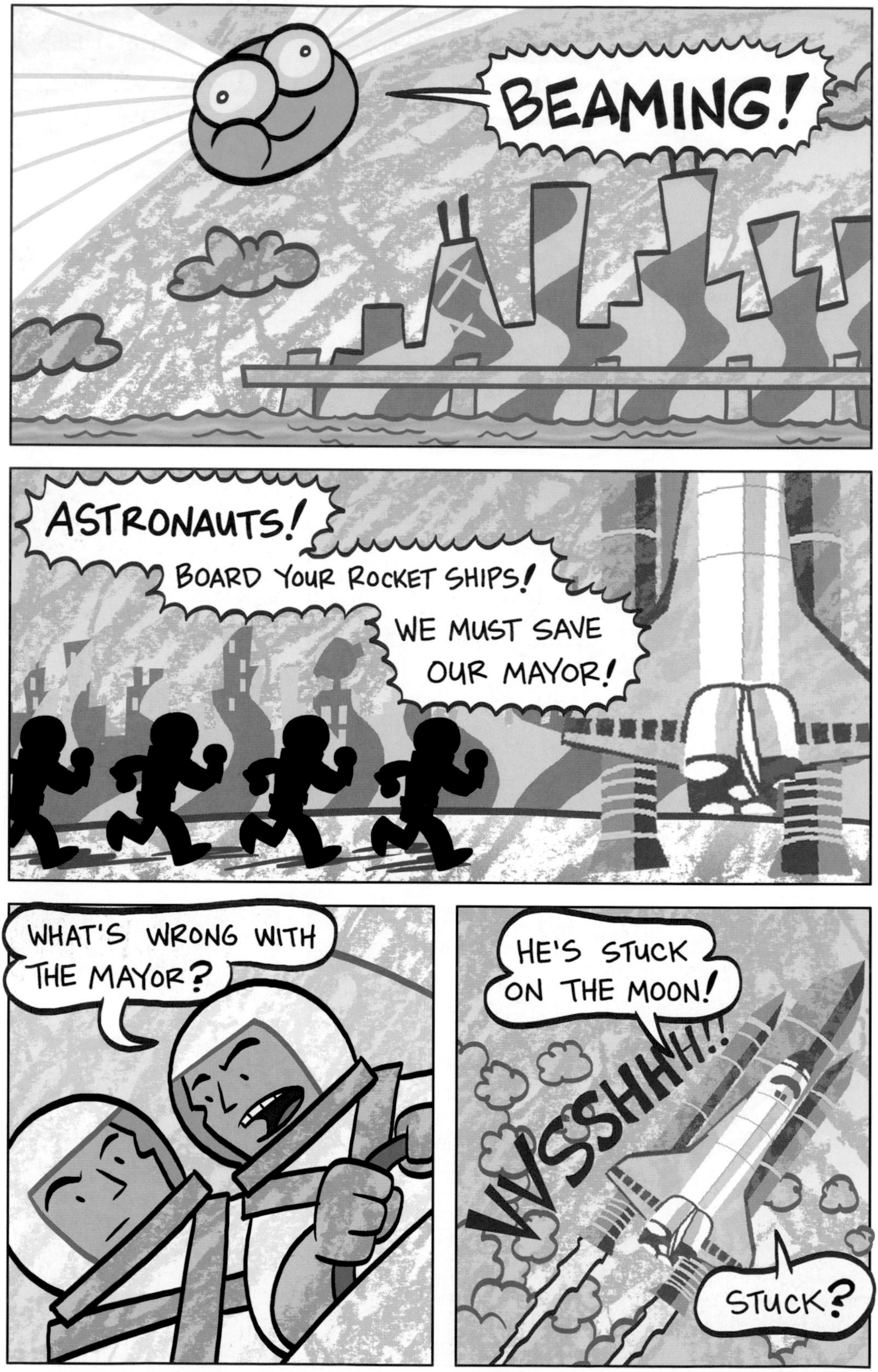
BEAMING!
ASTRONAUTS!
BOARD YOUR ROCKET SHIPS!
WE MUST SAVE OUR MAYOR!
WHAT'S WRONG WITH THE MAYOR?
HE'S STUCK ON THE MOON!
VVSSHHH!!
STUCK?

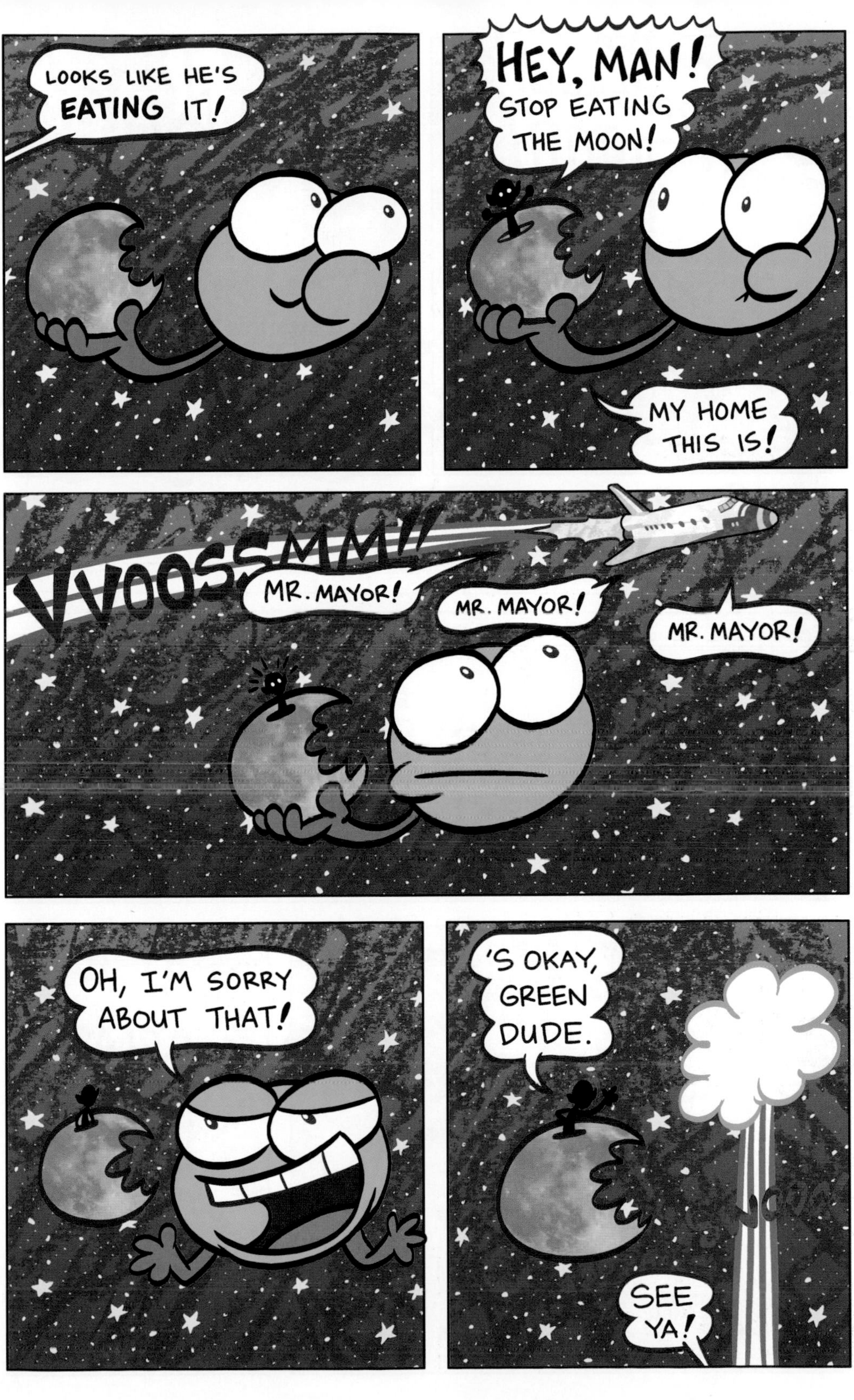
LOOKS LIKE HE'S EATING IT!
HEY, MAN! STOP EATING THE MOON!
MY HOME THIS IS!
VVOOSSMM!!
MR. MAYOR!
MR. MAYOR!
MR. MAYOR!
OH, I'M SORRY ABOUT THAT!
'S OKAY, GREEN DUDE.
SEE YA!

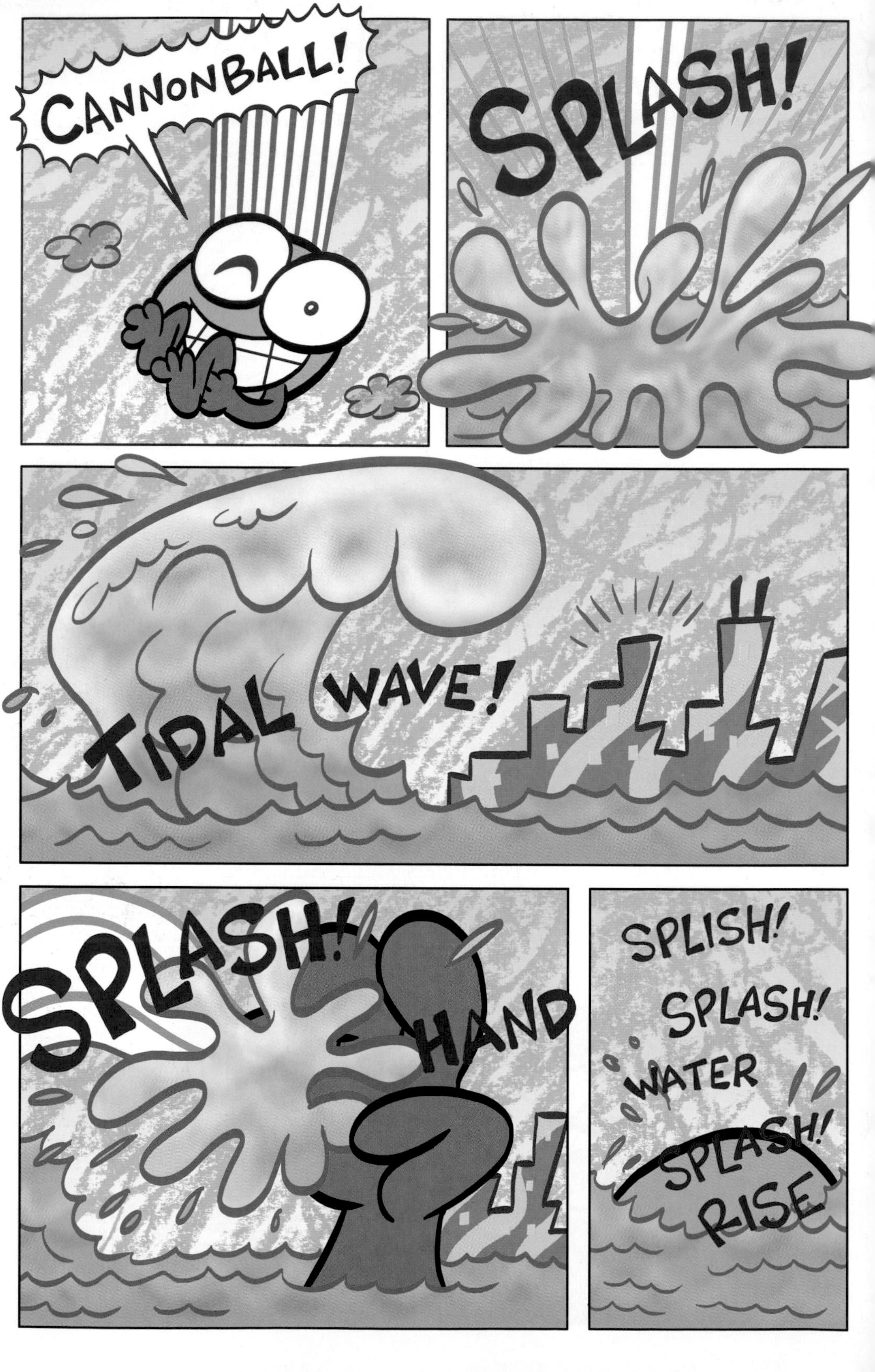
CANNONBALL!
SPLASH!
TIDAL WAVE!
SPLASH!
HAND
SPLISH!
SPLASH!
WATER
SPLASH!
RISE

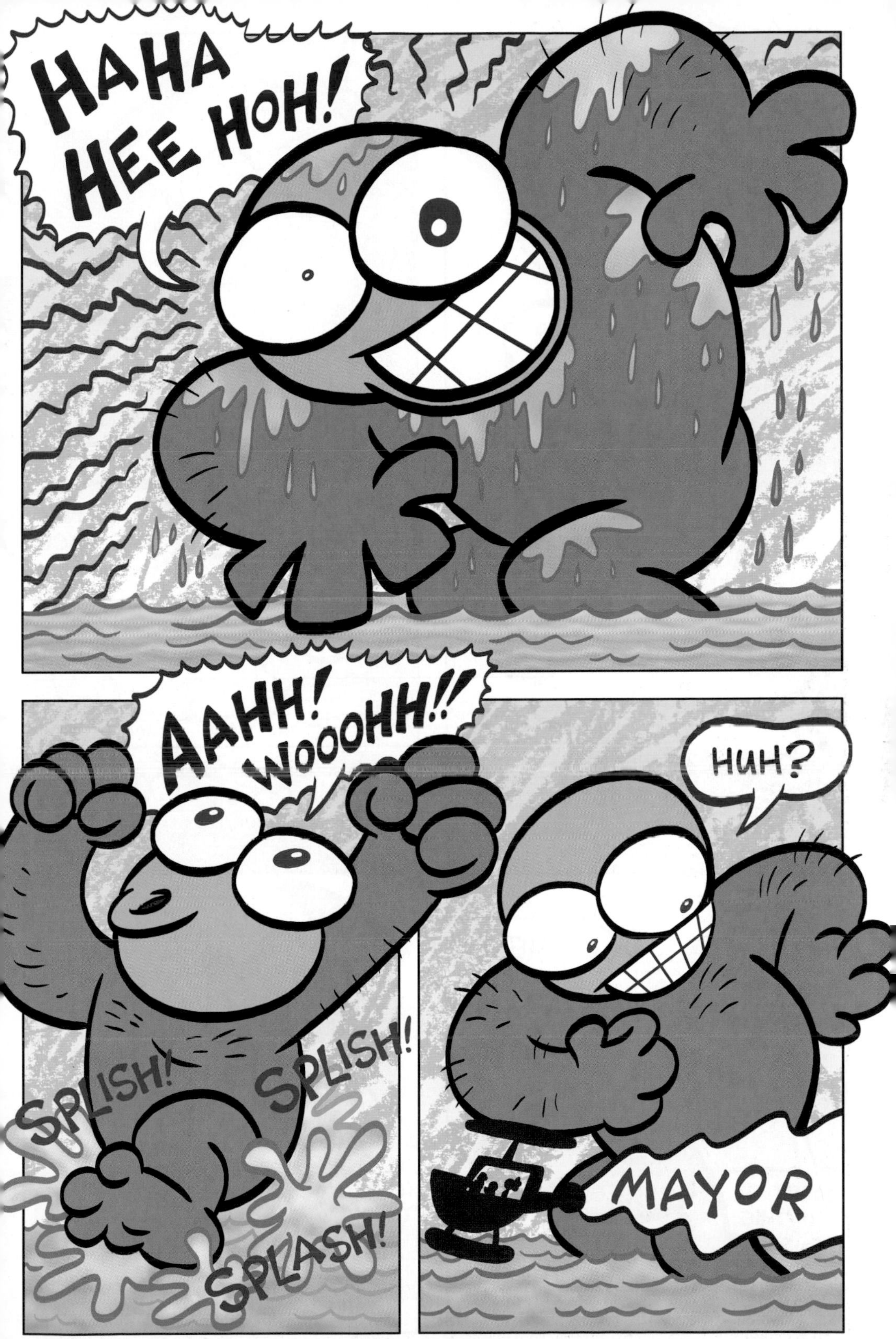
HAHA HEE HOH!
AAHH! WOOOHH!!
SPLISH!
SPLISH!
SPLASH!
HUH?
MAYOR

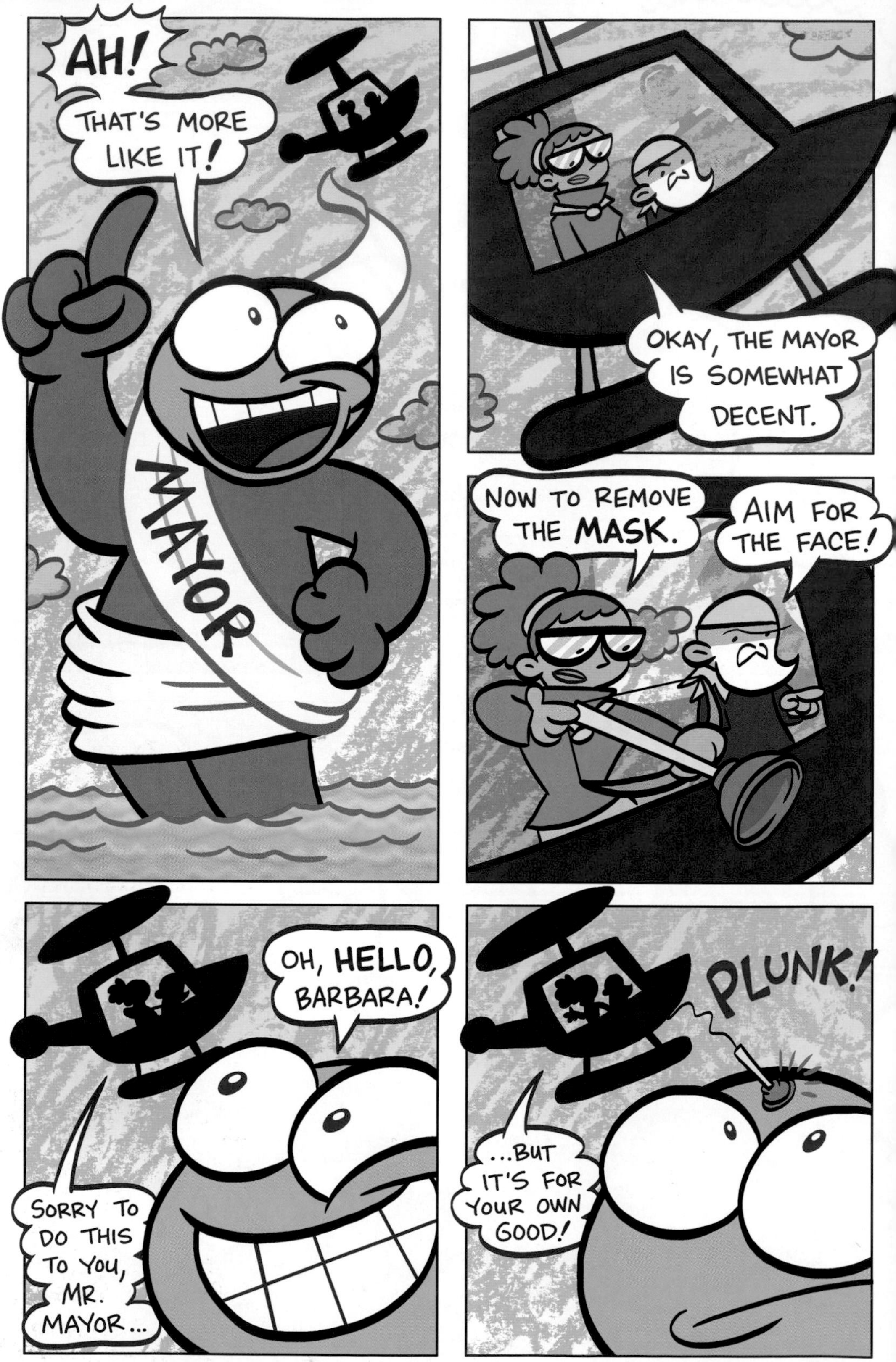
AH!
THAT'S MORE LIKE IT!
MAYOR
OKAY, THE MAYOR IS SOMEWHAT DECENT.
NOW TO REMOVE THE MASK.
AIM FOR THE FACE!
OH, HELLO, BARBARA!
SORRY TO DO THIS TO YOU, MR. MAYOR...
PLUNK!
...BUT IT'S FOR YOUR OWN GOOD!

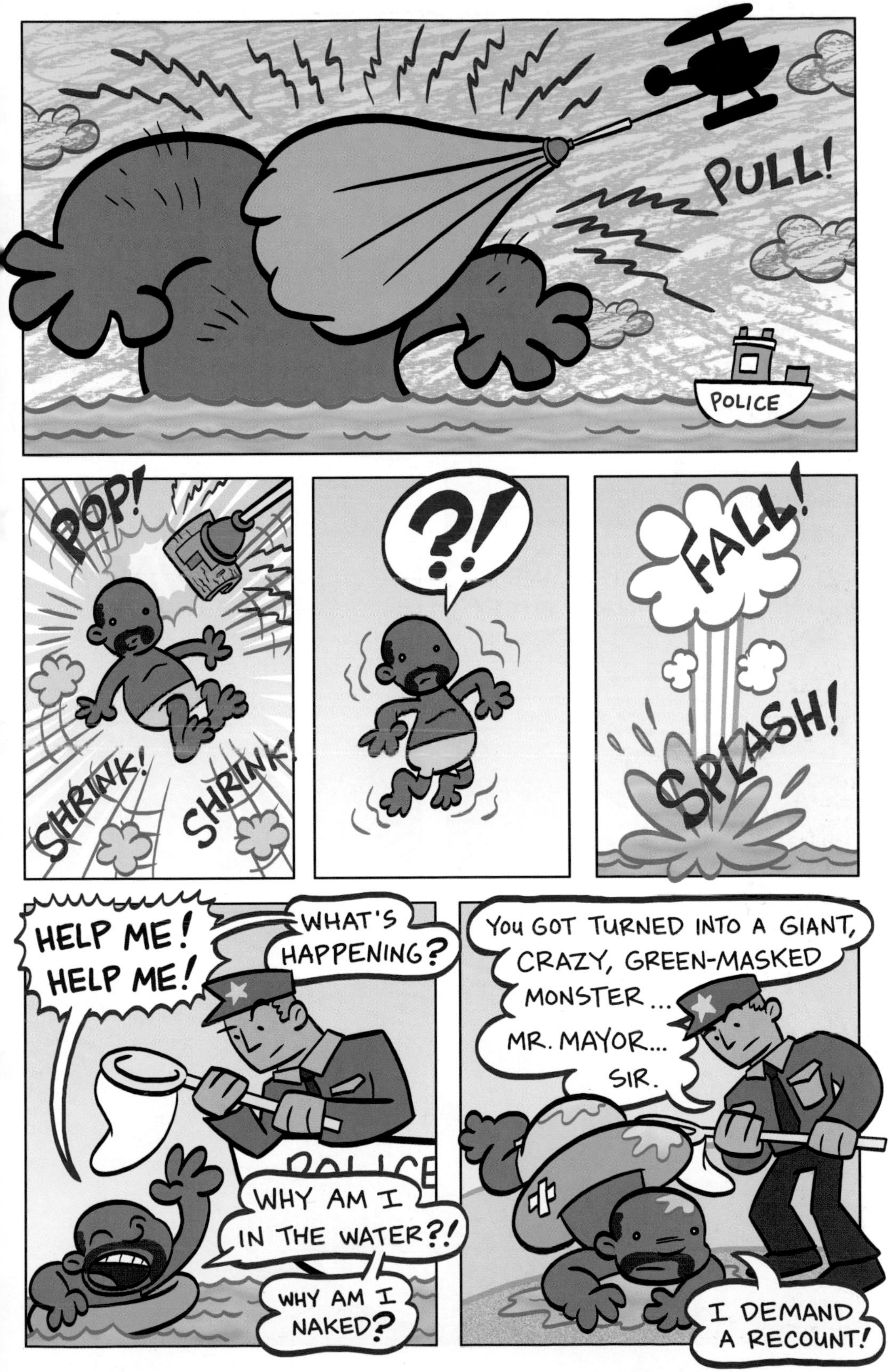
PULL!
POLICE
POP!
SHRINK!
SHRINK!
?!
FALL!
SPLASH!
HELP ME! HELP ME!
WHAT'S HAPPENING?
POLICE
WHY AM I IN THE WATER?!
WHY AM I NAKED?
YOU GOT TURNED INTO A GIANT, CRAZY, GREEN-MASKED MONSTER...
MR. MAYOR...
SIR.
I DEMAND A RECOUNT!

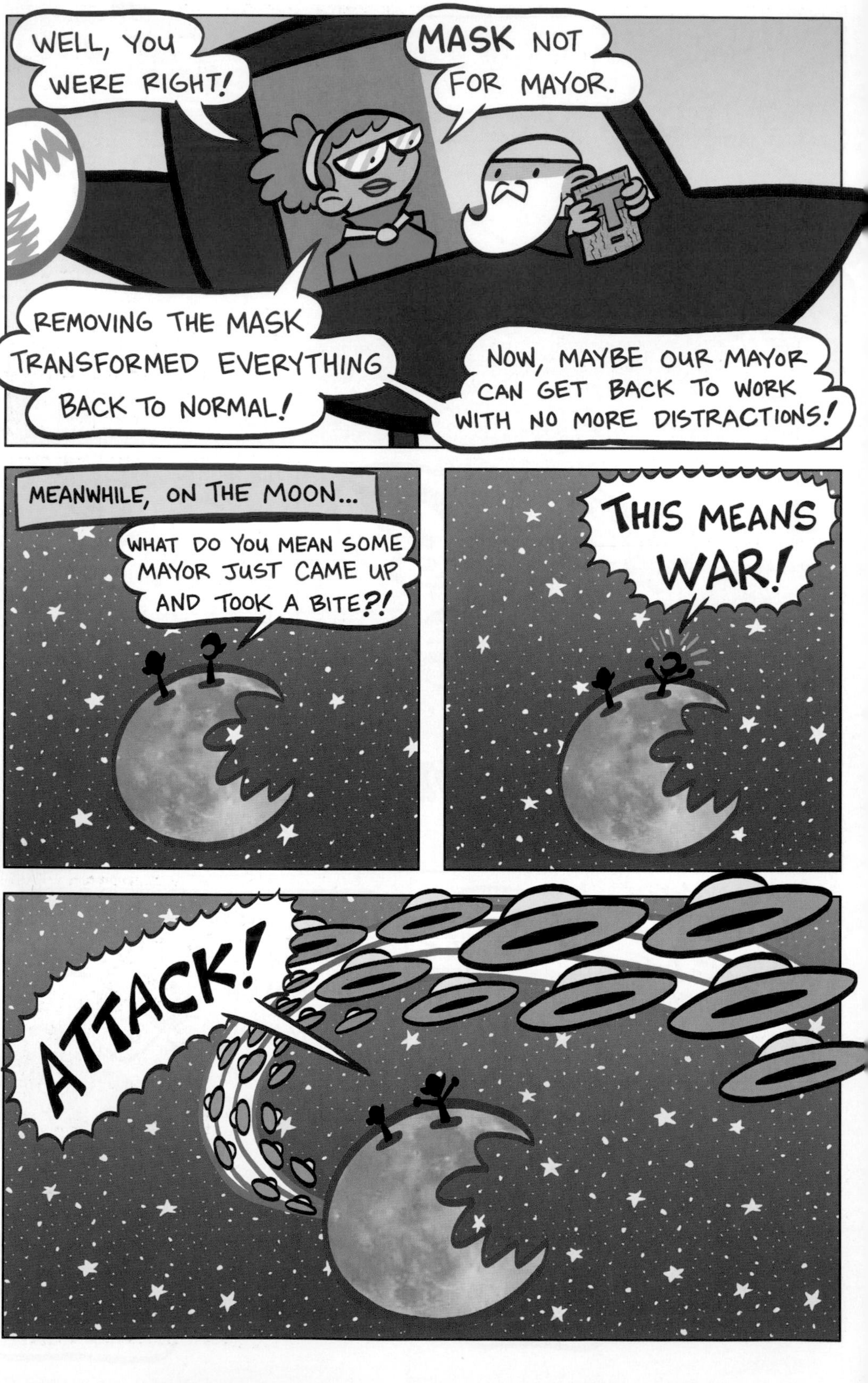
WELL, YOU WERE RIGHT!
MASK NOT FOR MAYOR.
REMOVING THE MASK TRANSFORMED EVERYTHING BACK TO NORMAL!
NOW, MAYBE OUR MAYOR CAN GET BACK TO WORK WITH NO MORE DISTRACTIONS!
MEANWHILE, ON THE MOON...
WHAT DO YOU MEAN SOME MAYOR JUST CAME UP AND TOOK A BITE?!
THIS MEANS WAR!
ATTACK!

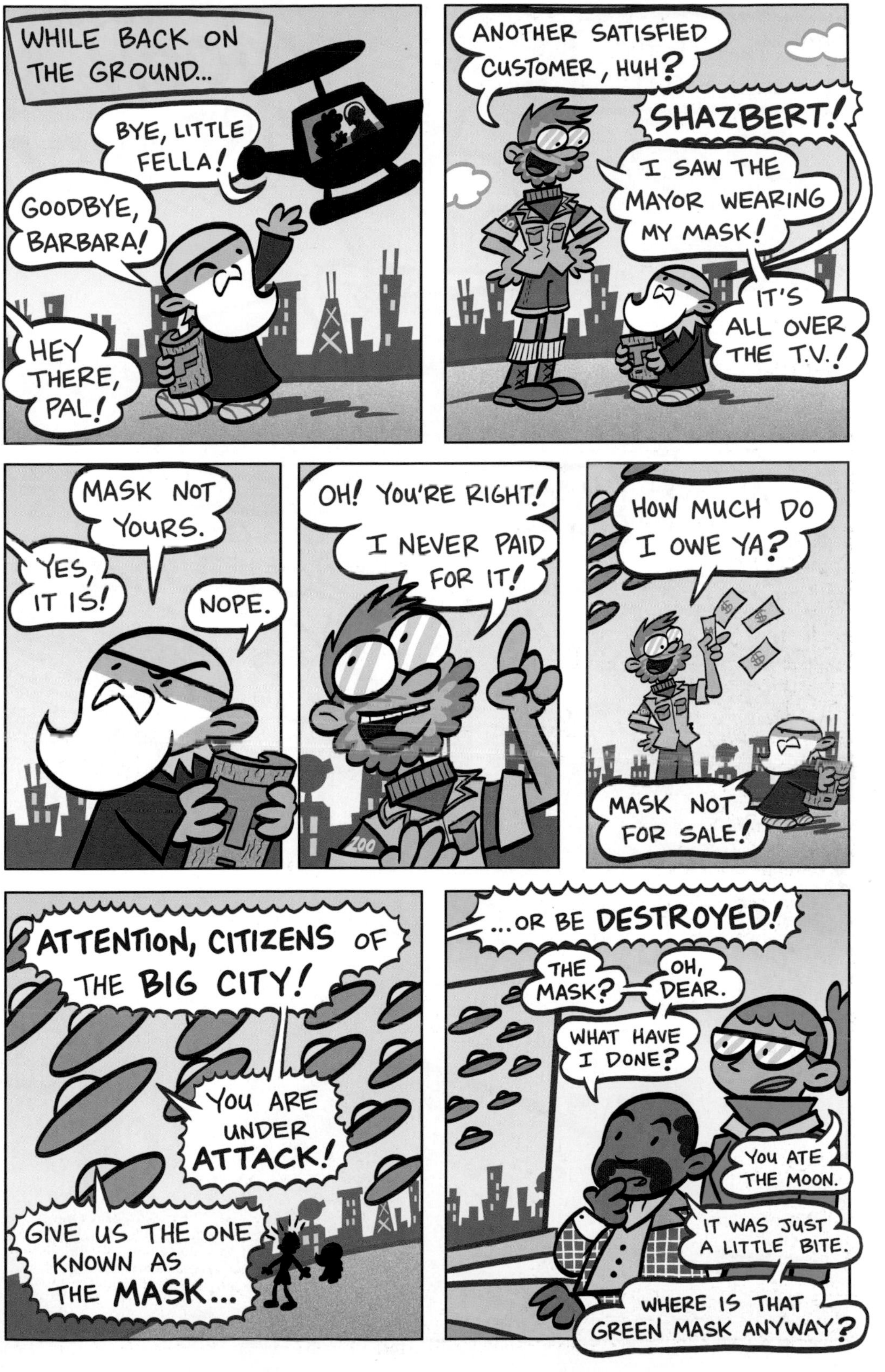

WHILE BACK ON THE GROUND...
BYE, LITTLE FELLA!
GOODBYE, BARBARA!
HEY THERE, PAL!
ANOTHER SATISFIED CUSTOMER, HUH?
SHAZBERT!
I SAW THE MAYOR WEARING MY MASK!
IT'S ALL OVER THE T.V.!
MASK NOT YOURS.
YES, IT IS!
NOPE.
OH! YOU'RE RIGHT!
I NEVER PAID FOR IT!
HOW MUCH DO I OWE YA?
MASK NOT FOR SALE!
ATTENTION, CITIZENS OF THE BIG CITY!
YOU ARE UNDER ATTACK!
GIVE US THE ONE KNOWN AS THE MASK...
...OR BE DESTROYED!
THE MASK?
OH, DEAR.
WHAT HAVE I DONE?
YOU ATE THE MOON.
IT WAS JUST A LITTLE BITE.
WHERE IS THAT GREEN MASK ANYWAY?

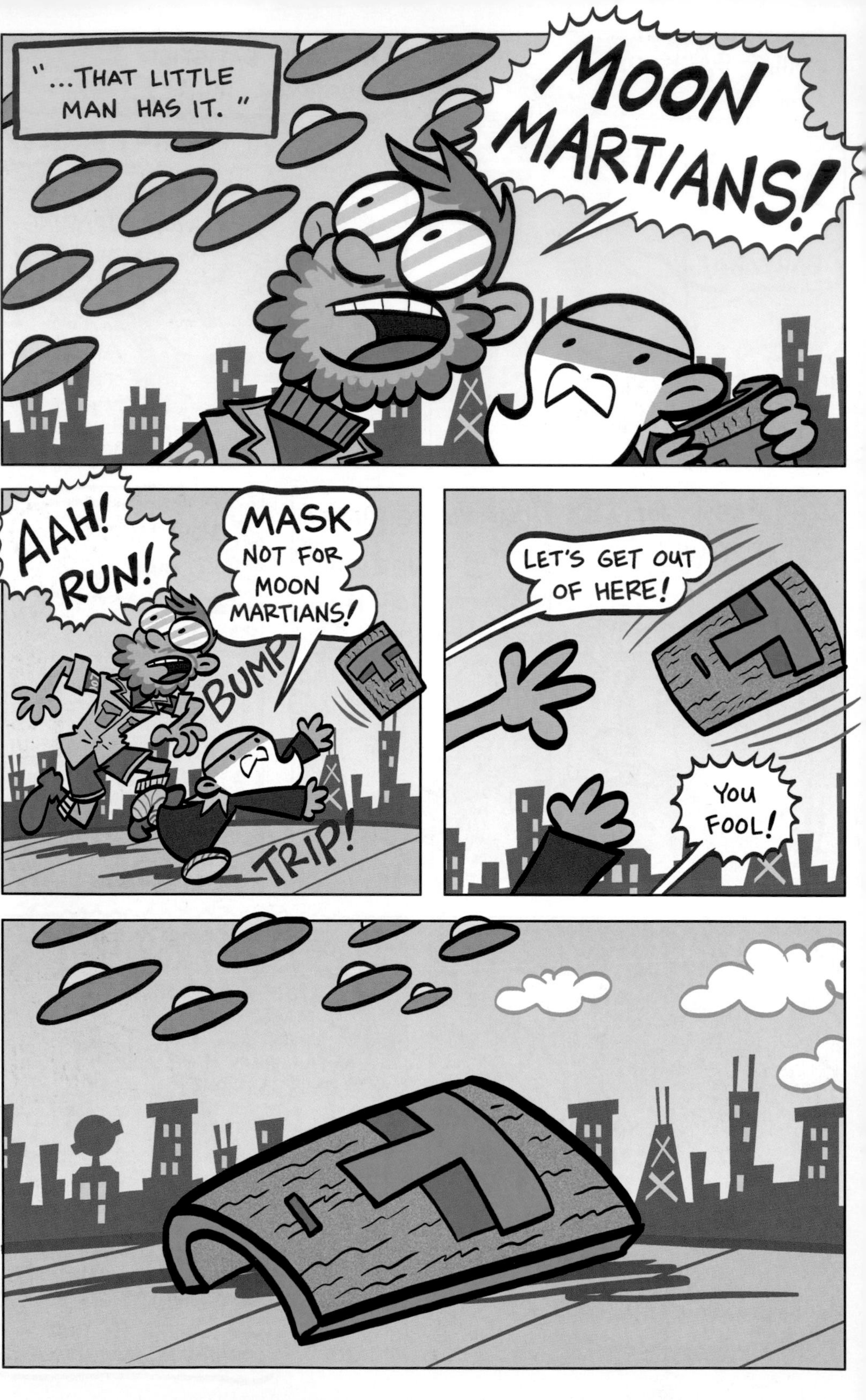
"...THAT LITTLE MAN HAS IT."
MOON MARTIANS!
AAH! RUN!
MASK NOT FOR MOON MARTIANS!
BUMP
TRIP!
LET'S GET OUT OF HERE!
YOU FOOL!

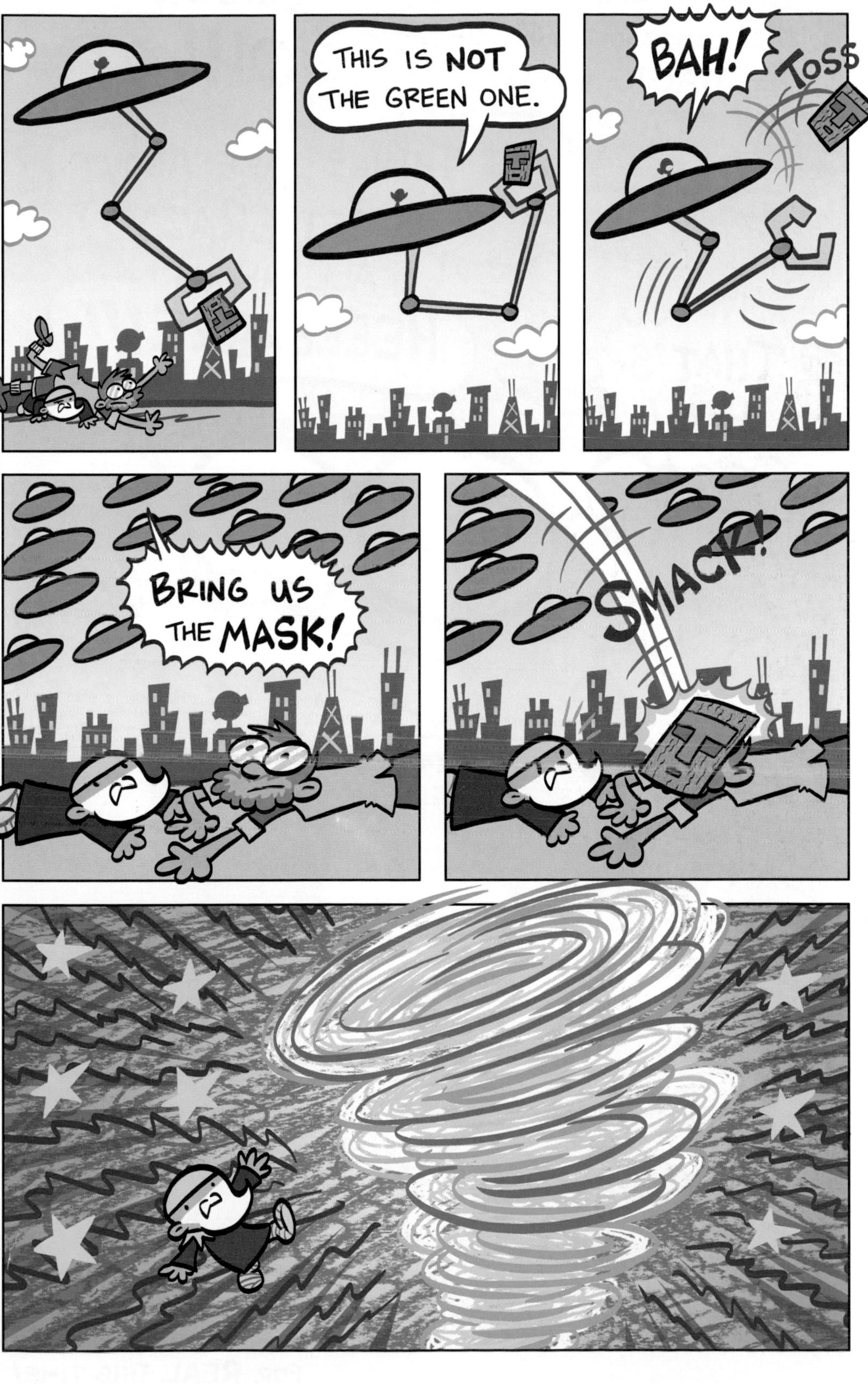
THIS IS NOT THE GREEN ONE.
BAH!
TOSS
BRING US THE MASK!
SMACK!

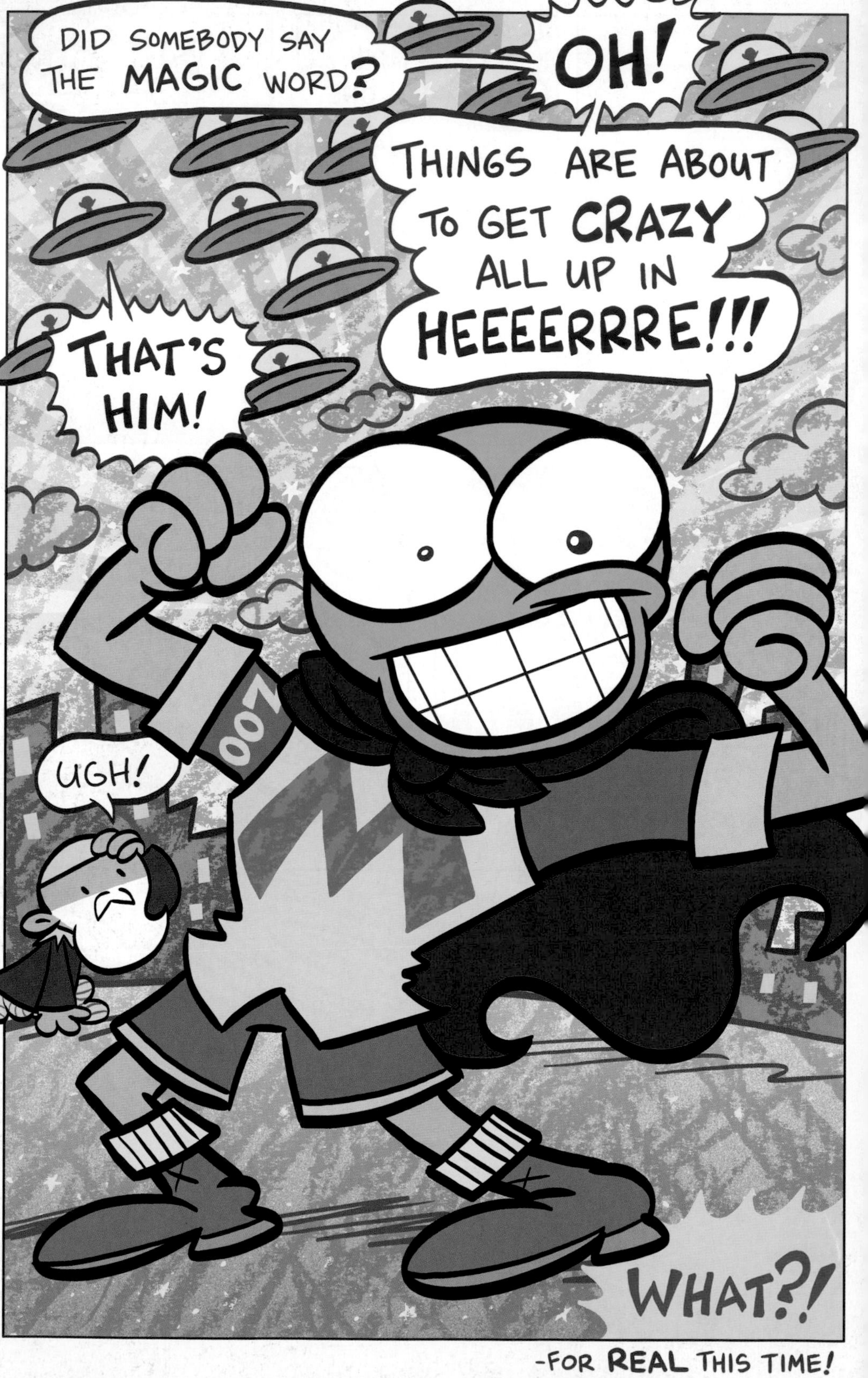
DID SOMEBODY SAY THE MAGIC WORD?
OH!
THINGS ARE ABOUT TO GET CRAZY ALL UP IN HEEEERRRRE!!!
THAT'S HIM!
UGH!
007
WHAT?!

-FOR **REAL** THIS TIME!

CHAPTER FOUR

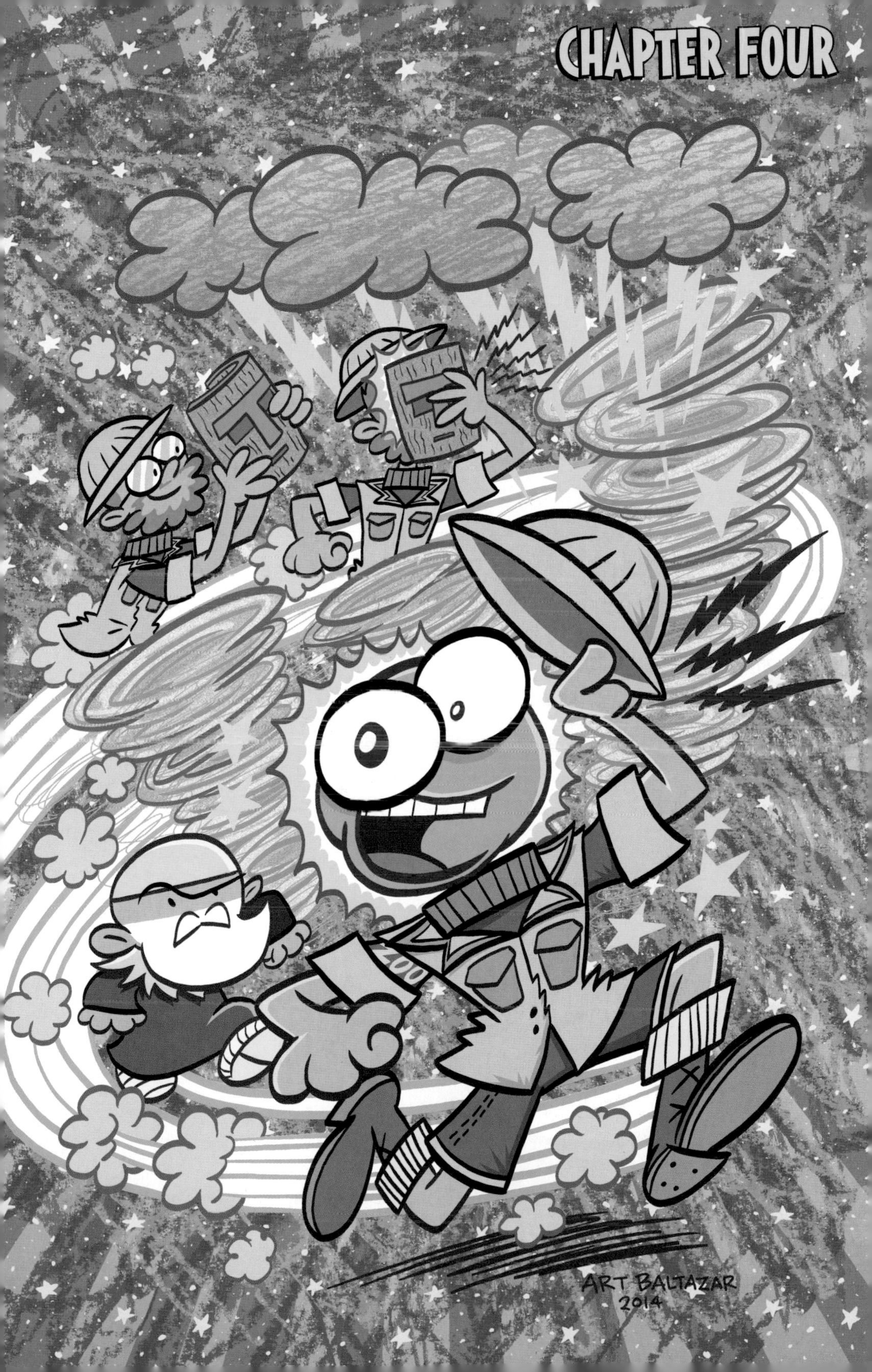
ART BALTAZAR
2014

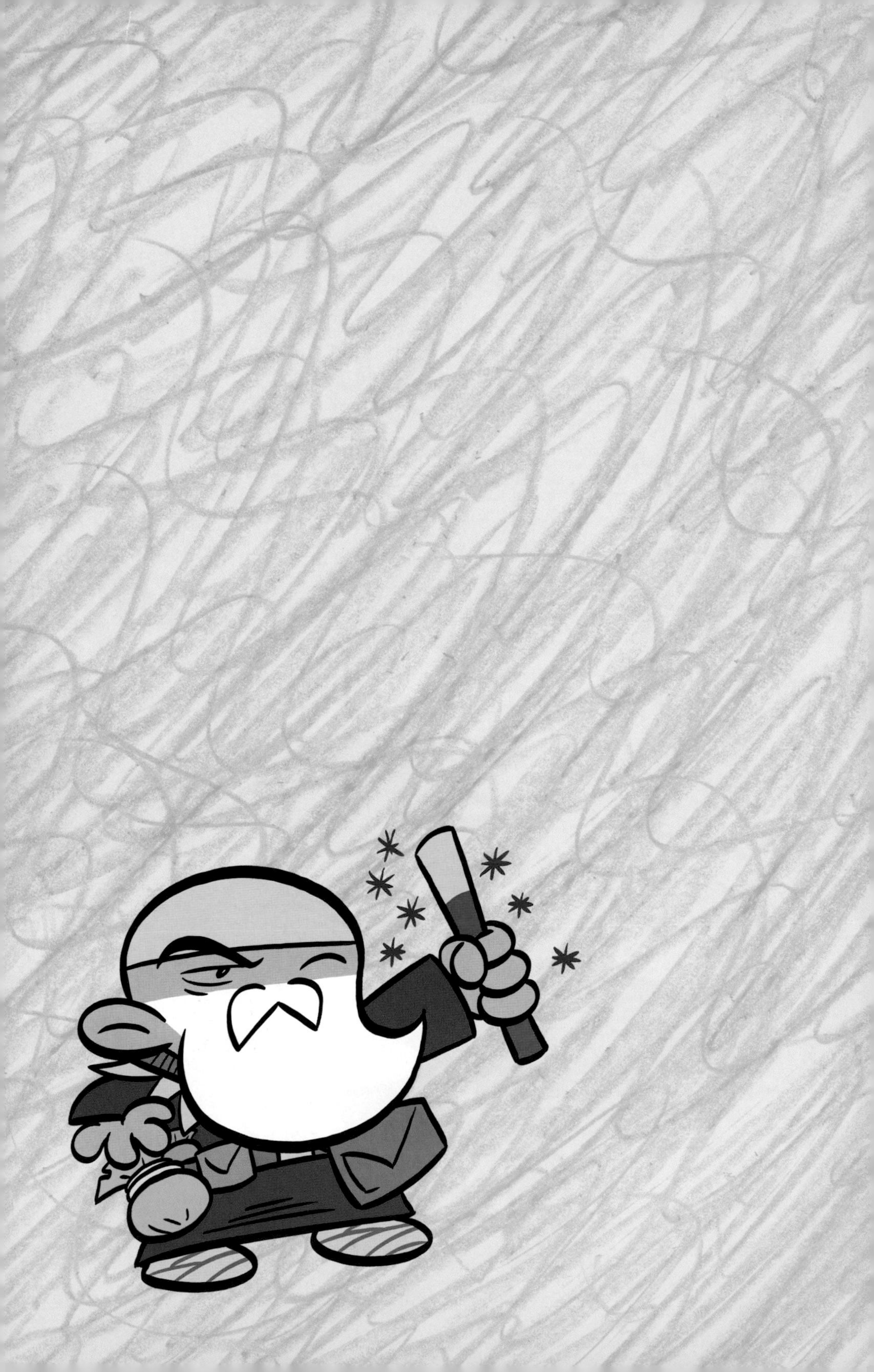

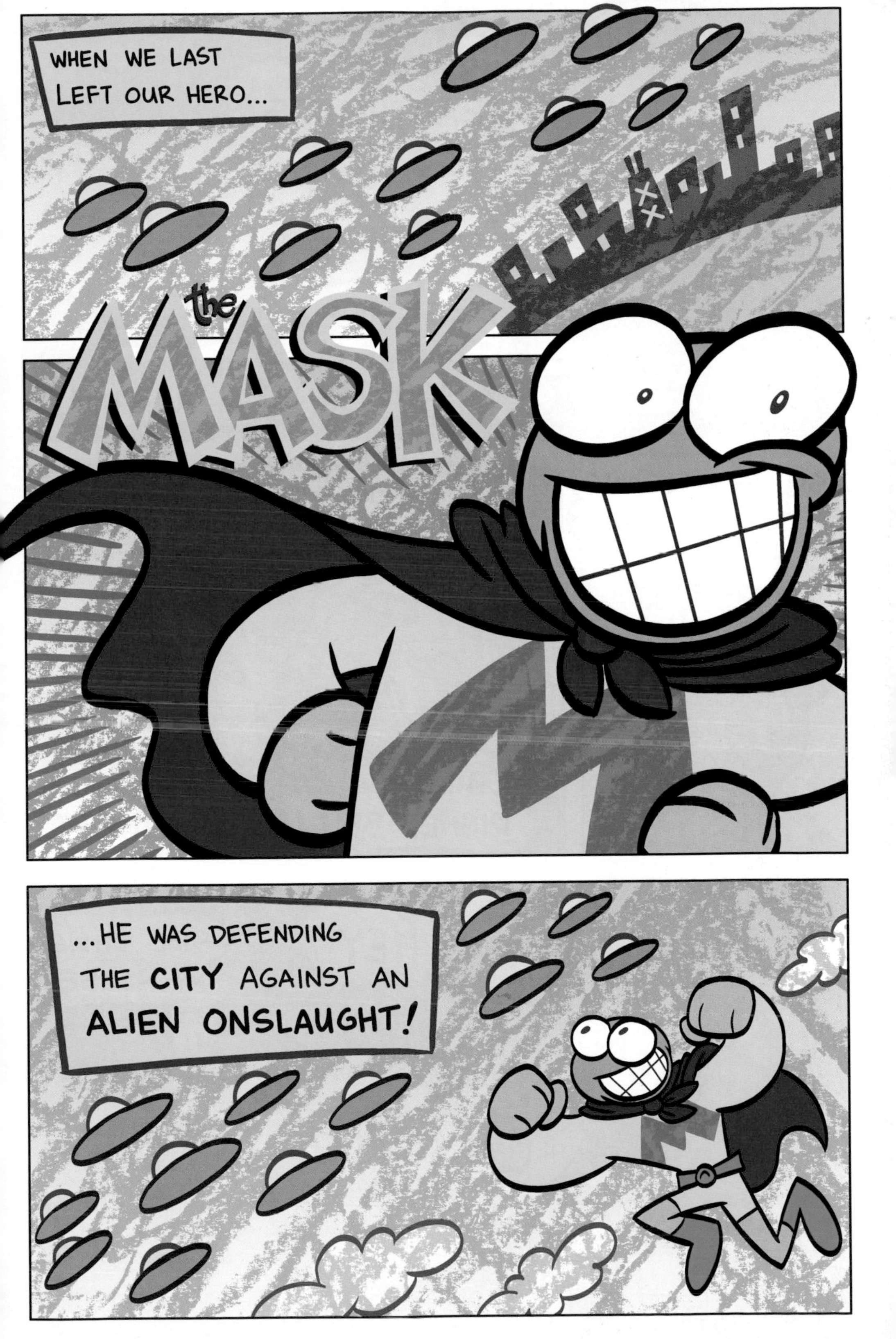
WHEN WE LAST LEFT OUR HERO...
the MASK
...HE WAS DEFENDING THE CITY AGAINST AN ALIEN ONSLAUGHT!

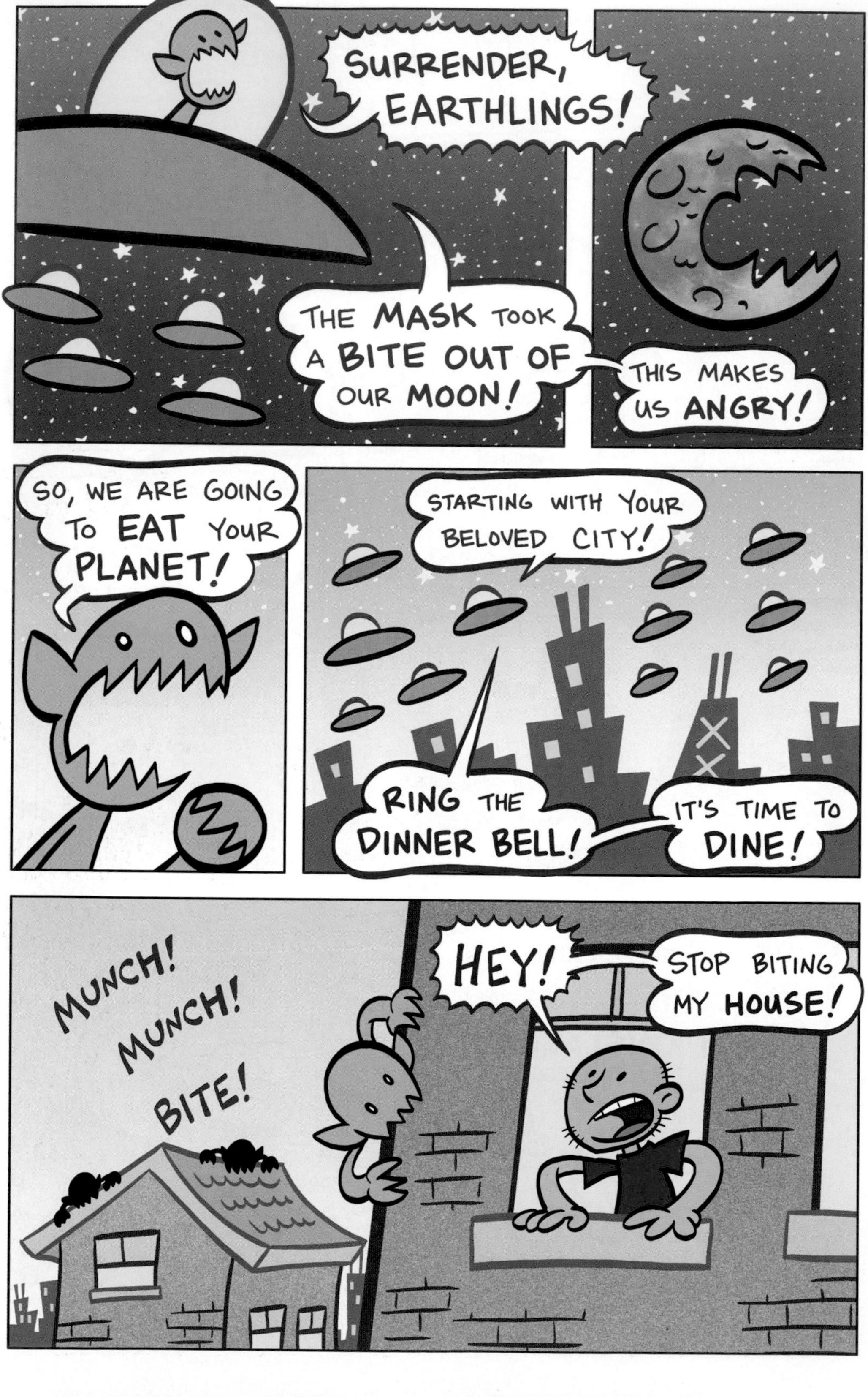
SURRENDER, EARTHLINGS!
THE MASK TOOK A BITE OUT OF OUR MOON!
THIS MAKES US ANGRY!
SO, WE ARE GOING TO EAT YOUR PLANET!
STARTING WITH YOUR BELOVED CITY!
RING THE DINNER BELL!
IT'S TIME TO DINE!
MUNCH! MUNCH! BITE!
HEY!
STOP BITING MY HOUSE!

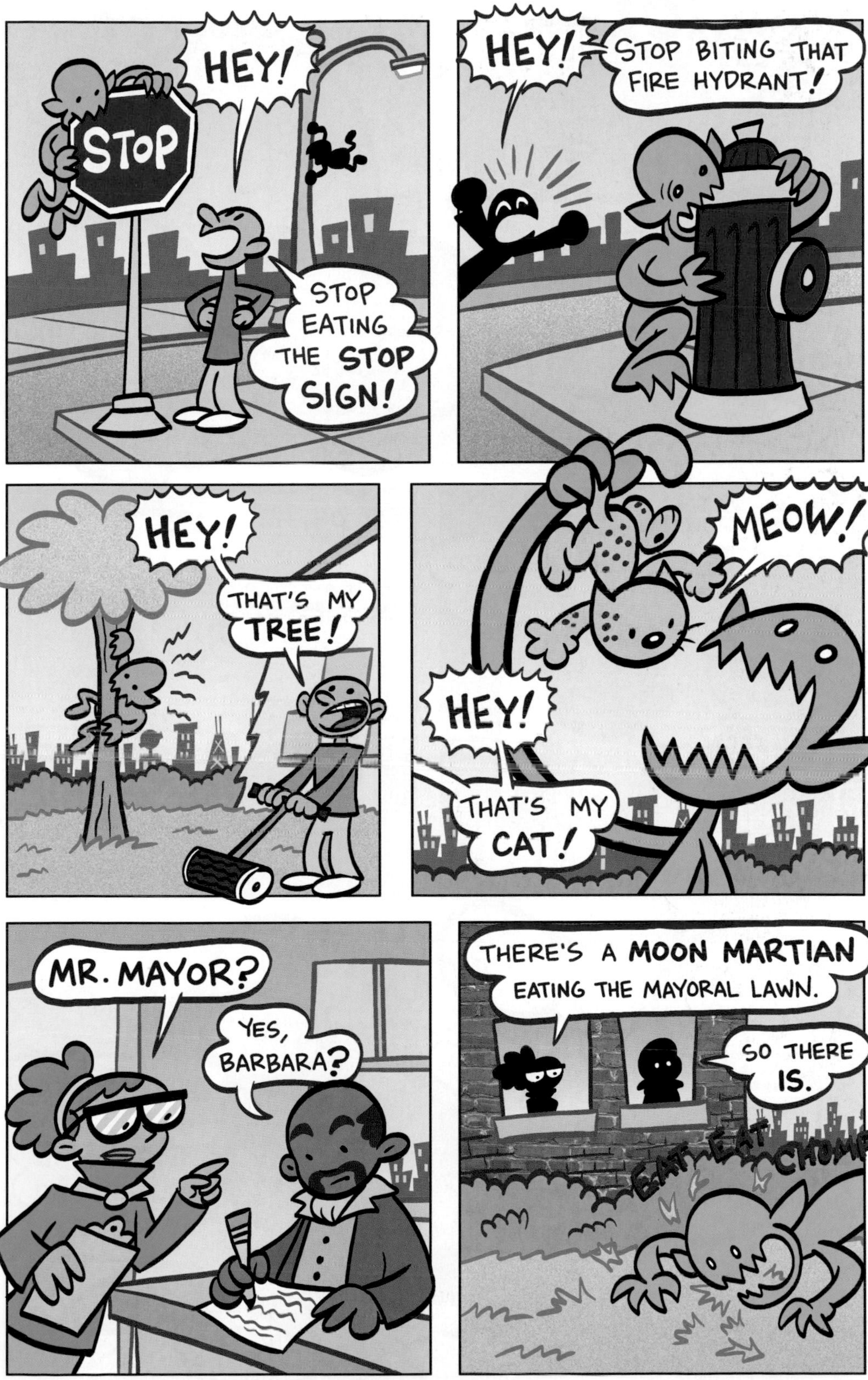
STOP
HEY!
STOP EATING THE STOP SIGN!
HEY!
STOP BITING THAT FIRE HYDRANT!
HEY!
THAT'S MY TREE!
MEOW!
HEY!
THAT'S MY CAT!
MR. MAYOR?
YES, BARBARA?
THERE'S A MOON MARTIAN EATING THE MAYORAL LAWN.
SO THERE IS.
EAT EAT CHOMP

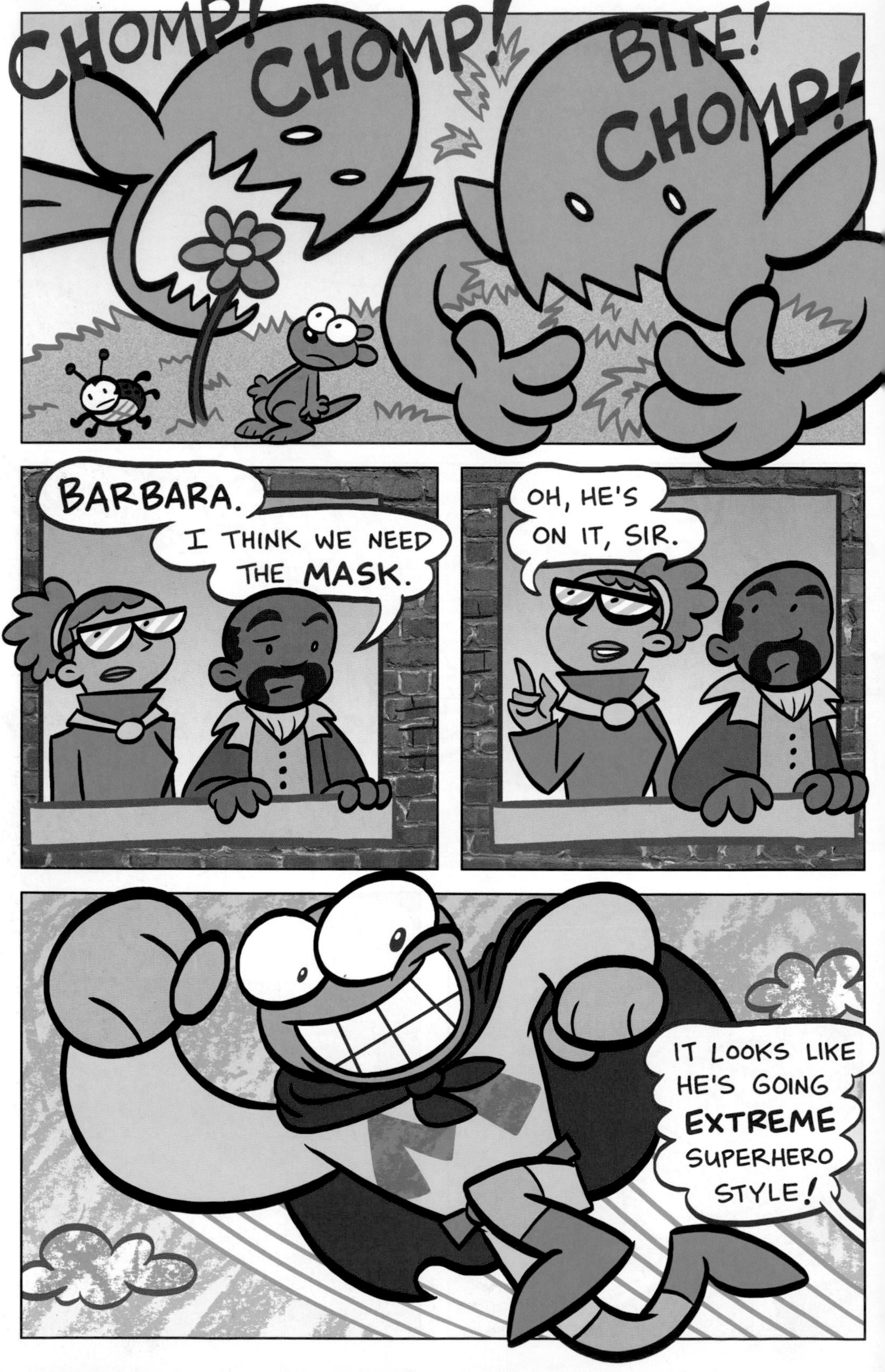
CHOMP!
CHOMP!
BITE!
CHOMP!
BARBARA.
I THINK WE NEED THE MASK.
OH, HE'S ON IT, SIR.
IT LOOKS LIKE HE'S GOING EXTREME SUPERHERO STYLE!

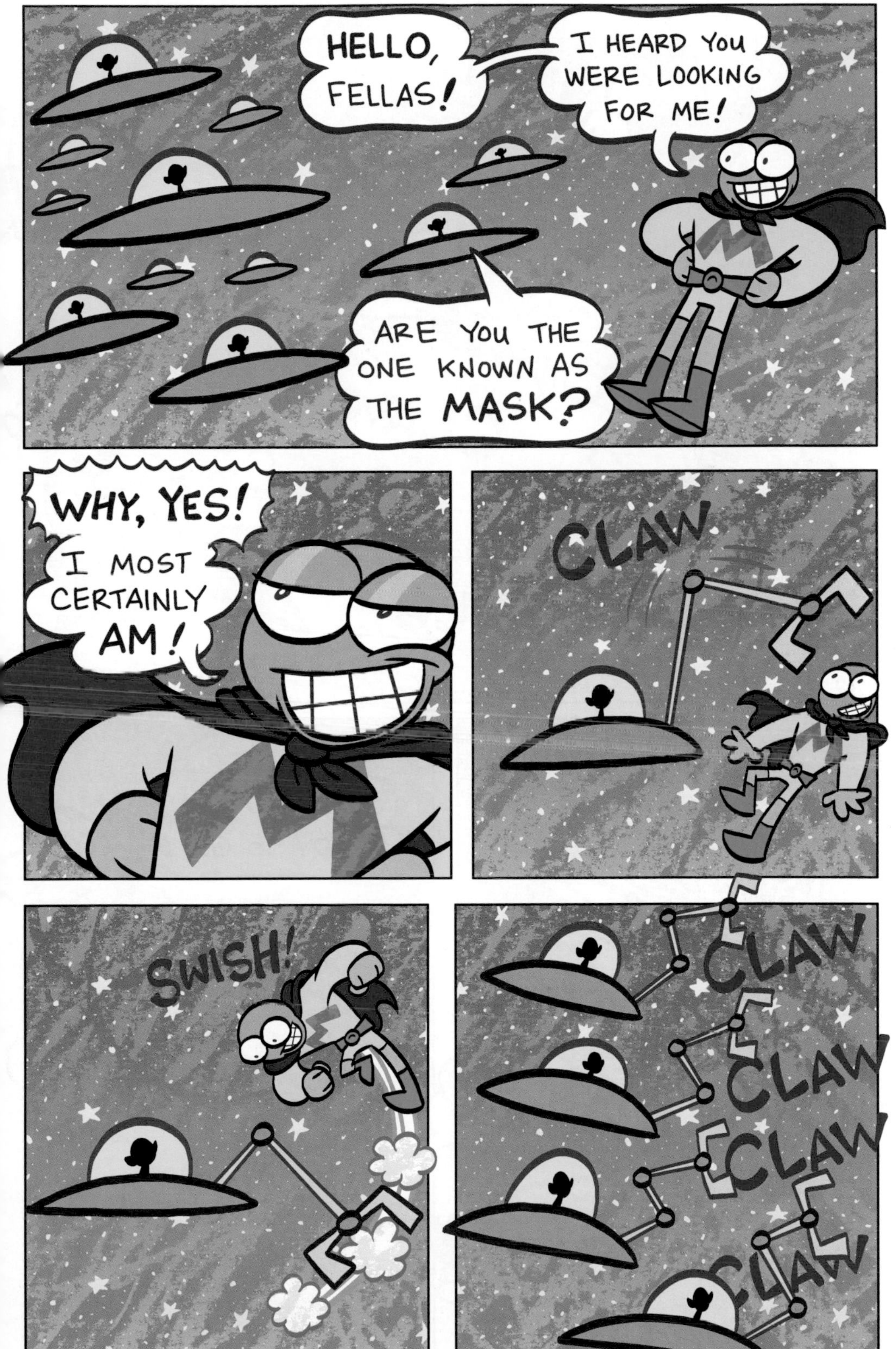

HELLO, FELLAS!
I HEARD YOU WERE LOOKING FOR ME!
ARE YOU THE ONE KNOWN AS THE MASK?
WHY, YES!
I MOST CERTAINLY AM!
CLAW
SWISH!
CLAW
CLAW
CLAW
CLAW

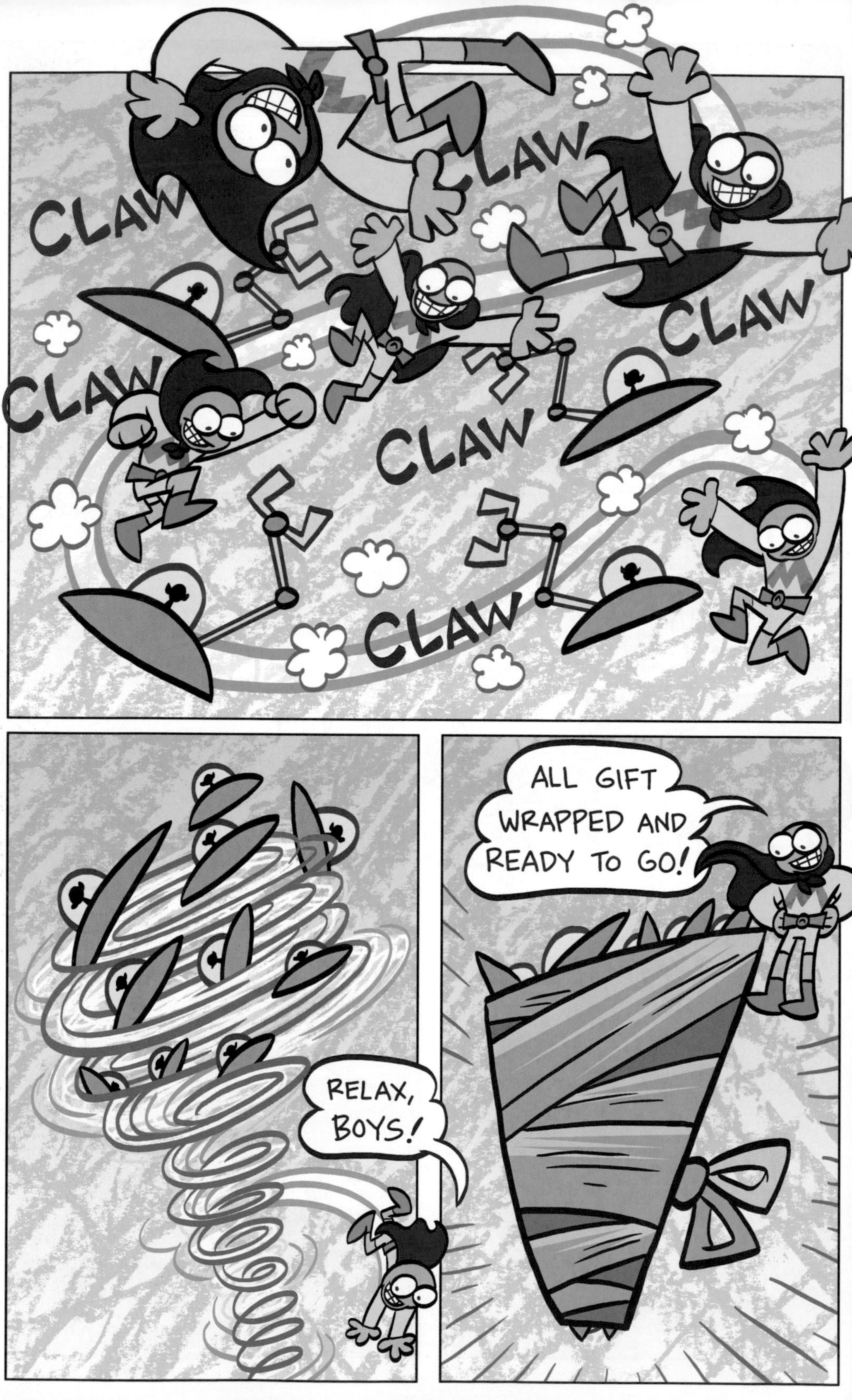
CLAW
CLAW
CLAW
CLAW
CLAW
CLAW
RELAX, BOYS!
ALL GIFT WRAPPED AND READY TO GO!

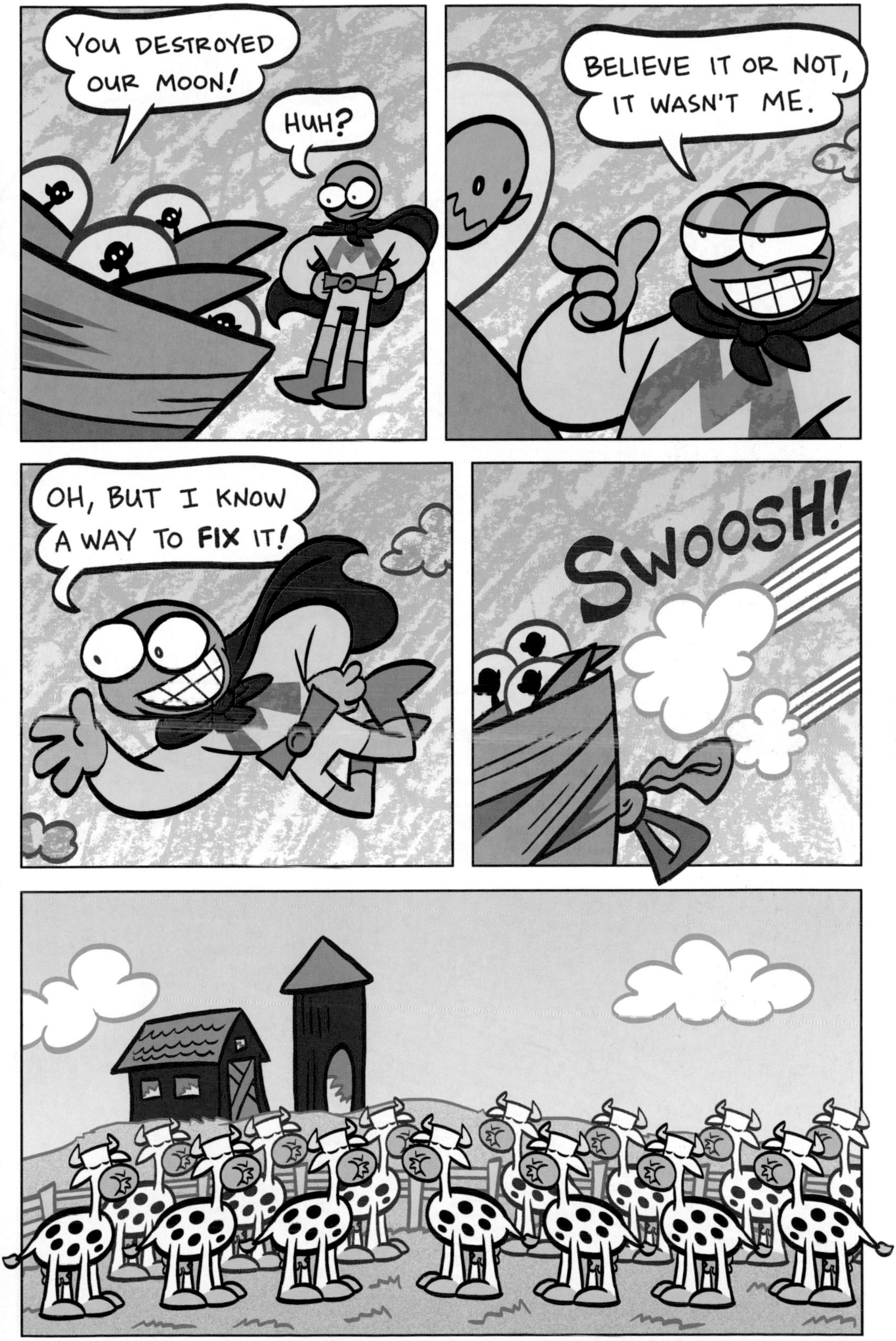
YOU DESTROYED OUR MOON!
HUH?
BELIEVE IT OR NOT, IT WASN'T ME.
OH, BUT I KNOW A WAY TO FIX IT!
SWOOSH!

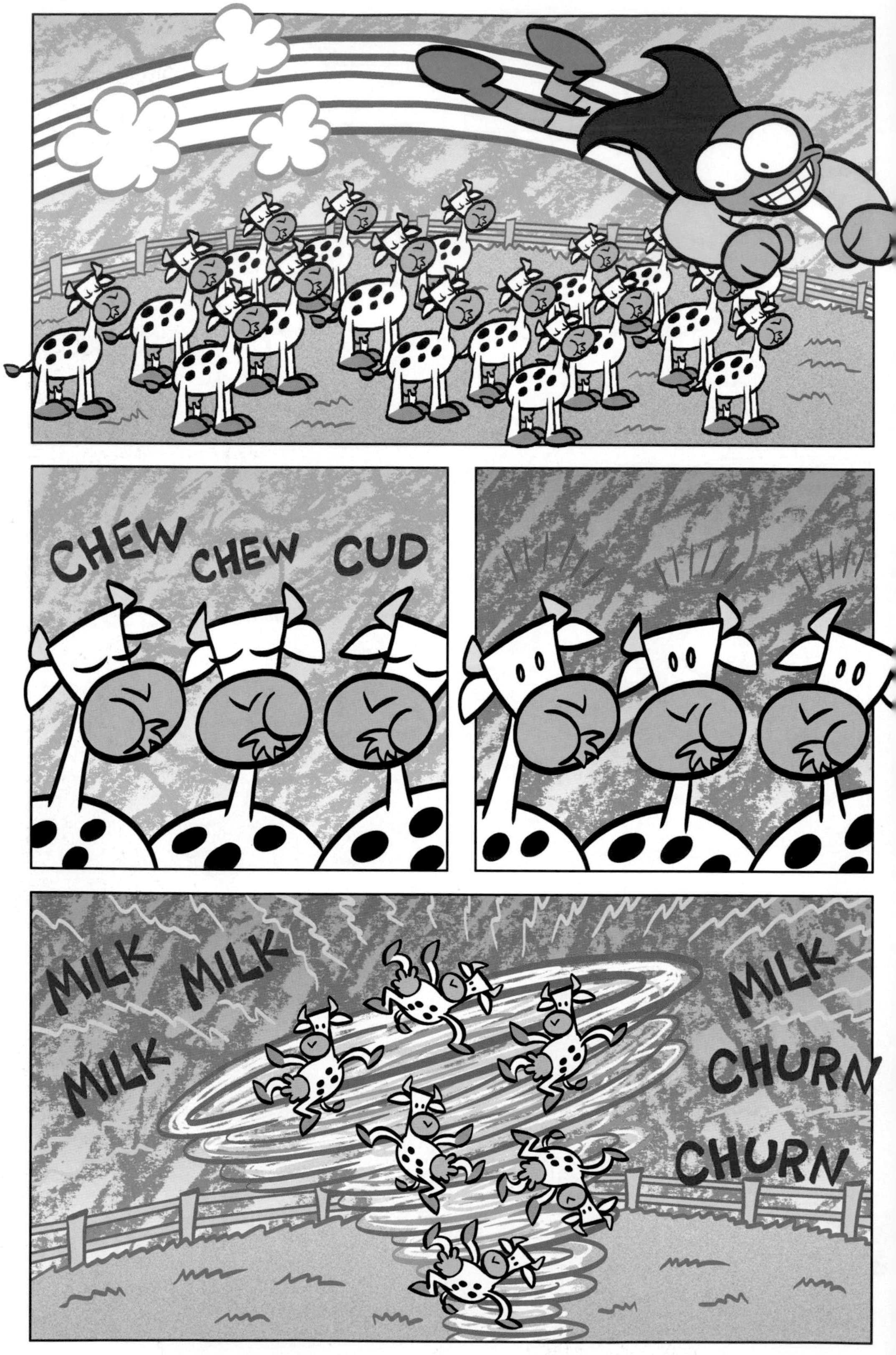
CHEW
CHEW
CUD
MILK
MILK
MILK
MILK
CHURN
CHURN

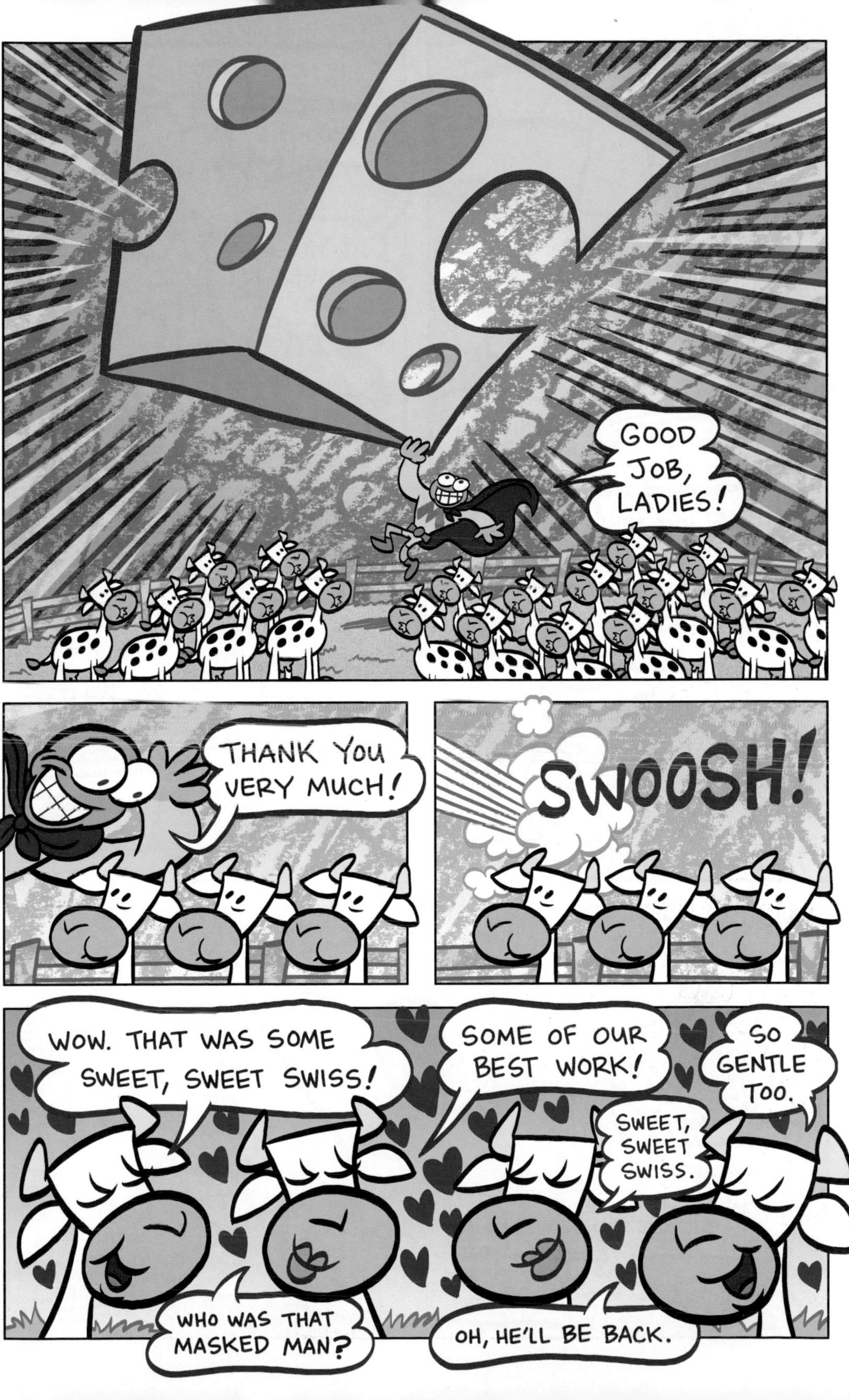
GOOD JOB, LADIES!
THANK YOU VERY MUCH!
SWOOSH!
WOW. THAT WAS SOME SWEET, SWEET SWISS!
SOME OF OUR BEST WORK!
SO GENTLE TOO.
SWEET, SWEET SWISS.
WHO WAS THAT MASKED MAN?
OH, HE'LL BE BACK.

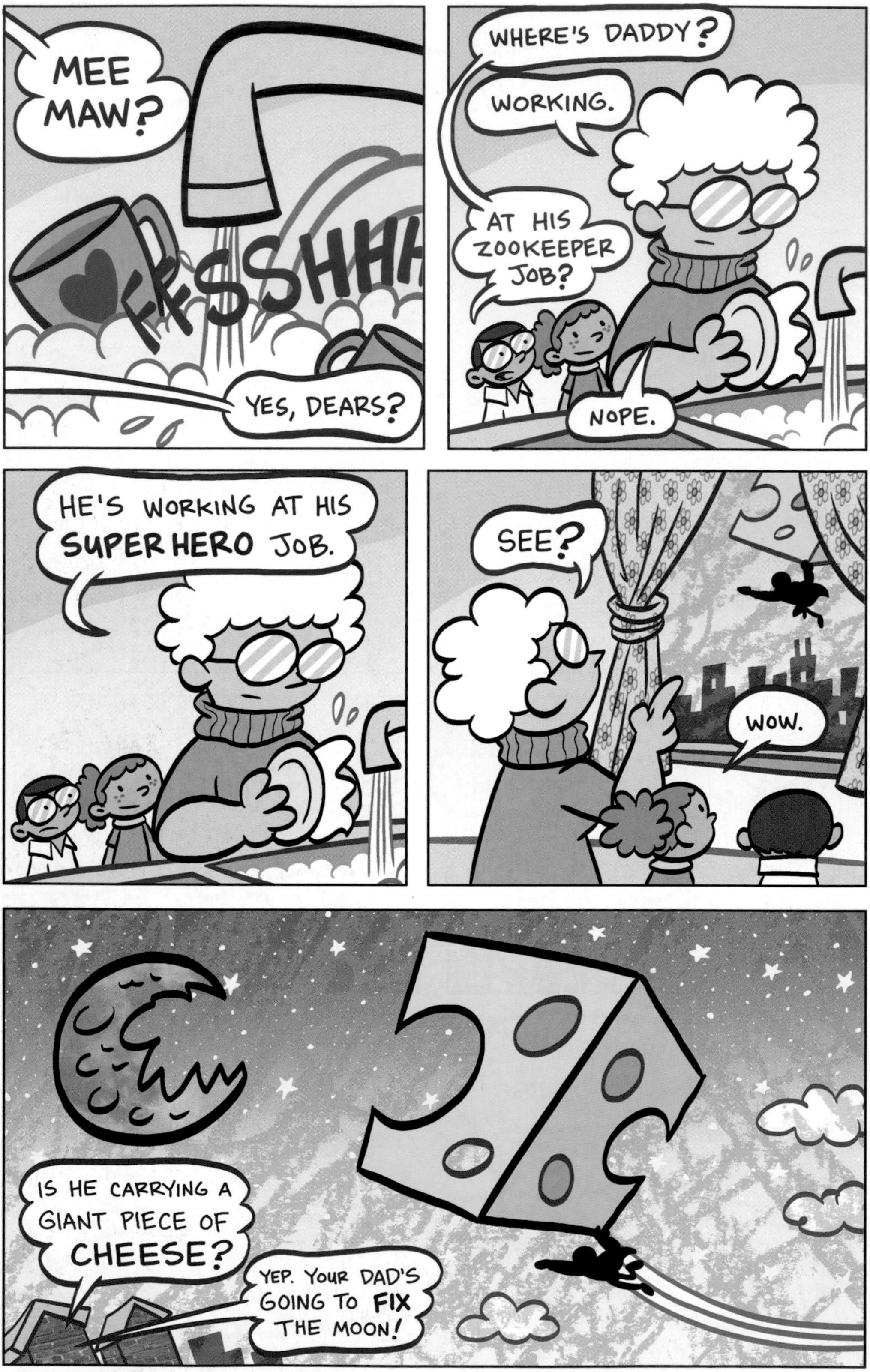
MEE MAW?
FFSSHHH
YES, DEARS?
WHERE'S DADDY?
WORKING.
AT HIS ZOOKEEPER JOB?
NOPE.
HE'S WORKING AT HIS **SUPERHERO** JOB.
SEE?
WOW.
IS HE CARRYING A GIANT PIECE OF **CHEESE?**
YEP. YOUR DAD'S GOING TO **FIX** THE MOON!

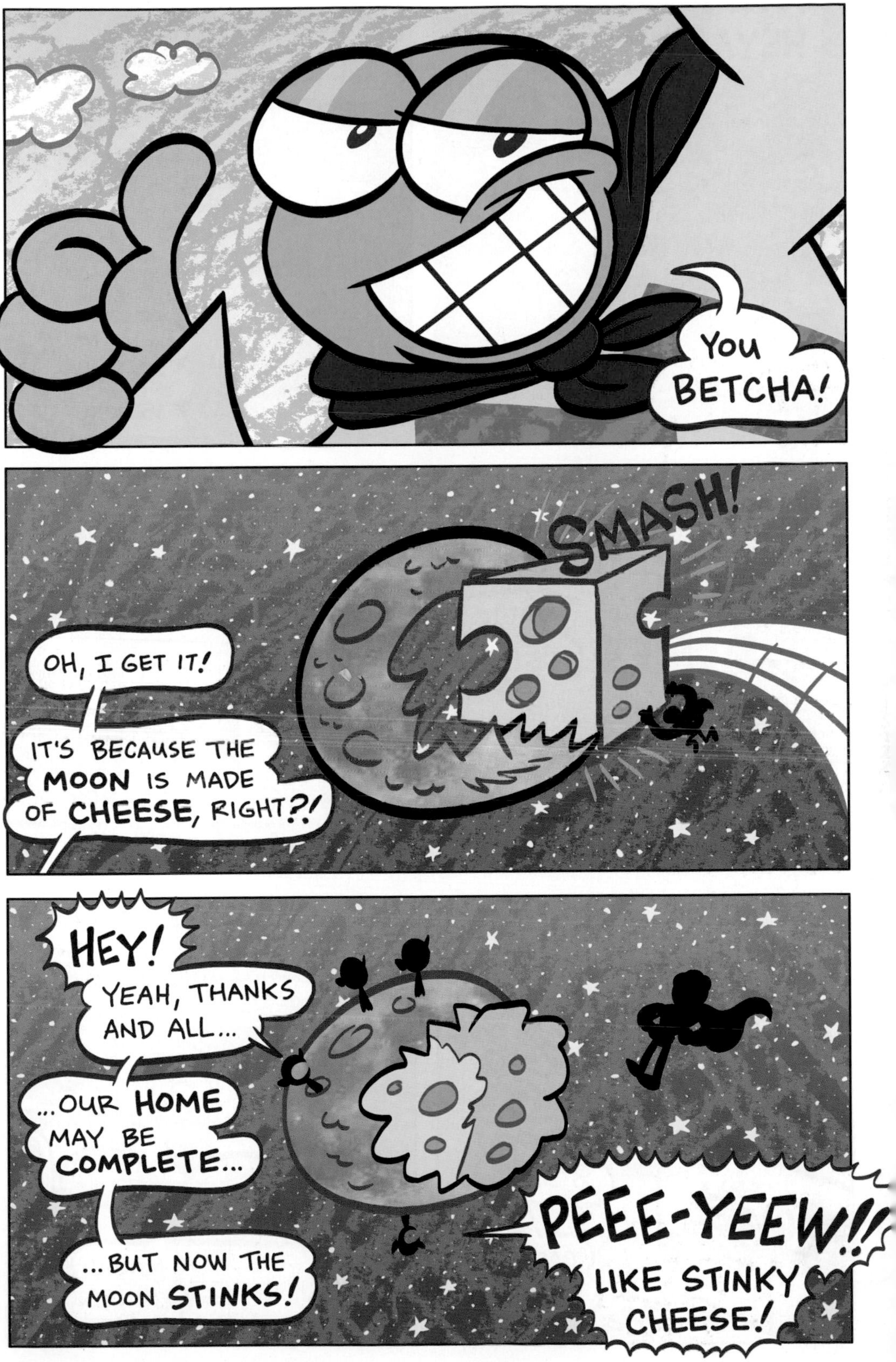
YOU BETCHA!
SMASH!
OH, I GET IT!
IT'S BECAUSE THE MOON IS MADE OF CHEESE, RIGHT?!
HEY!
YEAH, THANKS AND ALL...
...OUR HOME MAY BE COMPLETE...
...BUT NOW THE MOON STINKS!
PEEE-YEEW!!
LIKE STINKY CHEESE!

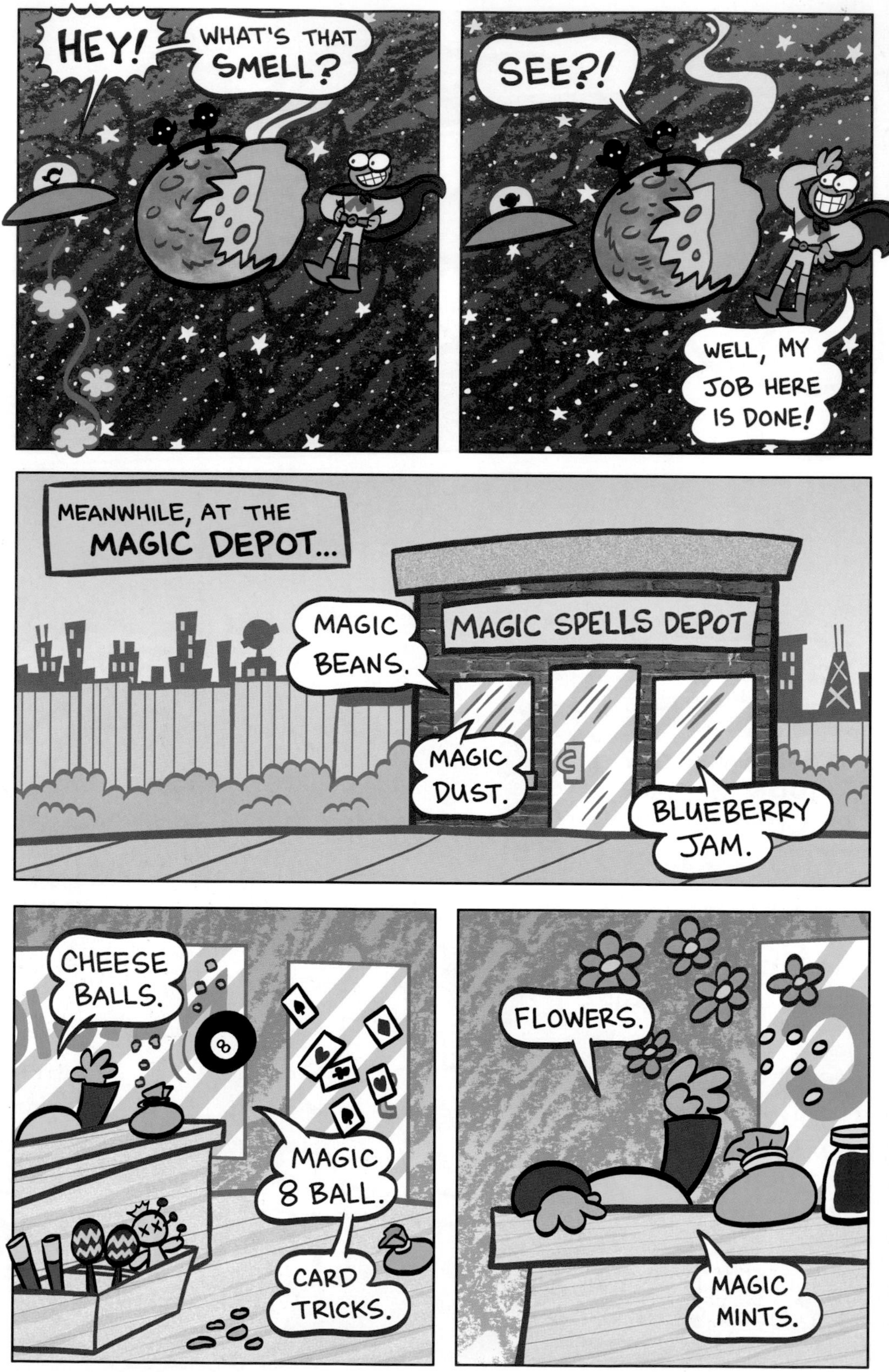
HEY!
WHAT'S THAT SMELL?
SEE?!
WELL, MY JOB HERE IS DONE!
MEANWHILE, AT THE MAGIC DEPOT...
MAGIC SPELLS DEPOT
MAGIC BEANS.
MAGIC DUST.
BLUEBERRY JAM.
CHEESE BALLS.
MAGIC 8 BALL.
CARD TRICKS.
FLOWERS.
MAGIC MINTS.

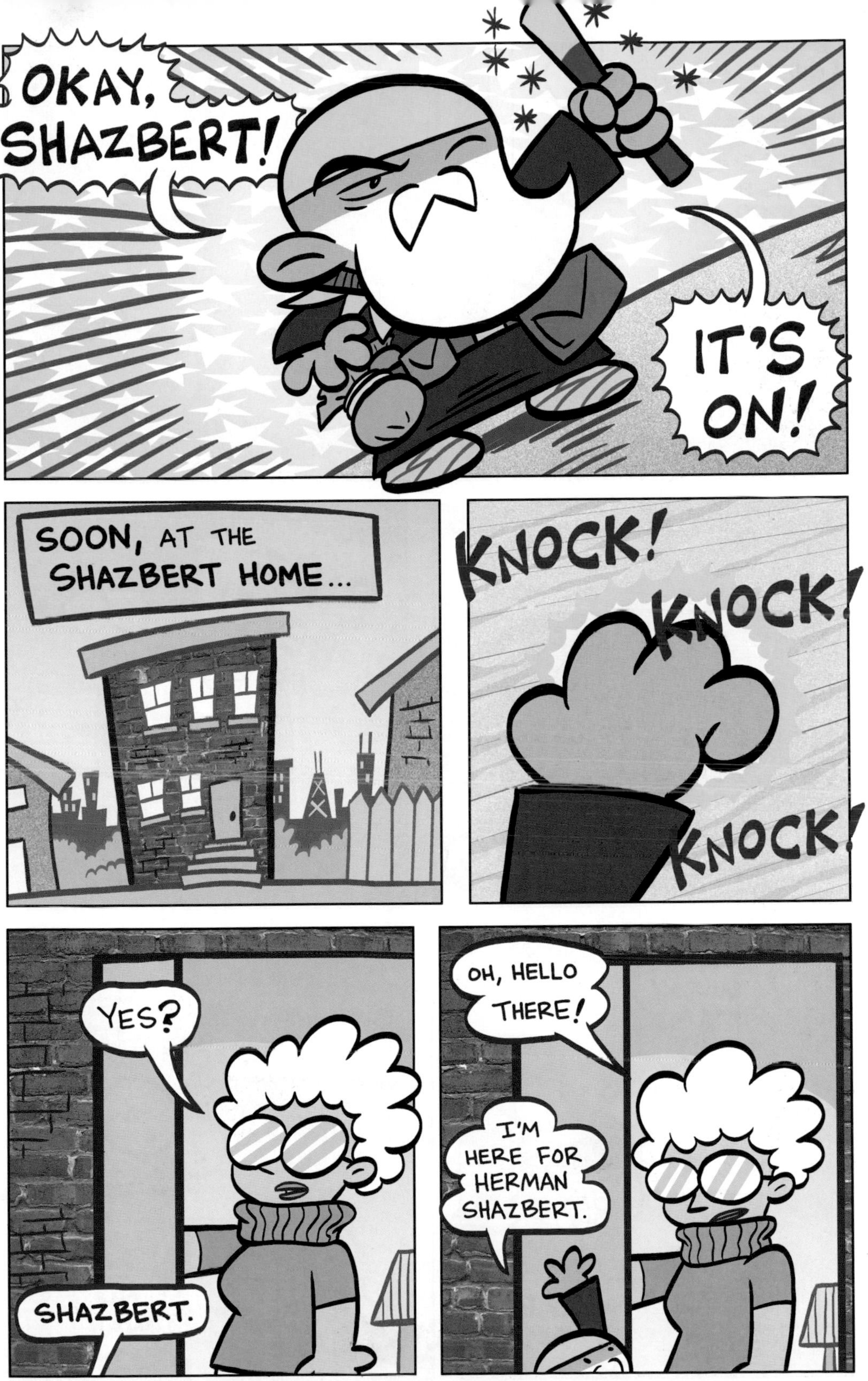
OKAY, SHAZBERT!
IT'S ON!
SOON, AT THE SHAZBERT HOME...
KNOCK!
KNOCK!
KNOCK!
YES?
SHAZBERT.
OH, HELLO THERE!
I'M HERE FOR HERMAN SHAZBERT.

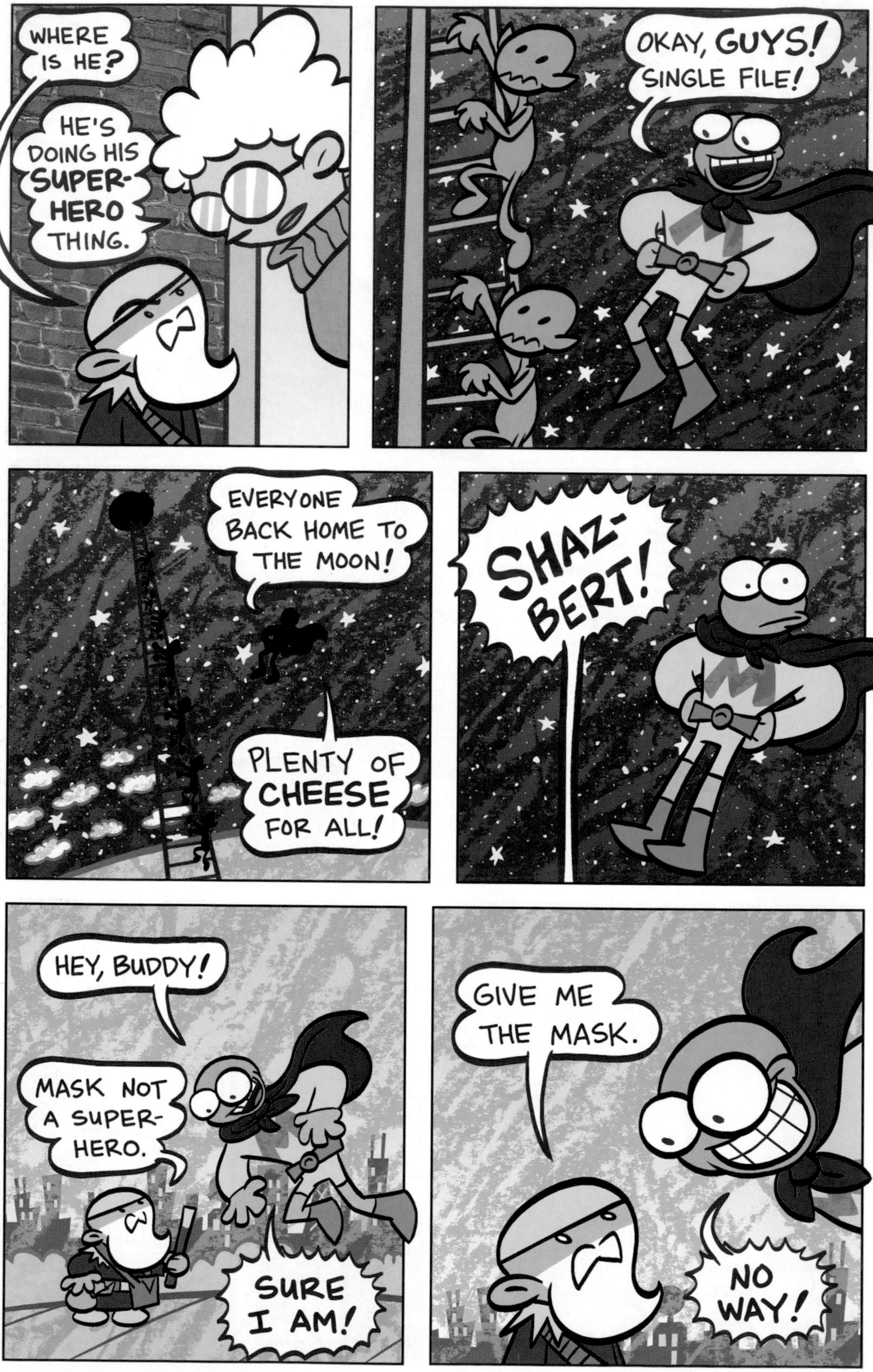
WHERE IS HE?
HE'S DOING HIS SUPER-HERO THING.
OKAY, GUYS! SINGLE FILE!
EVERYONE BACK HOME TO THE MOON!
PLENTY OF CHEESE FOR ALL!
SHAZ-BERT!
HEY, BUDDY!
MASK NOT A SUPER-HERO.
SURE I AM!
GIVE ME THE MASK.
NO WAY!

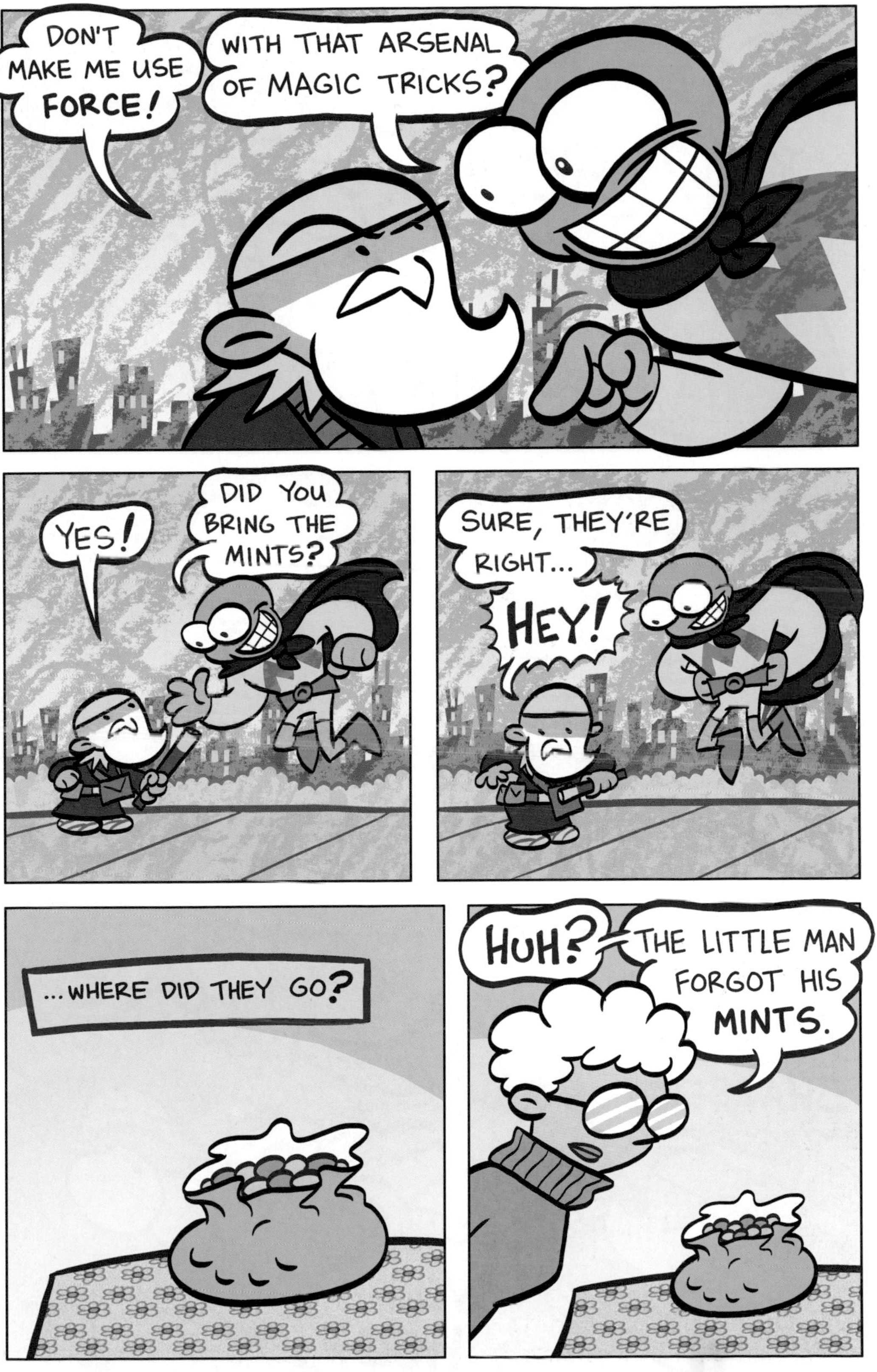
DON'T MAKE ME USE FORCE!
WITH THAT ARSENAL OF MAGIC TRICKS?
YES!
DID YOU BRING THE MINTS?
SURE, THEY'RE RIGHT...
HEY!
...WHERE DID THEY GO?
HUH?
THE LITTLE MAN FORGOT HIS MINTS.

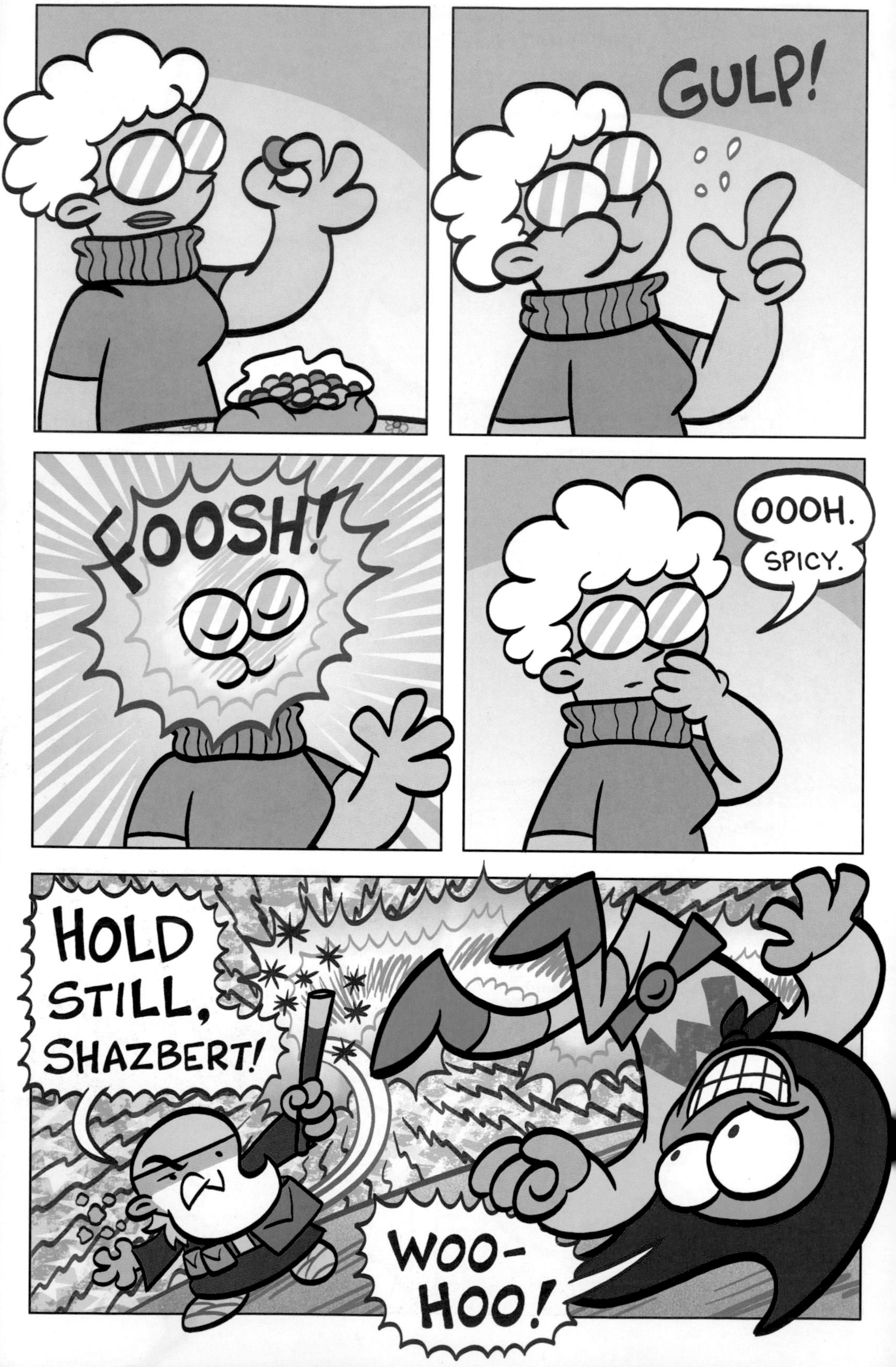

GULP!
FOOSH!
OOOH.
SPICY.
HOLD STILL, SHAZBERT!
WOO-HOO!

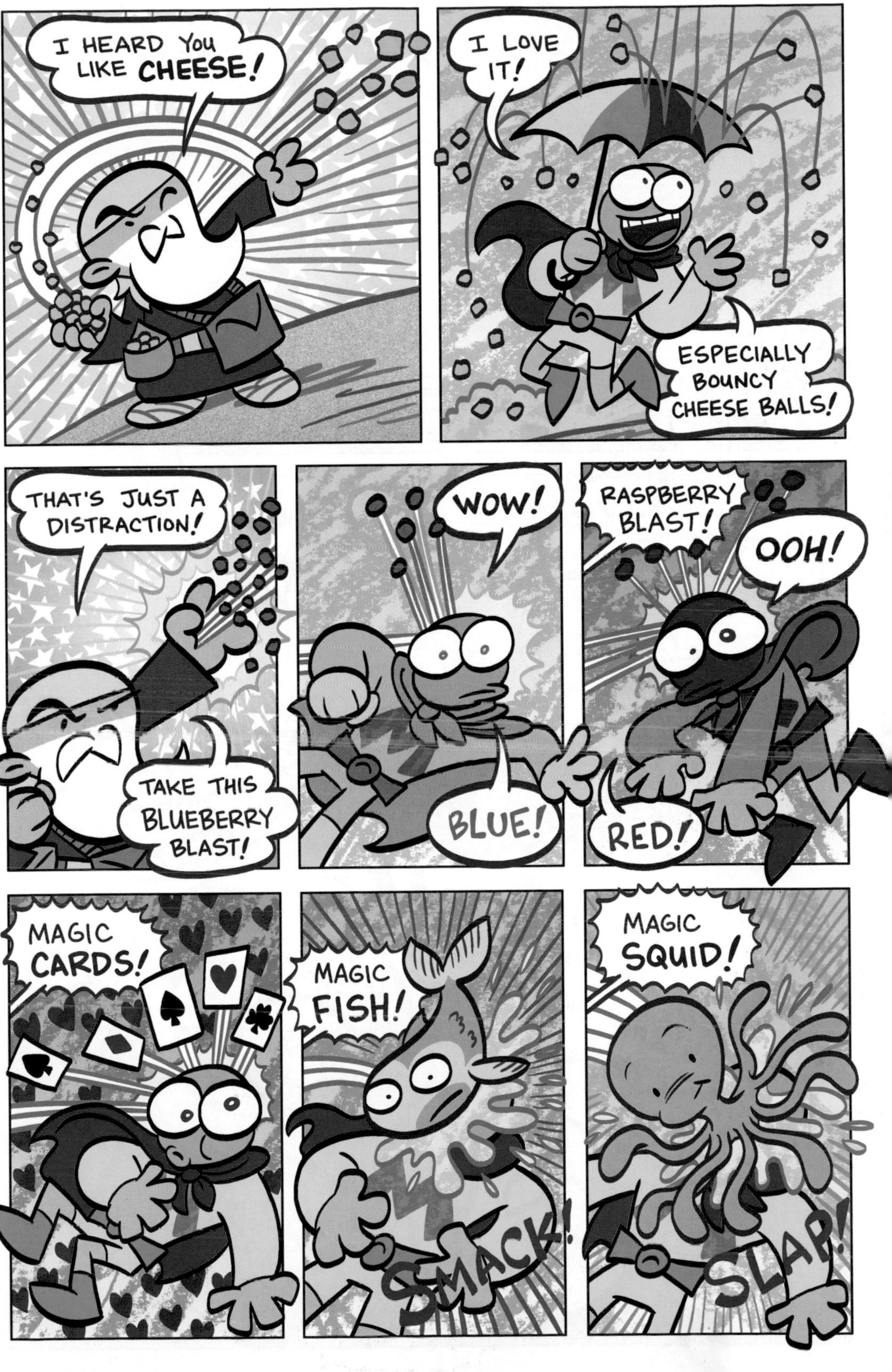
I HEARD YOU LIKE CHEESE!
I LOVE IT!
ESPECIALLY BOUNCY CHEESE BALLS!
THAT'S JUST A DISTRACTION!
TAKE THIS BLUEBERRY BLAST!
WOW!
BLUE!
RASPBERRY BLAST!
OOH!
RED!
MAGIC CARDS!
MAGIC FISH!
SMACK!
MAGIC SQUID!
SLAP!

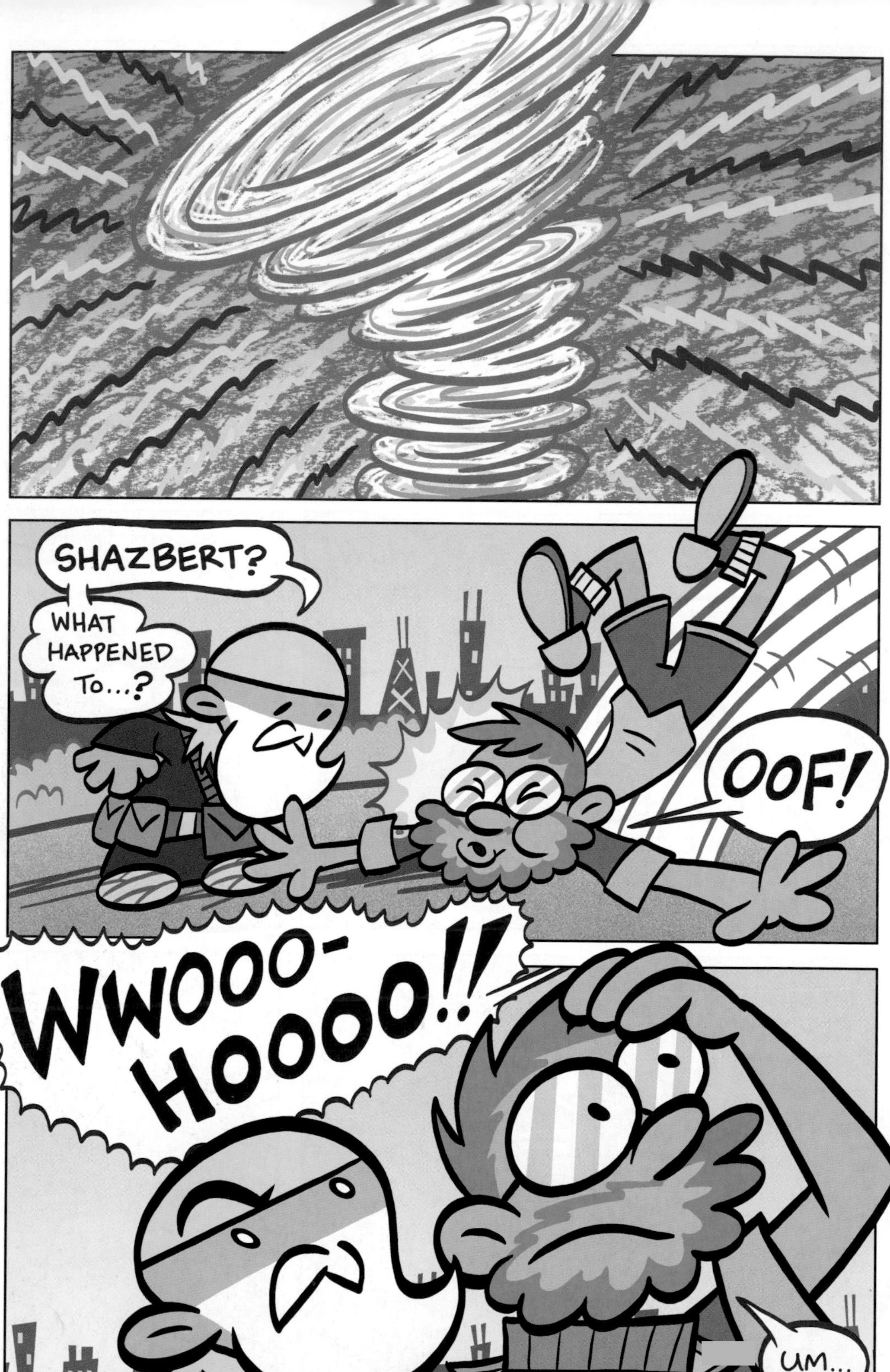
SHAZBERT?
WHAT HAPPENED TO...?
OOF!
WWOOO-HOOOOO!!
UM...

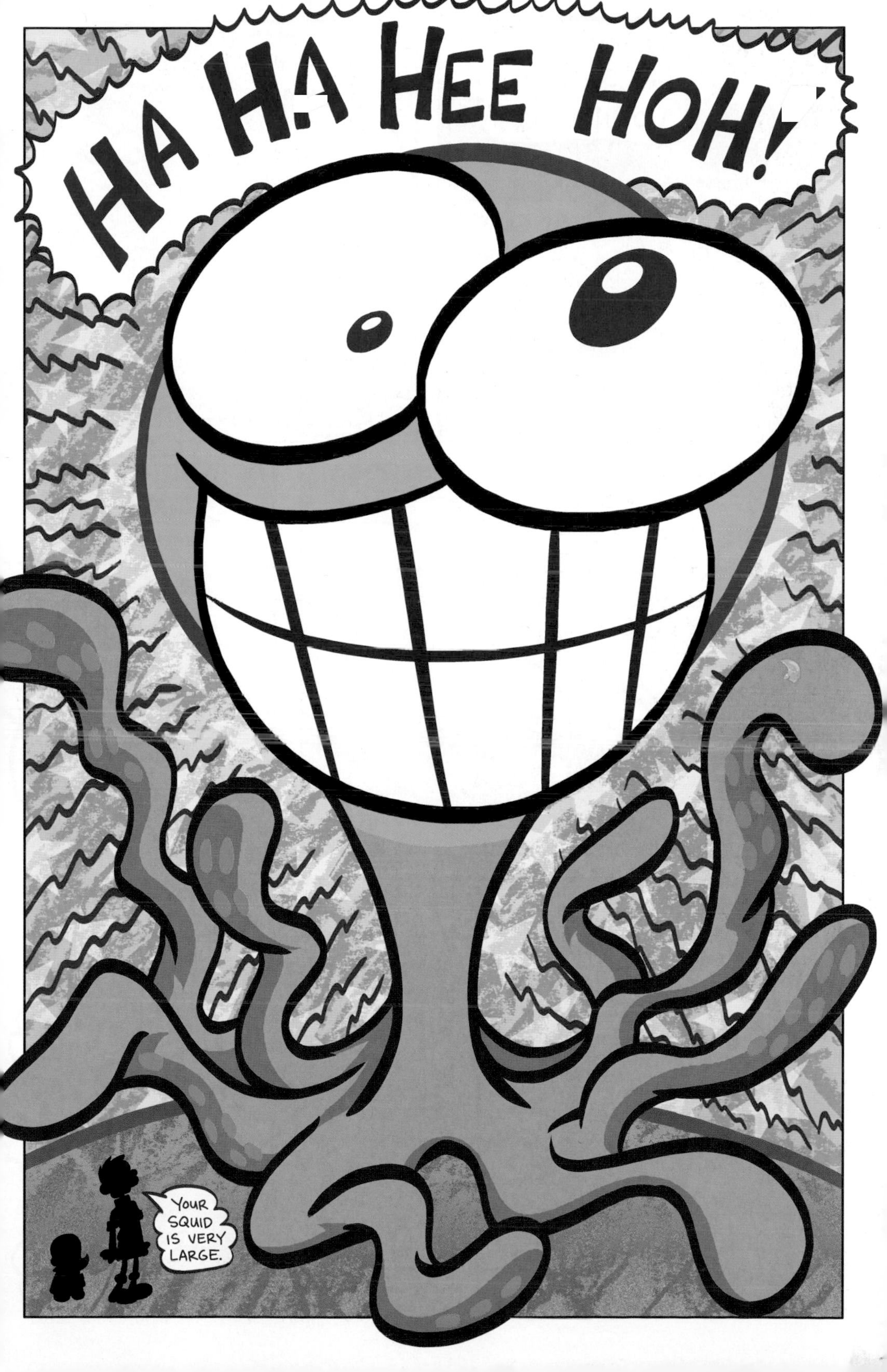
HA HA HEE HOH!
YOUR SQUID IS VERY LARGE.

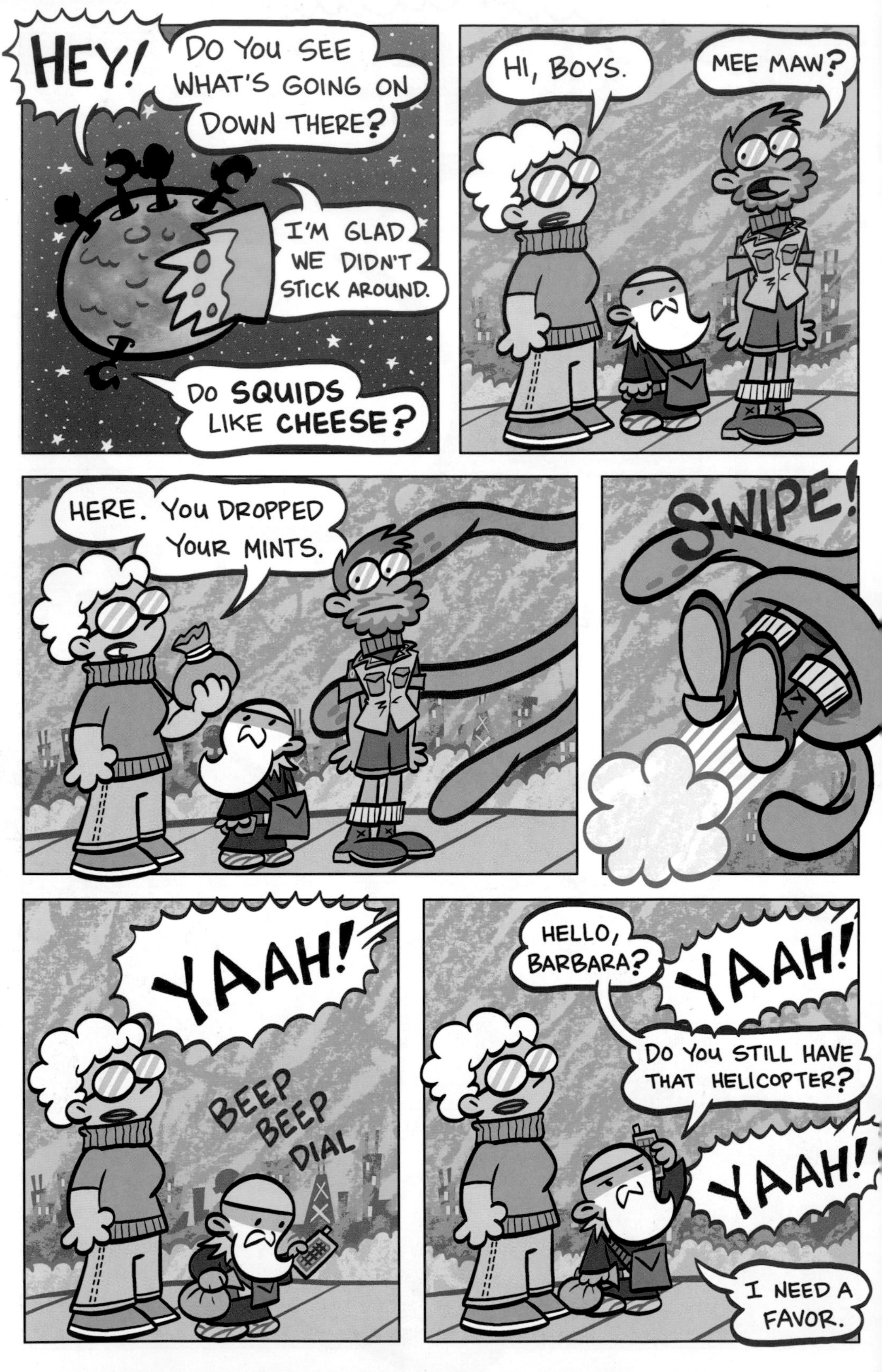
HEY!
DO YOU SEE WHAT'S GOING ON DOWN THERE?
I'M GLAD WE DIDN'T STICK AROUND.
DO SQUIDS LIKE CHEESE?
HI, BOYS.
MEE MAW?
HERE. YOU DROPPED YOUR MINTS.
SWIPE!
YAAH!
BEEP BEEP DIAL
HELLO, BARBARA?
YAAH!
DO YOU STILL HAVE THAT HELICOPTER?
YAAH!
I NEED A FAVOR.

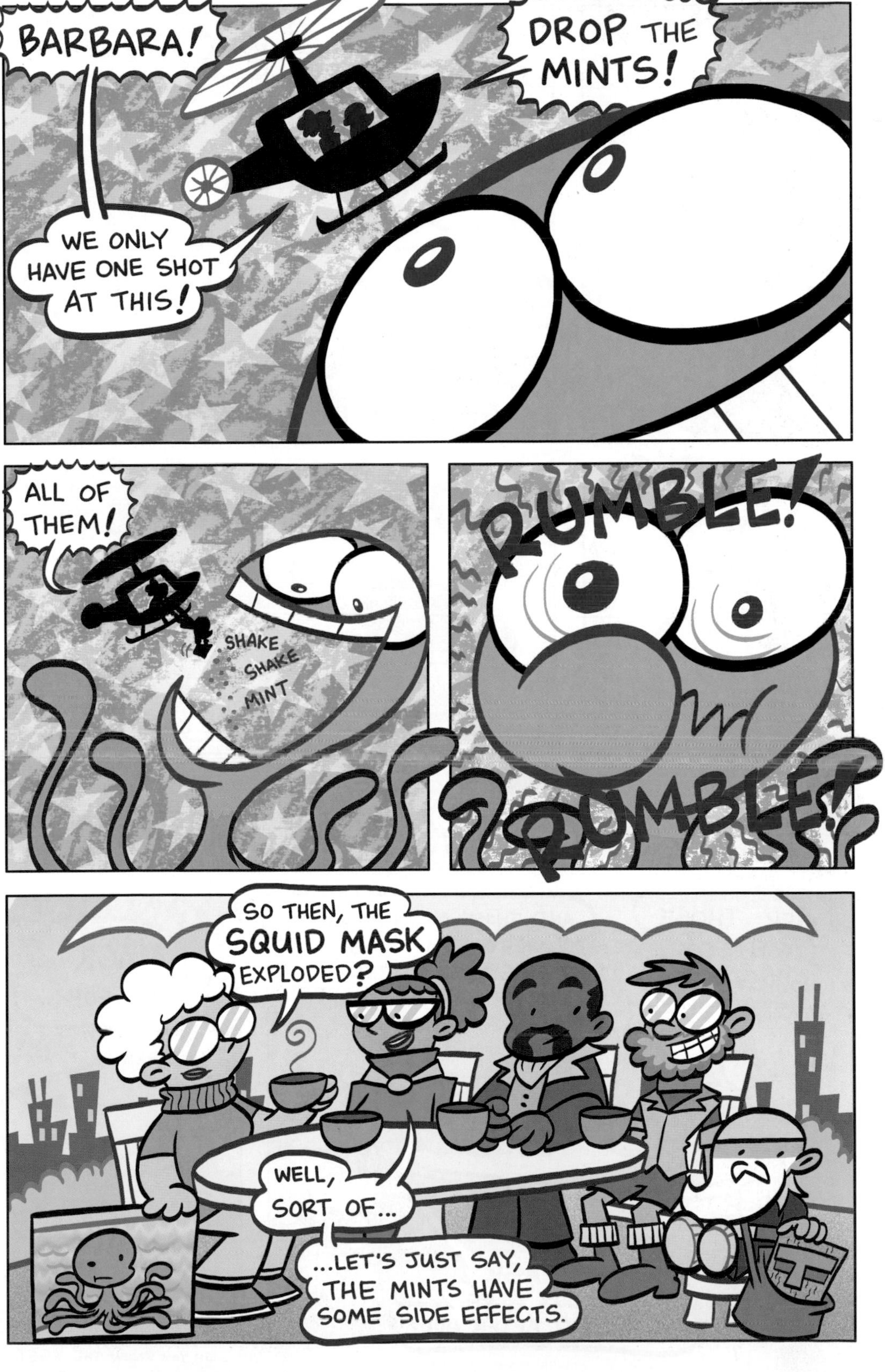
BARBARA!
DROP THE MINTS!
WE ONLY HAVE ONE SHOT AT THIS!
ALL OF THEM!
SHAKE
SHAKE
MINT
RUMBLE!
RUMBLE!
SO THEN, THE SQUID MASK EXPLODED?
WELL, SORT OF...
...LET'S JUST SAY, THE MINTS HAVE SOME SIDE EFFECTS.

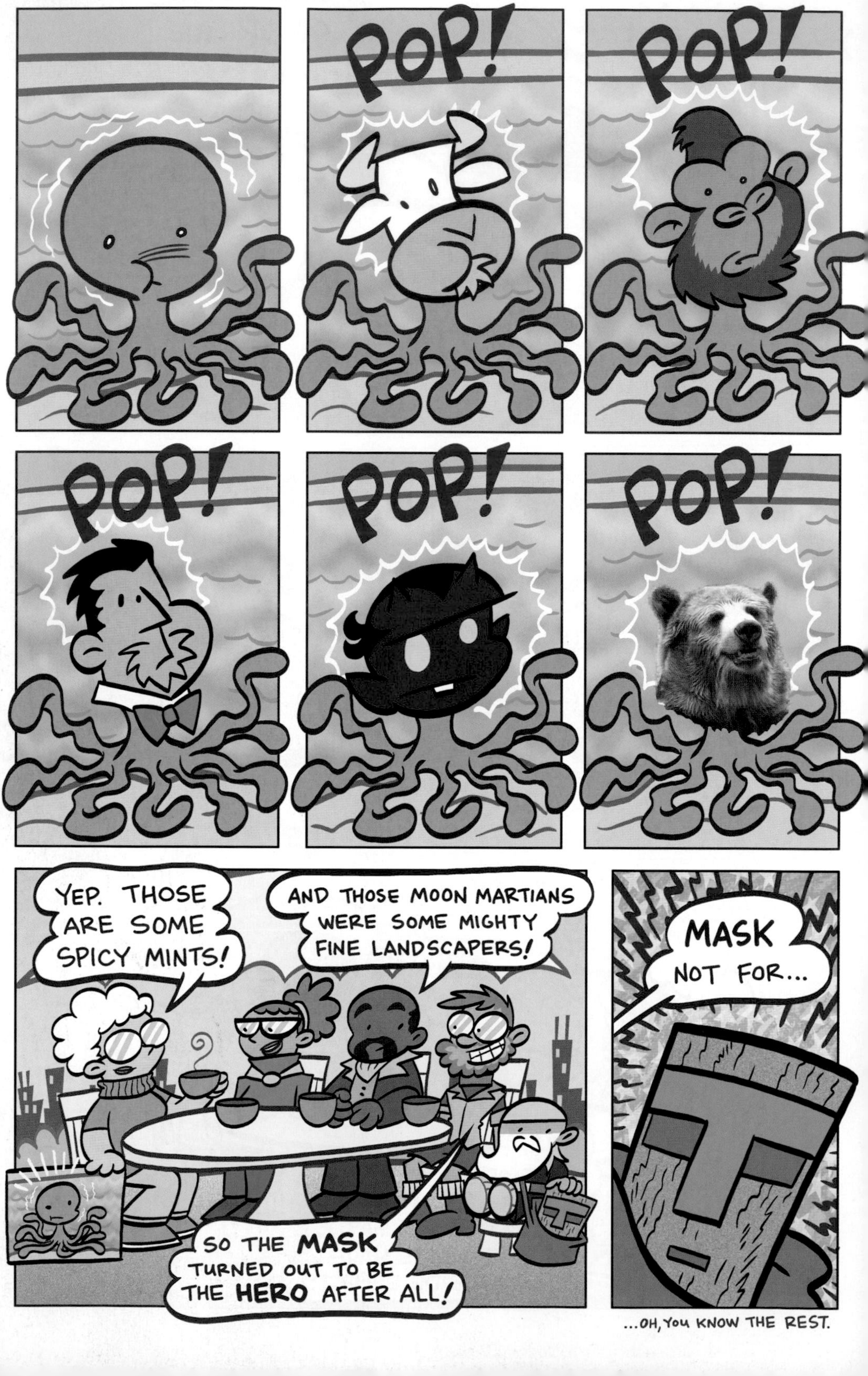
POP!
POP!
POP!
POP!
POP!
YEP. THOSE ARE SOME SPICY MINTS!
AND THOSE MOON MARTIANS WERE SOME MIGHTY FINE LANDSCAPERS!
SO THE MASK TURNED OUT TO BE THE HERO AFTER ALL!
MASK NOT FOR...
...OH, YOU KNOW THE REST.

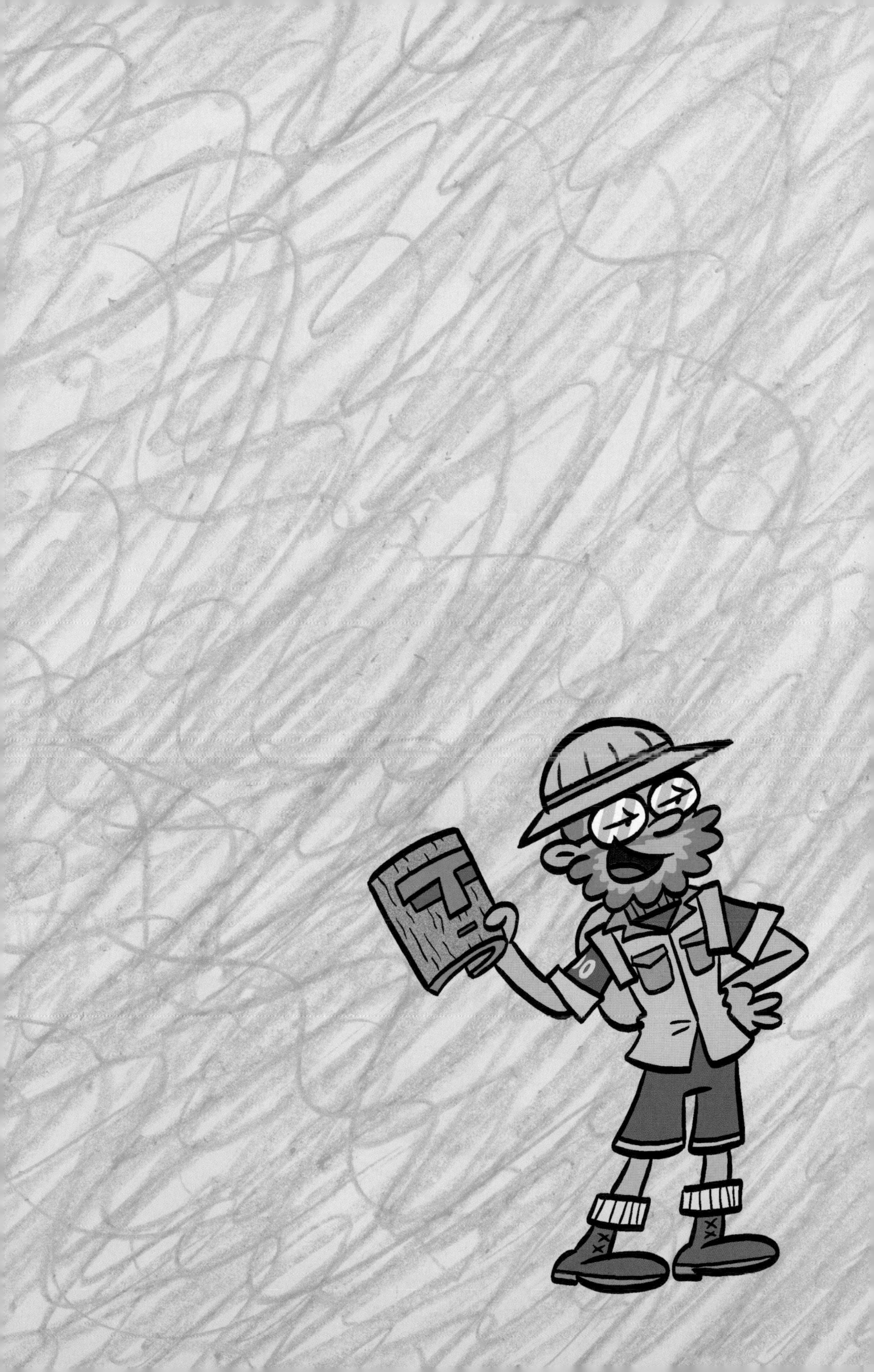

HALLOWEEN MASKS!

To celebrate the release of *Itty Bitty Mask*, Dark Horse created four super-awesome Halloween masks featuring the series' new character Herman Shazbert and a bunch of the zoo animals! AW YEAH HALLOWEEN!

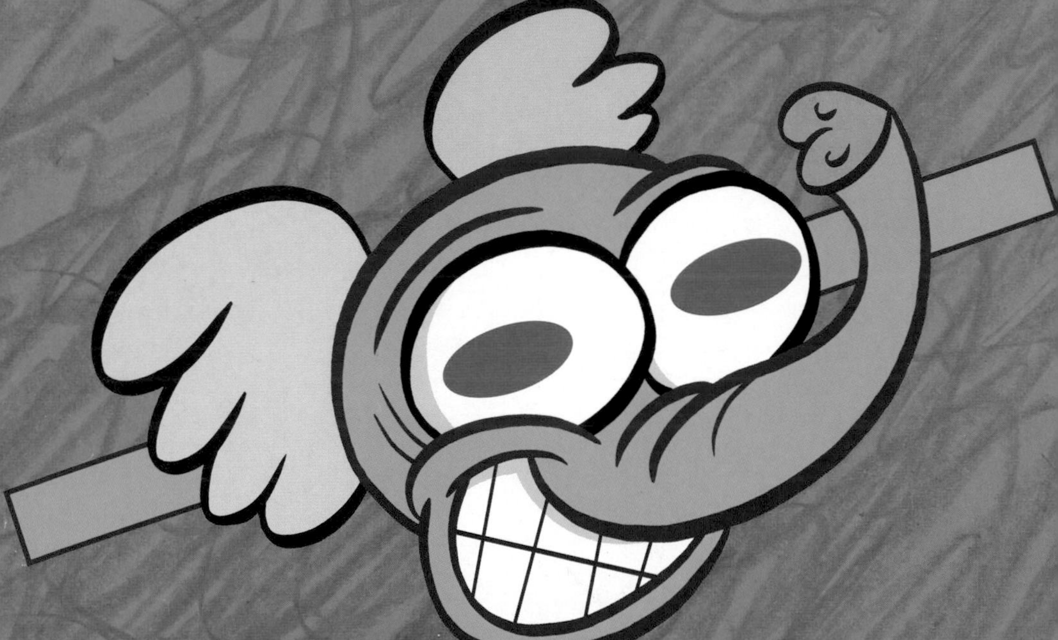

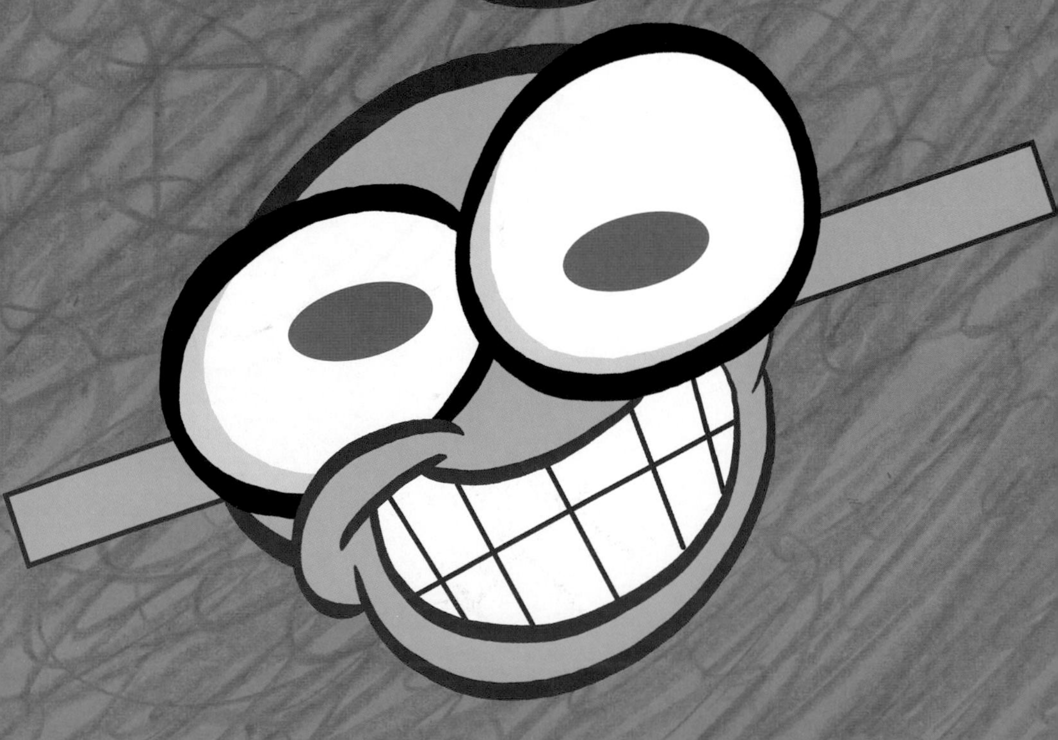

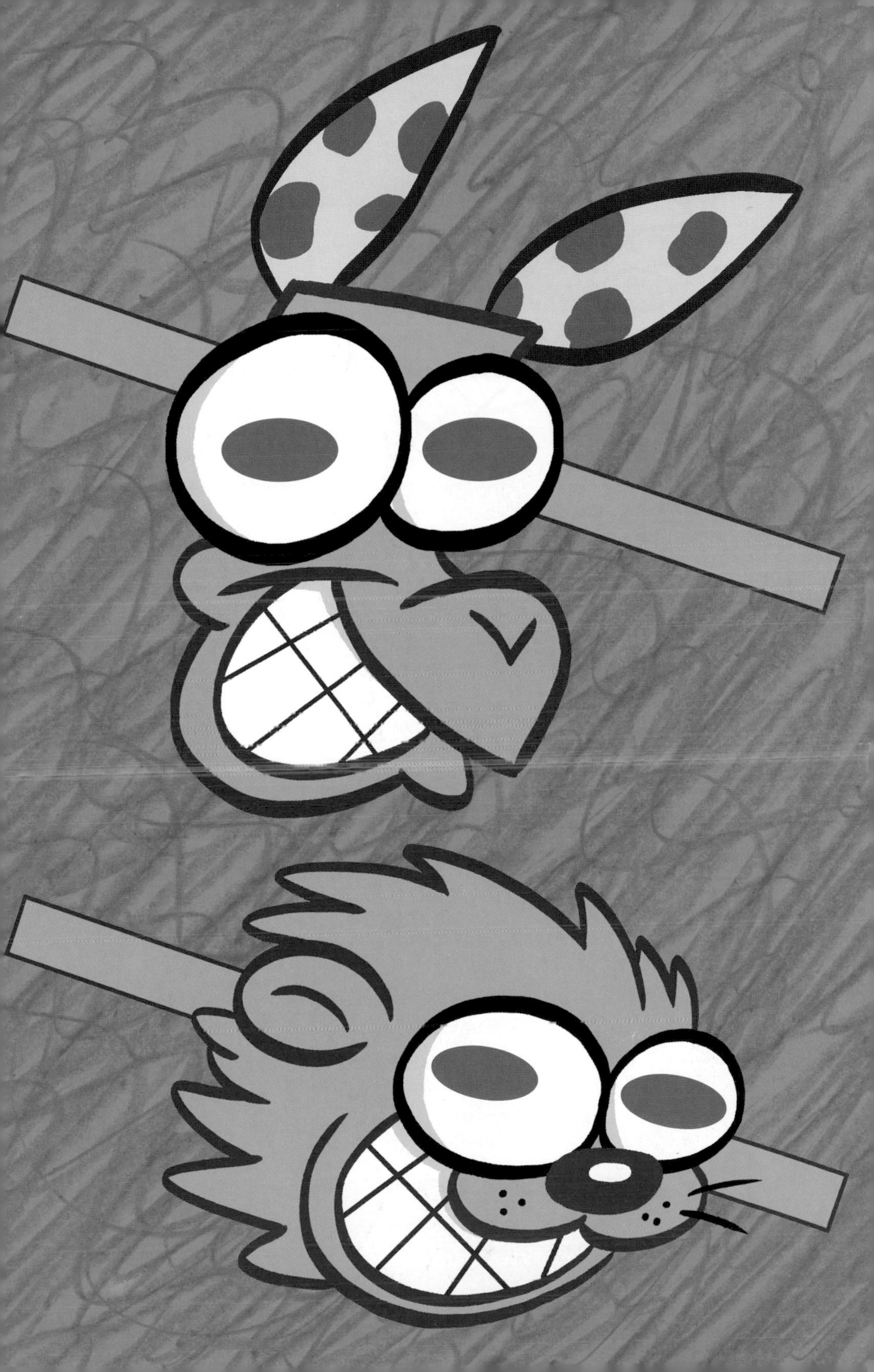

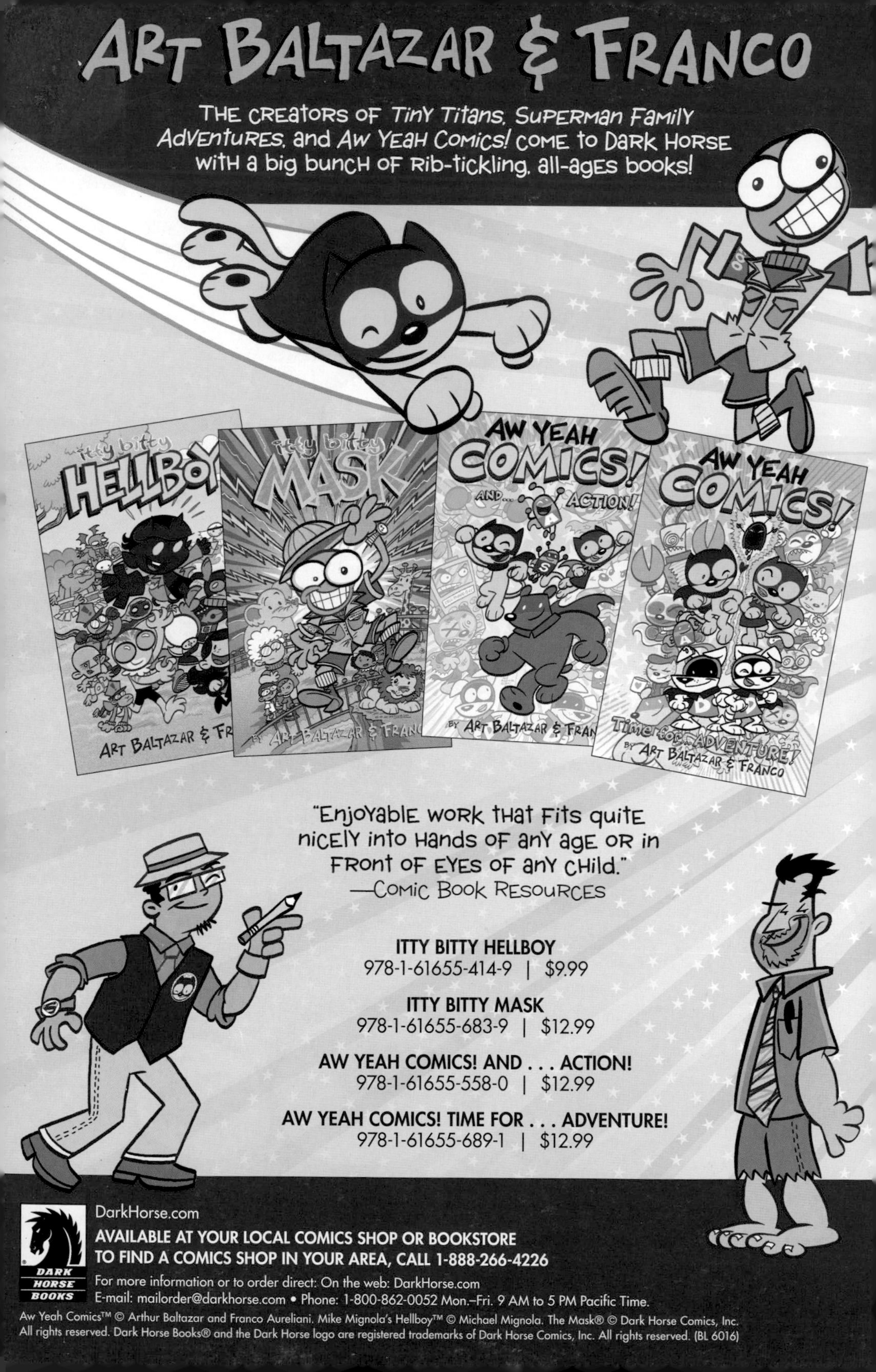

ART BALTAZAR & FRANCO
THE CREATORS OF TINY TITANS, SUPERMAN FAMILY ADVENTURES, AND AW YEAH COMICS! COME TO DARK HORSE WITH A BIG BUNCH OF RIB-TICKLING, ALL-AGES BOOKS!
ITTY BITTY HELLBOY
ART BALTAZAR & FR
ITTY BITTY MASK
BY ART BALTAZAR & FRANC
AW YEAH COMICS! AND... ACTION!
BY ART BALTAZAR & FRAN
AW YEAH COMICS!
TIME FOR... ADVENTURE!
BY ART BALTAZAR & FRANCO
"Enjoyable work that fits quite nicely into hands of any age or in front of eyes of any child."
—Comic Book Resources
ITTY BITTY HELLBOY
978-1-61655-414-9 | $9.99
ITTY BITTY MASK
978-1-61655-683-9 | $12.99
AW YEAH COMICS! AND . . . ACTION!
978-1-61655-558-0 | $12.99
AW YEAH COMICS! TIME FOR . . . ADVENTURE!
978-1-61655-689-1 | $12.99
DARK HORSE BOOKS
DarkHorse.com
AVAILABLE AT YOUR LOCAL COMICS SHOP OR BOOKSTORE
TO FIND A COMICS SHOP IN YOUR AREA, CALL 1-888-266-4226
For more information or to order direct: On the web: DarkHorse.com
E-mail: mailorder@darkhorse.com • Phone: 1-800-862-0052 Mon.–Fri. 9 AM to 5 PM Pacific Time.
Aw Yeah Comics™ © Arthur Baltazar and Franco Aureliani. Mike Mignola's Hellboy™ © Michael Mignola. The Mask® © Dark Horse Comics, Inc. All rights reserved. Dark Horse Books® and the Dark Horse logo are registered trademarks of Dark Horse Comics, Inc. All rights reserved. (BL 6016)